WINTERSTAR

STAR TRIBES, BOOK ONE

BLAZE WARD

KNOTTED ROAD PRESS

WinterStar
Star Tribes, Book One
Blaze Ward
Copyright © 2020 Blaze Ward
All rights reserved
Published by Knotted Road Press
www.KnottedRoadPress.com

ISBN: 978-1-64470-071-6

Cover art:

ID 69092951 © innovari | DepositPhotos.com

Cover and interior design copyright © 2020 Knotted Road Press

Never miss a release!
If you'd like to be notified of new releases, sign up for my newsletter.

I will never spam you, or use your email for nefarious purposes. You can also unsubscribe at any time.

http://www.blazeward.com/newsletter/

ALSO BY BLAZE WARD

Star Tribes

WinterStar

SeekerStar

SeptStar

SwiftStar

MorningStar

The Handsome Rob Gigs

Can't Shoot Straight Gang

Can't Shoot Straight Gang Returns

Hunting Handsome Rob

The Jessica Keller Chronicles

Auberon

Queen of the Pirates

Last of the Immortals

Goddess of War

Flight of the Blackbird

The Red Admiral

St. Legier

Winterhome

Petron

CS-405

Queen Anne's Revenge

Packmule

Persephone

Additional Alexandria Station Stories

Siren

Two Bottles of Wine with a War God

The Story Road

The Science Officer Series

The Science Officer

The Mind Field

The Gilded Cage

The Pleasure Dome

The Doomsday Vault

The Last Flagship

The Hammerfield Gambit

The Hammerfield Payoff

Shadow of the Dominion

Longshot Hypothesis

Hard Bargain

Outermost

Dominion-427

Phoenix

Princess Rualoh

Earth Force Sky Patrol

Birth of the Star Dragon

Flight of the Star Dragon

Call of the Star Dragon
Shadow of the Star Dragon
Trial of the Star Dragon

PART I

COOK

1

"*ENCULER*," Daniel slammed the receiver of the *vox* down onto the base unit and watched out his office window as the skytaxi lifted off, climbing past him and into the night sky.

Inside that sleek, yellow hull was the woman that he had been sleeping with off and on for the last two years, although it wasn't so serious as to contemplate a wedding. Oh, and she was with the Captain of the professional Forceball team for the capital city of Golden Harbor.

She hadn't answered on her skyvox, even though she absolutely knew it was him calling. Just ignored it and probably shut it off for the evening. He could leave a message. Or type her one. Or…something.

Daniel took a deep, teeth-grinding breath and blew out rage over his desk like a dragon that the *salauds* had woken up from a good nap, smiting them with its fiery breath.

He considered a cigarette.

It was an image thousands of years old, clear back to the planet Earth itself, for a chef to smoke, even though it was usually rare on the colony worlds. He had given up the filthy habit years ago, when the very first *Chef de Cuisine* he ever

3

worked for had explained that it altered the way you tasted things, depending on the flavor of the tobacco, and you could never be sure what you were actually serving if you smoked.

But he really wanted to reconsider it right now, watching his girl fly off with the jock.

The man was everything Daniel wasn't. Tall, athletic, golden, beautiful.

Daniel doubted the man would be any good in bed, but Angel would be smitten. Or something. Forceball players had to be huge, powerful men, and reached their physical peak by twenty-five, but that barely gave them any time to even discover how to properly pleasure a woman. Plus, they probably all had groupies throwing themselves at the future stars since they were fourteen, so they had never had to bother to learn.

It took time, like a good cassoulet, to learn those skills. Years spent in a kitchen perfecting the delicacy of your art. Years in the bedroom listening and working slowly.

And Angel was going off with the man. Worse, she had shown up tonight with that *salaud* to Daniel's own restaurant, flaunting things right under Daniel's nose where he couldn't dare make a scene.

Letting everyone know she had apparently moved on.

Daniel considered rekeying the security system to his flat, just to lock her out, but he suspected that by the time he got home in another hour or three, all her stuff would already be gone. Angel was never the flighty one.

No, she would be deliberate, in her insults as well as her social climbing.

Daniel Lémieux, *Chef de Cuisine* of the evening bistro *Pain du Soir*, lucky possessor of a *Golden Diamond* from *Gastropode*, the magazine for the discriminating, traveling gourmand. One of the top chefs on the planet of Genarde, since only three other restaurants in this entire sector had made it into the most recent edition of The Guide, and nobody had yet earned a second Diamond.

Those were few and far between, once you left Earth. Homeworld bias and vanity, and all that, tended to award diamonds to the oldest colonies instead of alien worlds that humans had settled on later.

But Daniel was apparently no longer good enough for Angel's intended social status. And she had to rub his nose in it, rather than a simple kiss on both cheeks as she left. Walk into his own restaurant with a date that she'd spent the entire evening flirting with.

And he had to smile while she did it.

The door to his office opened slowly and his human *Sous Chef*, Lucrèce, peeked in.

"Is safe?" the man asked carefully.

Daniel supposed that anyone outside this office, in the main space of the kitchen, had probably heard him cursing and ranting in here. And slamming a vox receiver down hard enough that it might be broken. Someone had called for an intervention and Lucrèce had drawn the short straw.

What else was a *Sous Chef* for, if not to protect the rest of the staff from the screaming madman in the corner office?

Daniel smiled and gestured for the man to enter.

His second in command was another one like the Forceball Godling. Tall, skinny, and possessed of a cleft chin that seemed to draw women (and men) like flies to honey.

All Daniel had going for him was wit, charm, and a face that didn't necessary curdle milk on a good day.

And ambition, but what good does it do a man to gain the world, just to lose his soul?

Even his thick, curly hair was rapidly moving from deepest brown to gray too early, as he was only thirty-seven years standard. It did lend him a bit of gravitas, but apparently made him too old for Angel, all of three years younger.

"Sit," Daniel gestured to the empty chair across the desk.

"You should have let me spit in her food," Lucrèce offered quietly.

Daniel shrugged and shook his head.

"It would have done no good, my friend," he replied sourly, trying to find something philosophical to the whole mess. "Tonight wasn't about the food."

"Then what was all that about?" Lucrèce asked, gesturing back over his shoulder at the dining hall. "I can already see the gossip pages and boards ramping themselves up for a good scandal over this. Why?"

"I do not know, Lucrèce," Daniel said, letting the exasperation bleed out instead of blowing dragon's fire. "And I will not ask her. If she returns, you will treat her just like any other patron. Those are my orders to you and the rest of the staff."

"Kill her with kindness?"

"Is that not better than putting drain cleaner in her mousse?" Daniel laughed.

"I will give both some consideration," Lucrèce laughed back before stopping to study his boss. "How are you doing?"

Daniel sucked a hot, angry breath into his chest and glanced back at the window, but the skytaxi was long since gone, vanished among the stars shining down. Probably going to the *salaud*'s place for a romp, assuming the two of them didn't just put on a show in the back of the cab itself.

Not that he and Angel had EVER done something like that.

Something crystalized in his chest. It wasn't low enough to be the ball of rage in his belly. Maybe closer to his soul.

Daniel studied Lucrèce for a long moment, as if weighing the other man's soul as well.

Over his *Sous Chef*'s left shoulder, the treasured announcement from *Gastropode*, awarding his restaurant that first, magical Golden Diamond and marking Daniel Lémieux as a man to be watched. Fawned over.

A superstar.

Who had just watched his girl walk into the bistro with her new boyfriend. Or at least boy-toy, as Angel had at least a decade on the young stud.

Something snapped.

Daniel found Lucrèce's eyes.

"How much cash do you have on you?" he asked in a dark, somber tone.

The *Sous Chef* flinched and almost recoiled in surprise, before he settled and pulled out his wallet.

"Just over one thousand Sept Crowns, I think," Lucrèce replied, looking up nervously as he flipped it open to check.

"So much?" Daniel was surprised himself. "I'm apparently paying you too well."

It was an old joke. The fastest way in the galaxy to go broke was to open a restaurant.

"Why?" Lucrèce asked.

"I'm done," Daniel decided aloud. "*Finis.*"

He pulled out a blank piece of paper and rooted around in his desk for a blue pen. Things like this should always be done in blue ink, not black or red.

Daniel started scribbling on the page in his compact, cursive hand, still trained from the old days of putting things on a chalkboard, as a true bistro would do it, rather than a printed menu that only varied seasonally.

Daniel looked at the outcome. *Bon.*

He signed the bottom left and dated it.

"Give me your wallet," Daniel said, handing the man the page.

"What's this?" Lucrèce took the page and simply handed the wallet over.

Such was the mark of trust you built up, running an excellent restaurant and only hiring the best humans and other species to work there.

"Daniel, you're nuts," Lucrèce continued as he read the page.

"*Oui*," Daniel agreed, counting. "And I'm done. Sign that. I'm selling you the entire restaurant and all associated components and corporations for…uh…one thousand, one hundred, and eighteen Sept Crowns. Write that number down at the top."

Lucrèce blinked, his face suddenly as pale as the page.

"Are you mad?"

"Yes," Daniel agreed. "Both angry and insane. What do you expect? I run a bistro."

The chuckle was a faint echo of the laughter of earlier.

"*Merde*, you're serious," Lucrèce barely breathed the words.

Daniel fixed his best friend with a hard smile.

"Done," he pronounced the doom. "You get the Diamond, the staff, the clientele, and the headaches."

"And your flat," Lucrèce pointed out. "That's paid for by the corporation."

"*Oui*," Daniel nodded. "I have enough clothes stored here that I can pack a bag. Plus the few papers I need. You can clean out everything in the flat and either burn it, keep it, or donate it. I won't be going back."

"But where will you go?" Lucrèce asked, finally finding some emotion to color his tones.

Anger, perhaps. A distant, pastel cousin to his own, at least.

"I don't know," Daniel said, feeling the weight of the entire galaxy slide off his shoulders. "And I don't really care."

No more concern that every meal that came out of his kitchen had to be perfect, on the off chance that THIS was the secret agent *Gastropode* sent to validate that his food was worthy of the Golden Diamond.

No more Angel and her rages, her flirtations, and her silly demands. He was rather looking forward to that part, although he might never tell a soul.

"I don't think this is a good idea, Daniel," Lucrèce countered.

"Sign it, or you're fired," Daniel made it easy for the man.

Lucrèce worked well with imperatives and demands. Thinking about himself, for himself, seemed to be the man's blind spot.

Daniel didn't want to consider what his own such idiocies might be.

Lucrèce stared at him hard for several seconds. Finally, he took a breath. Nodded to himself. Picked up the pen and scrawled across the page.

Daniel pulled out all the bills and handed the man back his wallet.

"There are about thirty thousand Crowns in the main account before tonight's deposit," Daniel said. "Another six or so for emergency capital expenses. I'll leave a message with the attorneys and the accountants before I sleep tonight, so you'll need to be up early tomorrow to talk to them. And you'll need to break in a new fish buyer, as you'll be too busy promoting people to fix all the mistakes I've made."

"The only mistake you ever made was hiring me," Lucrèce replied in an arch tone, another old joke.

"Ah, but I've fixed that," Daniel chuckled with an evil gleam in his soul. "Starting tomorrow, everything is your fault."

"And you'll be gone?" Lucrèce asked. "Just like that?"

"*Oui*," Daniel contemplated for a moment. "Perhaps I

will return and eat here someday. Perhaps not. I do not know who that man is yet."

He rose and held out a hand. Lucrèce shook it, and then Daniel stepped around the desk and pulled him close enough for a fierce hug and the traditional kisses on each cheek.

Daniel guided the new owner of *Pain du Soir* around to the other side of the desk and sat him down. The desk was unlocked, as were the file cabinets and the computer. Lucrèce had all the keys and passwords anyway, so he could run things if something happened to Daniel. Or if Daniel had ever taken a day off.

"Yes," Daniel nodded, studying the new tableau. "That will do."

Quickly, he pulled a few documents from a file and folded them into the inner pocket of his jacket.

He turned and opened the door to the tiny office that had been his home for nearly five years. Outside, much of the staff was waiting in a tiny bundle of nervous energy.

Daniel walked down the line, shaking hands, hugging folks, and kissing cheeks, but never saying a word.

When he reached the end, he turned, smiled, and opened the locker where he kept a bag. He pulled it out, closed the metal door, and walked right out the front door of his life.

"What just happened?" one of the cooks poked his head into the office.

"The galaxy just changed," Lucrèce replied quietly.

2

<hr>

"You're nuts. You know that, right?"

Kathra looked up as Erin, her own wingwoman, leader of her comitatus, stomped in to her command office and sat down without a by-your-leave or even a polite knock on the frame.

But then, that wasn't Erin's style, which was part of the reason this young woman led the rest.

Kathra let her dark face fall into something neutral enough that an outsider might be fooled into thinking she wasn't angry.

"Why?" Kathra finally asked after Erin had sat still long enough to fidget in her chair.

"It's bad enough to hire an outsider, Commander," Erin groused. "But now you're going to bring in a male? And a *Rabic* one, at that?"

That the potential victim wasn't black like the rest of them was probably what had set Erin off, moreso than hiring a *man*. Unlike most of the crew, Erin's skin was much lighter, a little darker than a tawny bronze with hints of duskiness under it. Unlike Kathra's nearly onyx flesh, or the range of dark browns the rest of the women in the comitatus had.

Erin's grandmother had been taken by slavers, and Erin's mother was mulatto. None of the fighters on this ship cared about your heritage, but Kathra knew Erin had been teased about it when she was young.

The barcode tattoo on the woman's right cheek was black enough to stand out cleanly. It was a sign of Erin honoring her ancient Grandma Ezinne, who still had the mark of the slavers on her own cheek to this day.

This woman's curly hair was clipped and shaved into a mohawk seven centimeters wide and nearly that tall. It fit awkwardly under her flight helmet, but Erin made it work. That was her signature, after all.

Making it work.

Kathra considered the other woman almost as a bright reflection to her own. Kathra's skin was so dark that it was nearly black. Full lips that never smiled, on a lean face that seemed at odds with her broad shoulders and muscles. High cheekbones and a narrow jaw made many consider her beautiful, but Kathra wanted none of it.

She was too busy building a new nation and protecting it from those bastards in the Sept, the empire of humans that had inherited Earth and apparently planned to subjugate the rest of the galaxy and all the aliens along the way.

Kathra was a warrior, not a model. In that, she and Erin were the same person.

"I have thought long and hard about this decision, Erin," Kathra fixed her gaze on her second in command like a cobra eyeing an intruder. "I have not yet heard a reason to doubt the decision."

"Can no one else do this?" Erin asked, hints of anguish creeping into her voice.

"Certainly," Kathra agreed. "Many could. You, even, if you decided that you were done flying. But none this well. Not even Grandma Ezinne."

She liked the way Erin recoiled at the suggestion, but Kathra liked to tweak her best friend and closest advisor from time to time. Kept them both on their toes, when facing a hostile galaxy.

"But a male?" Erin asked again.

"There are other men in the tribe, Erin," Kathra pointed out starkly. "To be white or male does not disqualify you if you wish to belong to the Mbaysey, even if you stand out from the rest of the tribe. And it's not like we're hiring him to be a warrior. Or even a mechanic."

"He will be the only male on this entire vessel," Erin pointed out, stretching for anything to deflect her commander's will.

"I'm sure there are a few women aboard who might be open-minded enough to consider him, for at least the odd tumble," Kathra replied. "The new flavor of the month, as it were. You will not be required to participate, or even notice."

Again the flinch. Absolute horror at such a visceral level, to consider being touched by a *male*. Kathra had dabbled, in her youth. As had many of the women, before Kathra managed to convince the clans to rise up and finally seize their freedom from the Sept by leaving planets behind. Not every woman on this ship was born Mbaysey, but all belonged today, down to the lowliest, *Anglo* crew member. Or a *Rabic* one, perhaps.

One of these days, even Kathra would need to go to the refrigeration station and pick out the sperm she would use to provide a new generation of Mbaysey leaders.

It would be filtered, spun, and verified, so she would bear a daughter who could take up her crown, as the others in the comitatus did when they reached the point where they no longer had the reflexes to fly with her. It hadn't been long enough since they were free, but there were a few, and there would be more over the next few years.

Modern science was a wonderful thing. The tribe could trade for the sperm they needed to remain viable, without ever needing all that many men around. Kathra had set the limit at twenty percent of births and members.

Of those males born, some would choose to leave the tribe later, seeking their fortune in a patriarchal galaxy more favorable to their kind. The rest would come out of the training crèches and find their place in the softer parts of the tribe. Teachers of the young. Artists. Nothing that required them to do anything physical or dangerous.

"Are there other complaints, Erin?" Kathra asked, watching the woman continue to fidget with extra energy.

"None that will likely sway you, once you're like this," Erin shrugged and grinned.

She had fired her shot and watched it bounce harmlessly off Kathra's armor. And they both knew it.

"Should I send someone else when we get to the station?" Kathra asked, studying the woman who was her right hand.

"No, I will do it," Erin stood. "Best this fool of a man learn his place quickly enough, if he's going to be serving the comitatus."

Kathra nodded and smiled as the woman departed without another word. That would be an interesting conversation, if she could but be a fly on the wall to watch.

Her command vessel, *WinterStar*, had a full crew, hundreds of hard working women doing everything necessary to keep such a warship functioning. Around them, were the myriad other ships that made up the Mbaysey tribal squadron. *ForgeStar*. *IronStar*. The *WaterStars*. The many *ClanStars* that each held a facet of her people.

Into this Kathra knew she would rile things, like a rock dropped into a still pond.

But how often does one get the opportunity to hire a mere cook with a Golden Diamond next to his name?

3

———

ERIN WOULD HAVE PREFERRED to do this in her fightership, *Spectre Two*, but she needed to pick up supplies for the fleet as well as retrieve the new cook, so she had flown in from *WinterStar* in an ugly SkyCamel, the stubby, boxy transports that were the complete opposite of her sleek dagger.

Two places up front for flying crew. A cargo area with flip down seats that could haul a dozen people or boxes in combinations. No particle cannons. Nearly blind. At least she had a lot of armor around her.

But she would not subject even one of the other women of the comitatus to an ignorant male.

The ship shifted into the airlock with a solid thunk as the station reached out and grabbed it with metal clamps. A moment later, the gravity field inducers extended their fingers and down became down again.

"SkyCamel Six docked," Erin announce tersely over the radio.

Neither of her escorts replied, other than to flash a green light on her piloting board, but Erin knew that Spectre Five and Eight would immediately move to dock as well, so that she would have her own wingwomen when she got onto the deck.

She didn't like Sept TradeStations, but they were a fact of life when you lived in deep space. At least she didn't have to do something stupid today and actually land on a planetary surface. Those were the worst, just imagining all the things that could go wrong with nowhere to flee.

Because she was also feeling extra feisty, Erin had worn her shorts today, instead of the long pants she normally had on when she was around outsiders. It let everyone see the cybernetic replacement that started at her right knee with a big, armored housing over the joint that was as much cosmetic as functional. The titanium post that was her shin. The secondary hinge across the back that looked like a calf muscle under long pants. The hoof-like foot, since she hadn't even bothered with the toe extenders she could attach when wearing boots.

There was a reason she had never let them talk her into the sleek replacements available back in the Sept Empire, the ones that looked just like a real leg with fake flesh over the top. Erin told everyone that she was concerned it would throw off her flying reflexes, having grown so used to the current, mechanical version.

That was a lie, but a good enough one that the Commander had never said anything about it.

Let this silly-ass white male see that he was dealing with warriors, rather than shuttle pilots. The pistol on one hip and the knife on the other would barely register, she knew, because everybody zeroed in on that leg and their mouths would drop open like fish.

Erin stepped onto the deck once the lock completed cycling and looked around for trouble. It was always weird, standing on a platform with artificial gravity. The builders tended to do silly shit like make square corners into geometric shapes.

WinterStar and all the rest of the tribal squadron vessels were too small for Grav Field Inducers, so they were just big, spinning disks rotating around an engine and power core in zero gee. Centrifugal forces kept your feet on the outer hull as it spun, and you could get anywhere by walking in a straight line long enough.

Here, the fools actually had slidewalks installed on perfectly-flat decks, to haul people around. Lazy gits.

Most of the folks in the immediate vicinity were human. That made sense, with the Sept Empire being centered on Earth and most of the early colonies. A few alien worlds had joined later, some of them even by an invitation not delivered from bolt cannons.

The others were generally just wanderers who had happened along.

There was a Vida slithering into a bar down the way, the creature's belly scales hissing on the rough, steel floor and the tail spikes tapping rhythmically. She couldn't see enough of the upright top half to determine if it was a male or female, but it was definitely a warrior, with a thin katana on a shoulder baldric and a pistol hanging off one hip. Or whatever you called the part where it stopped looking like a scaly human and started looking like a big snake.

Erin didn't really care. The Mbaysey were mostly human, although Kathra would probably be willing to accept any warrior or mechanic that wished to join the tribe and showed enough competence or potential.

As long as they were female. The men could go elsewhere. Or learn to cook. There was always that.

Two figures approached from beyond the bar the Vida had disappeared into. Joane and Iruoma. Spectre Five and Eight. Her backup.

Joane had taken the time to pick her dark, kinky hair up into the sort of huge, poofy halo that shouldn't fit under any flight helmet. Iruoma just got up every morning and shaved her head smooth to show off the complicated tattoos.

Good enough.

Erin pulled out her commbox and sent off a message to the *package*. Station authorities already knew she was here, and everything had been negotiated, so work crews would soon board the SkyCamel and fill it with cargo.

She still had a man to deal with.

There was no response, which really put sand in her gears right now. Hopefully the stupid bastard wasn't drunk somewhere, or asleep. She had docked and stepped onto this deck within seventeen seconds of the scheduled time. Stupid git should have been waiting for her to arrive.

Then he stepped out of that same bar the Vida had entered. She knew him as soon as they locked eyes across the distance.

Short. Swarthy. Not an African genotype like her, but too dark and reddish in skin to be *Euro* or *Anglo*. *Spanic*, she might have guessed, had she not known he was actually *Rabic*.

He had a bag slung over his shoulder that was smaller than she had been expecting. Maybe thirty centimeters in diameter and twice that long. Semi-rigid. Anonymous. Like the man.

Erin considered meeting the man halfway as he started walking towards her, but that might suggest a willingness to do exactly that, so she just watched him walk towards her. Joane and Iruoma took up corner positions where they could cover all approaches. Sept authorities generally didn't bother the Mbaysey, but that wasn't the same as saying no gendarme troopers wouldn't suddenly get punchy.

Still, this was a TradeStation, not an Outpost. The rules were different here.

Iruoma wasn't the shortest woman in the comitatus at one hundred and seventy centimeters tall, but most of the rest were taller than most of the men around. Erin was one hundred eighty-five in height, organic and metal appendages included.

This male was two or three centimeters shorter than Iruoma. Maybe. Depending on the heel on his boots. And not a muscle-bound dwarf either. It was like someone had taken an average male and just shrunk him down with magic, keeping all the proportions. Black, wavy hair starting to gray, but the face was largely unlined.

And it wasn't expensive rejuvenation treatments. Those left the skin on the neck loose. No, he was just going gray young.

Dark eyes that didn't miss a thing. Scanned her foot just enough to nod to himself, before moving on to study her face, her tattoo, and her mohawk. Glanced at the other two woman, dismissed them as her wings, and addressed himself to her.

"Daniel Lémieux. Am I in the right place?"

Voice was a little rough. Like talking quietly was a new thing to him, when he wanted to yell. Kitchens on planets must be loud places.

Erin nodded.

"Gear?" she asked.

He pulled the bag around front and tapped it with a palm.

"All set."

"That's it?" Erin was a little shocked.

Most fools traveling in deep space had trunks of crap, because they had never sat down and thinned their needs to the true basics.

Or never faced the poverty of a renegade star tribe trying to make a living without gravity.

"Yes," Lémieux replied. "I left the rest on Genarde for them to burn."

Erin had wondered. Most people had baggage. Physical as well as the rest.

Top chefs like him didn't just come on the market like this one had. Must be having a mid-life crisis early and gone off to reinvent himself.

Or some other stupid, upper-middle-class-mysticism bullshit that rich white people indulged in.

Being the smallest person here didn't cause him to flinch though, or get aggressive. Small men usually did, but he seemed poised and self-contained in ways she hadn't been expecting.

What had she been expecting?

Male.

Territorial dominance games. Sexual innuendo and boundary pushing. Stupid crap she would have to break him of quickly, maybe using enough blunt force to get through to the pinhead's brain if she was lucky.

Mbaysey didn't tolerate men. Didn't even need them, beyond a duty they could fulfill alone in a quiet chamber with a small pump.

Chef-boy just watched her without fidgeting or rocking. Eyes stayed on her face, instead of wandering down her curves. As if a man was ever touching those.

"The station will need an hour to load my shuttle," Erin looked at the man.

"The bar I was just in has food I would rate above poisonous, but below adequate," the cook said. "There is a burger joint in a nearby corridor that seems better run, but I've had to stretch my funds to get here and didn't feel like indulging in the expense while I waited."

He fell silent and watched her.

What had she been expecting?

He had offered two suggestions to kill time, rated them, and waited patiently for her to decide, as if she was in charge.

She was, but most men outside the Mbaysey never seemed to grasp that they weren't.

Erin glanced at Joane and Iruoma. Both nodded and twitched in the silent language that said they preferred the burgers.

Meat was a rare delicacy in the tribal squadron. The ClanStars produced all manner of fruits and vegetables in their hydroponics operations, but anything more than a few miniature cattle for milk required too much space and feed.

A good chunk of the cargo she was hauling, by mass but not value, included frozen chubs of ground meat. Several different kinds. None of the cuts particularly choice, but compact protein that a young girl needed if she was going to be tall and strong when she grew up.

"Burgers," Erin decided.

The cook nodded sharply.

"Do you know the place, or should I lead?" he asked.

Again, offering information, without assuming that he would decide.

Erin gestured for him to walk and listened as the other two women fell in behind her.

Maybe this punk could be made to fit in with the rest of the females on *WinterStar*, if he could be trained well enough.

They'd see.

4

WHAT THE HELL had he been expecting?

Daniel didn't have a good answer to that one. While Angel had been petite, around half the women he had encountered in his adult life were taller than he was, even if they weren't wearing heels, but these three were all big, tough, *dangerous* women. Break him in half if they felt like it.

Inwardly, he shrugged as the concierge sat them in a corner booth and dropped laminated menus before departing.

It was easier to not think of them as women at all. He'd done enough research on the public boards to understand that the Mbaysey were almost as close as you could get to the ancient Amazon warrior legends of Central Asia, back on Earth. Not that he'd ever been there, but one picked up all sorts of odd tidbits when researching food and recipes.

Almost no men. Women filled all the traditionally-masculine roles that he had grown up with, except that they considered cook to be a lesser role, which was apparently why they were willing to hire him.

Since Angel, Daniel wasn't all that interested in female

dalliance right now. Not that he liked men, but he was going to need time to get over his broken soul to consider a woman.

She hadn't broken his heart, but certainly had uncorked a rage he had forgotten about, buried deep beneath the need to run a perfect bistro. Seven months wandering in deep space hadn't done more than perhaps shave the thinnest slice of prosciutto off the top of that anger.

Still, he was here. Seated at a table with three impressive women. Fighter pilots and warriors. Calm, silent, and hard as freaking nails.

He might have forgotten what the other end of the female spectrum was like, after dealing with Angel for so long.

"Joane?" he said, pointing a finger at the tall one with the enormous hair.

She nodded silently, with perhaps the faintest hint of a smile.

"Iruoma?" he turned to the one next to him, with tattoos on her skull that told him just how tough this woman was, because someone had once explained to Daniel how much something like that hurt.

"Iruoma," she corrected his pronunciation with a hard, cold face.

Daniel nodded gratefully and went back to the menu. Erin was easy to pronounce, hard to miss, and apparently not the least bit willing to engage in idle chitchat today.

He could work with that. His life probably hinged on these women having a reasonable opinion of him, because he'd be on their ship soon, deep in space, with no place to go if they got angry.

At least nobody from *Gastropode* magazine was likely to send a spy out to rate his food when he wasn't prepared.

Starting with a clean slate, like mornings back with that

first bistro he had ever worked at. Buy whatever was available at the market today, figure out how to work magic with it, wipe the board clean when you run out of something.

Start over again tomorrow.

He contained a hollow sigh and tried to keep himself as compact as possible, physically as well as emotionally. Good kitchens were so tight that brushing people as you went by was unavoidable. He had never stood for bad touching from anyone on his staff, but his inner crew had been together for years, so physical contact as one went by was natural. People had bad days and needed a hand on a shoulder or a hug. People had good days and a high-five was a way to celebrate.

Daniel was pretty sure he'd pull back a bloody stump if he tried to touch these women.

He listened as they ordered, coming around to him last not because of courtesy, but relevance. The waitress knew these women, by reputation if not sight. He was the afterthought.

Each of the three had different tastes, but cataloging something like that was second nature by now.

"Number seven," he said simply when it was his turn. "With cold, sweet tea to drink."

That got him an interesting look from the leader, Erin. Black eyes bored in on him, making Daniel wonder if he'd missed something in his research. Not that there was much information available about the tribe, but he'd consumed it.

He stared back, working hard to keep his face neutral. But also not backing down from something so basic as what he liked to eat.

Madam, I am a chef. That will be my kitchen and you will be my customer. And you will be satisfied with your food.

He didn't snarl, or even move. The other two had picked something up and grown the faintest bit restive, and either could stab him or punch him from where they sat.

Daniel understood knives. He had lived in a kitchen for twenty years. His kind had an old, inside joke about trying to tell the difference between a tattooed psychopath with a knife; and a cook.

Not every tattooed psychopath with a butcher knife you encountered was a cook, but…

Dead silence at the table.

Understanding that this was a test just as deadly as first earning his right to call himself a chef had been.

Eight prospects in a teaching kitchen. Each handed a box of random ingredients as a timer started. Seven fools immediately starting to throw things into pots and pans while Daniel sat with everything around him on the counter and had a nice, pleasant smoke, listening to the soul of the food.

One of the instructors had even come over to make sure nothing was wrong. Daniel had smiled then. He smiled now.

Three of the other seven had eventually made the cut and put on the hat. Only Daniel's results had earned praise from the judges.

Be calm. Plan ahead. Then act.

Be a chef.

His smile seemed to convey something useful to Erin. She calmed. The other two did as well.

"Have you ever attempted something like a comitatus meal?" Erin asked in a voice that had apparently softened from a sharp sneer before it exited her throat.

"Weddings, bat mitzvahs, and holiday parties," he replied in a professional, almost professorial tone. "A group of close friends eating from communal dishes, with a dozen options to cover tastes and potential food allergy needs. I suspect stir fry and ancient, *Sinofied*, American food will probably be a good opening gambit as I learn. Especially as meat is not common and vegetables are."

"Allergies?" Iruoma asked, perking up.

Must have something she might be too embarrassed to discuss in the open. Warrior mentality and all that. Too tough to cry.

"I had a friend back home for whom mushrooms of all types were a violent, almost lethal allergy, and onions a lesser one," Daniel turned his attention to her. "Garlic was fine for the man, but it was necessary to reshape certain dishes to avoid killing him over dinner. Especially with French cuisine. That, in turn, became a welcome challenge for me as an artist, because then you are working with a palette of flavors, brightening things or softening them down into more earthy tones as heat, acid, and time work their magic."

He saw the twinkle in the woman's eyes that promised a quiet conversation later. But he'd be doing that with all of them anyway in short order. That was what professionals did.

"And you won't grow bored?" Erin asked dryly.

"I ran a bistro for five years," he replied. "I have worked in kitchens for twenty. Boring would be having to cook the same menu for years on end, like a fast-food restaurant. I took this job because of the challenge of the larder."

"Really?" she looked at him closer. "I was under the impression that you were unemployed and running out of money."

"Whoever told you that was a fool," Daniel couldn't hide the sharp side of his tongue. "I left my personal skyvox behind because I knew there would be so many investors suddenly interested in backing me for a new gig that I would never sleep. Reporters wanting to know where I'm cooking next. I could have taken several more years to find a job, if I wanted."

"Then why *WinterStar*?" Joane leaned closer from directly across, staring at him from close enough she could have kissed him if she wanted.

"Nobody will ever find me," he turned to her and said quietly. "There will be no demands on me other than to cook good food. No investors will rattle my window at dawn trying to fund my next establishment ahead of the others."

"Are you really that good?" Erin leaned forward as well.

Daniel found himself in some bizarre form of verbal combat with these women, when they would perhaps have preferred the blades on their hips, but it couldn't be helped. This was the challenge that they understood. Three hard women, all trained warriors with disdain for the capabilities of a mere man.

"Yes," he growled quietly. "And I shall prove it when we get there."

For the briefest moment, he wondered if a fist or knife would be the reply, but he wasn't about to back down to that sort of gauntlet.

Commander Kathra Omezi had found him, in ways Daniel still wasn't sure how, and offered him a truly unique path forward. But he understood that he would have to cross a minefield of these women, and all the rest like them, to prove that he belonged.

Daniel let his gaze slide across all three with the sort of utter disdain that he would have unleashed on a reporter who came to an interview unprepared and asked the same, inane questions.

"Bring it," he whispered.

5

———

Kathra had read the reports all three women had filed when they returned, and it filled her with a cold, evil joy to consider the impression the tiny man had made on three of her best, most aggressive warriors.

As if only women could be warriors. As if being a *Gastropode*-rated chef was somehow a lesser responsibility. And from the descriptions, they had all been surprised to find the man capable enough, secure enough to stand up to the three of them in public.

Kathra was pleased as she and her new cook toured *WaterStar One*.

Her few agents remaining in the Sept Empire had reported what little was known of the man. One had even been able to talk to the new owner of the old restaurant, *Evening Bread*, and get that person's impression of the possibility of hiring Daniel Lémieux to serve the Mbaysey.

Kathra suspected that her mother's ghost was probably laughing right now, in between cursing her fool of a daughter for ever relying on any man. But seriously, she was looking forward to being served something better than stew on a regular basis.

It was one thing to declare your independence from the humans and odd aliens of the Sept. To break your tribe off from the slavery and servitude they had endured for generations, and then escape, as her mother had done.

It took twice the gall to simply detach one's self from the Sept altogether and flee into deep space with all her people. Twenty-two ClanStars. One *ForgeStar*. One *IronStar*. Two *WaterStars*. And the *WinterStar* itself.

She had put the chef into her personal strikefighter, *Spectre One*, and ferried him over to *WaterStar* One, with him crammed into the space in front where a weapon's officer would fly, if she ever had any missiles for her squadron, rather than just the particle cannons she would use to chase off pirates or fools.

And Sept patrols, but they had long learned the folly of pursuing the Mbaysey into deep space, well away from their support bases.

So she had taken this Daniel Lémieux and carried him over to one of the two gigantic aquarium ships that kept her squadron fed. It was a massive cylinder, turning on a central axis, like the rest of her tribal squadron, to provide the illusion of gravity when gravity field inducers were so massive and expensive to run.

Cheaper to just spin.

Eight ring tanks, filled with all manner of freshwater fish and other aquaculture, as she and the cook made their way along a catwalk overhead. The ClanStars produced all the fruits and vegetables, trading between ships and paying tithe and taxes for protection and support. But none of them had the space to haul this much water, or grow this many fish.

"Thoughts?" she asked the tiny man who barely came up to her jaw.

"Do you ever trade caviar out?" he asked, pausing to stare down at the gigantic lake beneath them. "Keep sturgeon and harvest half their eggs?"

"Too much work, even with the prices we could probably command, this far from the few planets where the fish were introduced successfully," Kathra replied, wondering how this man's mind worked. "Sturgeon take decades to mature, and we don't have the right environment for them, without a renovation."

He nodded absently and began to walk again. She followed silently in his wake.

"Almost no land-based herbivores for meat?" he asked after a few steps.

"Functionally none," Kathra said. "We do trade frozen fish for such things with several of the more remote TradeStations, since they have to get them from planets otherwise."

Again the absent nod, like a computer taking input passively.

"Have you considered sacrificing one of the tanks for salt-water species?" he looked up at her. "Seaweed has already been modified to provide an excellent source of vitamins and minerals on many worlds, since oceans are common. Plus it makes *maki* easier to make."

"Maki?"

"Nihon rolls, formed of a dried seaweed to contain it, pressed rice, and raw fish at the center," he smiled at some memory she was not aware of from her spies. "Tuna can grow huge, so you can get enormous amounts of *otoro*, a prime source of protein and fat."

"At a loss of over twelve percent of my fresh water supplies?" she asked.

"Just over six percent, unless you were to decide to modify both vessels," the cook answered with a serious face.

"Or perhaps you could consider building an *OceanStar* at some point?"

Here less than a week, and he was already planning next year's meals. Yes, she had chosen well when she had decided to look outside the Mbaysey for help. Idly, Kathra wondered if she should look for a competent sushi chef next. The kind that had traveled all the way to Earth to learn her craft over years, and could train a new generation here.

Fish was never really in short supply in the tribal squadron, because of the two *WaterStars*, but the look in the man's eyes promised whole new levels of gustatory exploration that they had perhaps never imagined in the poverty of deep space.

"So what made you accept my offer?" Kathra asked when the man fell silent and began to walk again.

Her longer legs made it easy to catch up, so she walked beside him on the metal platform now. His head was tilted forward, but she caught the glimpse to one side filled with all sorts of silent emotions.

They walked several more paces in silence.

"It was not one thing," he finally answered, probably when he realized she would outwait him. "The escape from my past. The excitement of a truly new challenge. Even the possibility to disappear into obscurity."

"I hardly doubt a famous chef from the civilized worlds could be obscure here," Kathra countered.

"Very few people will like me here," he almost grinned as he continued forward. "Men are a rarity and only a necessity in certain circumstances I do not foresee myself being involved in."

She watched him without comment.

"For the last several years I have been famous, Commander Omezi," he said. "The center of attention, the object of ridicule or gossip columns, the cover of magazines, depending on the day. Challenged to never serve a single bad meal. Never have a day off, except for the traditional First Days when all bistros such as mine are closed and the restauranteurs get together to lie and drink wine. If I have notoriety here, it is because so many of the women of your tribe will openly disdain me, but it will not be personal. And they will have to come into my kitchen to do it, which most will not do, after they have a chance to appreciate better cuisine."

"And when you want to go back to Genarde?" Kathra asked.

"I am already past the man who lived there for fifteen years, Commander," the chef intoned like a low bell ringing. "At this point I have a hard time even remembering who he was. Yes, everyone will know who I am, but that cannot be helped out here, and it will be contained within your people. I will cook, sleep, and relax with a few thousand good books."

"Books?" Kathra felt herself perk up. "What kind?"

"All of them," the man said as he continued to pace remorselessly forward. "I loaded my e-board up when I decided to leave Genarde, Commander, perhaps knowing that I would be departing the Sept at some point and would need to haul the better parts of it with me."

"The better parts?" she probed.

This man didn't spout like the sort of chauvinistic patriotism too many of the Sept Empire's citizens absorbed in their socialization.

"The literature of several thousand years," he paused to look up at her, almost craning his head back as he did.

There was nearly thirty centimeters of difference between them.

"What sort of library does the Mbaysey keep?" he asked, face suddenly inscrutable.

"Each of the clans maintains their own," she said with a sharp eye. "Without looking, I would presume that a book finds its way to all of them eventually."

Daniel Lémieux, Sept Chef, nodded and began to walk again.

"Then we will need to upload all my books to your system, so you have something interesting to trade with the rest," he almost laughed.

She followed, and considered what she could get out of some of the more stubborn groups with a whole new collection of books.

The vox on her hip beeped.

"Omezi here," she replied as she pulled it out with one hand and put the other on the chef's shoulder to stop his pacing.

"Signal, Commander," Joane Obiakpani replied. She must be holding the command watch right now. "Sept frequencies and heavily encrypted. Looks like they found us again."

"Understood," Kathra said. "Launch *The Haunt* and tell the clans to prepare to flee. I will join you shortly."

"Understood."

Kathra turned to the chef, taking his measure silently. He stood perfectly still, relaxed and calm, staring up at her.

"Come," Kathra decided. "You need to see what it is we face."

Kathra began to jog past the man, looking for the next staircase up to the core of the ship. Behind her, the chef pounded loudly along, but didn't seem to lose much distance as they moved.

Hopefully, it would be nothing more than a scout ship that had blundered into the wrong system. The Sept did not build long-range cruisers that could chase her people, especially since the Mbaysey didn't live on planets, or even stations anymore. Simply step back and let the dark of deep space hide you, until you had to emerge again at a TradeStation for supplies she couldn't yet fabricate out here.

The Sept would never catch her, but she also knew they would never stop trying.

6

———

He managed to keep pace with the crazed, Amazon warrior, up three decks, across and into the *WaterStar*'s core. From there, Daniel just had to remain perfectly still and rigid with his arms held in as Commander Omezi had emerged into zero gravity, grabbed him by the hips, and shotput the two of them down a long, open corridor.

She did it much faster than he suspected he would ever be able to, even when she was hauling along an extra sixty-eight kilograms of heavily-gasping baggage.

Spectre One sat perched in a small bay forward like a harrier hawk, clamped to the deck with magnets and joined to the ship by the short umbilicus of an airlock. Daniel didn't try to help, other than to listen to and obey the giant woman's commands as she thrust him along the soft-sided tube and into her ship.

Turn left to go forward. Feet first into the front well where this design apparently kept a gunner. Buckle himself in tightly.

Not touch anything on the boards in front of him, nor on the armrests.

Around him, the fightership came live with a hum of quivering power. His board even lit up, showing what his mind interpreted as a scan of nearby space, maybe looking down from the top of the solar system.

Wylanne system's star off in one corner. The planet itself on the top edge, with several lights that maybe represented orbital platforms and TradeStations.

A cluster of lights over here, but not all that tightly bound. ClanStars up in the rings of the ice giant the squadron was orbiting, out in Wylanne's darkness, mining for rocks and ice. Others below, deeper into the atmosphere, sucking vast amounts of gas off the atmosphere to be refined later. Two *WaterStars* off to one side, waiting. *ForgeStar* had been crawling through the planetary rings, pulling loose chunks of metallic ore into its maw with a magnet on the bow.

Overhead, *WinterStar* was disgorging fighterships like a tree in spring casting seeds into the wind. *Spectre One* was suddenly catapulted off the deck and into space with a force that drove the breath from his lungs for a moment.

Idly, Daniel wondered why nobody wore spacesuits when flying, but then he supposed that it went against the hard-ass, warrior mentality. You lived to fight, or died from it.

Stupid, but nobody had asked his opinion.

Plus, suits would be expensive, especially with the varied sizes and shapes of women he needed to cook for. That was money that either didn't exist, or could be put to better uses.

Books would be the same way. A newcomer would bring things like that, and contribute them to the common cause, just like they did their skills and knowledge. It wasn't like he was going to get rich from what they were paying him, but he had room, board, and people that didn't bother him much, so it worked out more or less even, as far as he was concerned.

On the board, a new dot appeared. It appeared to be moving closer to the tribal squadron, even as the other twenty-two craft that made up *The Haunt* moved to intercept it. Twenty-three *Spectre* fighterships. Not much to defend the tribe, but all they had, and he'd spent enough time around those women the last week to know they wouldn't break or back down.

But what the hell was he doing out here? Besides having been with the commander, on the wrong ship, when it happened? Doing it this way would save her having to come back for him later. And keep him out of trouble with the *WaterStar* locals, when she wouldn't be around if they decided that they didn't like the thought of a lone male running loose without adult supervision.

"Signals?" Kathra's voice suddenly brought Daniel back to the present tense.

"He was trying to be quiet," Erin's voice came over the radio. "That kind don't understand the concept, so we caught him not long out of jump, just as his engines lit and started the burn to bring him to us."

"Do we know what it is?" the commander asked.

"Negative, *Spectre One*," Joane spoke. "Passive scans only. Didn't want him knowing that he'd found the whole tribal squadron if it was Sept. Figured we could sneak up on a pirate or prospector otherwise."

"Good call," Commander Omezi said.

Daniel watched the dot grow closer on the screen without himself moving more than necessary to breathe and blink. He looked up and spotted the ship in the distance.

"There it is," he said. "Three fingers to the right off the bow and down a little."

"He's too far away to see!" somebody snapped on the radio.

"Then what's that?" Daniel held out a finger to point,

only then realizing he was almost alone in a cockpit and nobody could see his hand.

"*Draka…*" somebody swore over the line. "That thing must be huge."

"Septagon," the commander seated behind him said in a most definitive voice.

Septagon?

Daniel considered the origins of such a word. *–agon* was ancient Greek. *Sept* was Roman and the name the Sept Empire had chosen for itself, representing the seven families on Earth that had formed the thing, as well as the traditional seven continents of humanity's homeworld.

Septagon was a bad mishmash of languages, but suggested a seven-sided structure. Why would you build a ship that way? Felt like all the bad elements of design decisions had been baked into the soufflé, just so you got to have the play on words.

Spectre One was idling. Coasting now. Closing, but without a hard burn to bring the two sides together quickly enough that all they could do was wave in passing.

No, this felt like the sort of speed a defender would take when forcing an attacker to waddle up into all of their guns if he wanted to engage them.

Or he could just blow by them at high speed while chasing the tribal squadron, but that required that he know that they were there.

Daniel's board changed, drawing his eyes down from the cluster of lights in the distance that represented *intruder*.

Huh. Septagon. Built by the Sept Empire. Specifications listed down the side.

"*La vache*. That thing is *huge*," he muttered.

"Indeed," the warrior in the rear seat replied. "They build to overawe the barbarians. It has a downside, however."

Daniel wasn't sure what sort of downsides there were

when you had a flying space station thirty-two hundred meters along a facing and over seven kilometers, nose to tail. Seventy decks tall on the main part of the ship, with a number of towers stuck out the top where members of the *Vuzurgan*, the Sept's nobility, might retire to, to escape the common masses.

The hollow space at the base of the septagonal shape was large enough to park *WinterStar* without touching.

"Tribal Squadron, this is Commander Omezi," Daniel heard her voice take on a layer of steel that had been missing before. "All ships flee immediately. *The Haunt* will follow once you are away, and rendezvous at the next Concursion point."

Concursion?

Daniel had no idea what the word meant, other than perhaps it bore a linguistic similarity to congress, or conclave.

The image of the Septagon on his screen shifted again, moving to one corner of Daniel's untouched board and bringing back a list of ships behind him.

One by one, they blinked out, disappearing from the chart, until only the fighterships and the Septagon remained.

"All Spectre ships, stand by," she said in a quiet tone.

Daniel heard a beep, and then other voices filled the cockpit. Male. Hard professionals talking to one another absently.

"What do you want?" Commander Omezi asked in a voice right on the verge of polite.

Daniel was reminded of a woman walking along the sidewalk that turned to confront you, in spite of the fact that you had just accidentally ended up going the same direction, rather than stalking her.

"This is *Septagon Vorgash*," a voice replied a few moments of silence later. "I am Naupati Amirin Pasdar, commanding.

You are trespassing in Imperial space and will surrender immediately."

Naupati? Daniel was impressed. That said that the man was one of the highest ranking naval officers there were in the Sept Empire, but that made a kind of sense, if he was in charge of *that*. A septagon was a large city floating in space. And being a Pasdar meant he was probably part of one of the main genealogical lines of the seven founding clans of the Sept itself.

A dangerous man to even know, let alone have as an enemy.

"I could say the same about you, Naupati Amirin Pasdar of *Septagon Vorgash*," Commander Omezi replied in an equally hard tone. "Wylanne is only a colony, and not a full member. You are outside your laws."

"I make the laws, Mbaysey," the man said grimly. "Surrender or die."

"Catch me if you can," she mocked the man.

Daniel felt a moment of pure panic at her words, but then the stars around them seemed to stretch and turn blue as he watched.

Daniel had never realized a ship this small might be equipped with a valence drive, capable of leaping between the stars.

One moment they were facing down a monstrosity of a ship, *Septagon Vorgash*.

The next, they were surrounded by streaks of light as he looked out the windows.

And Daniel was surrounded by the laughter of an Mbaysey warlord.

What the hell had he gotten himself into?

7

ERIN DIDN'T LIKE the way the rest of the group had sort of organized themselves into a pair of wings around her in the dining hall, but she didn't really have a good argument about her innocence.

Someone had managed to track the tribal squadron to the outer fringes of the Wylanne system. Worse, a major Sept warship, and not just a patrol force that her sisters of *The Haunt* might have chased off or even defeated.

No, a Septagon had arrived.

Erin had heard it on the radio. Everyone had. Just before the jump, that naupati over there had called Kathra *Mbaysey*. Had known who he was dealing with, even without a word from the Commander.

They'd known who they were facing. Knew where to find them.

Erin and her two wingwomen had been the most recent team out. Naturally, everyone else suspected them of being spies.

Or worse, being so amateur that they got followed home from Renneth.

The eating hall was quietly ostracizing them. Erin sat with Iruoma and Joane at a corner table after she filled her plate from the troughs by the kitchen window. The little cook was so fast that he had managed to land with the rest of the team, get here, and prepare pasta in sauce with steamed veggies on the side before the women of *The Haunt* had finished showering and getting dressed.

Erin had taken longer to get here, because Kathra had wanted to ask her something. The rest of the room had gotten surly by the time she arrived.

Kathra stepped through the door now and glanced around, meeting Erin's eyes with shadows of anger and laughter hooded inside. That made Erin feel a little better, because she had the feeling she was going to be at the sharp end of a lot of insults and jabs over this. Not enough for a true challenge, but she still might have to give way as Kathra's Second In Command. At least for a while.

If it was her fault.

Erin had her doubts.

The cook arrived with coffee, served the three of them silently before moving on to the others. They were all big girls, able to serve themselves, so she supposed he was making a statement.

Or at least trying to diffuse things. The quiet anger in here almost had a smell to it.

Everyone fell silent as Kathra made her way to the buffet and loaded up with food. Pinched hexagon noodles that reminded Erin of hourglasses. A red pesto sauce rather than a marinara, so extra chewy with stewed tomatoes rather than just the soupy bits. Peppers and something she couldn't identify by taste or texture, but might have been celery chopped extra fine.

That sweet, cold tea that was the commander's favorite, as well as the cook's, apparently.

Kathra made her way to the open spaces on this communal table, the space next to Iruoma and across from Erin and Joane much wider than necessary, unless one of them was giving off a particularly foul odor. Not necessarily rare, right after combat, which was why everyone had showered after they made it through jump and back to the mothership.

Kathra looked around the room like a proctor with a class of recalcitrant seven-year-olds, before the genders were separated off a year later so the females could study the harder things they would need, like military art or mechanics, and the males could take up less dangerous vocations. Art. Farming.

Cooking. But she wouldn't tease him about that. Not anymore. This dinner was simply amazing, especially considering how quickly he had done it and the limited amount of ingredients in his world.

But if Daniel Lémieux turned out to be a spy, she'd put him out the airlock personally.

Kathra Omezi, Commander of the Mbaysey tribe, ate in a bubble of silence that only seemed to pop when she took her second bite. The women around them began to murmur again in subdued tones.

There was little laughter today.

"Renneth to Vorgash to Wylanne is probably eight days, best case," Kathra announced in a voice too loud to just be speaking across the table to Erin. "And that assumes patrol craft. A Septagon probably requires an extra day for that last bit, even over a short jump like Vorgash to Wylanne."

She went back to her bowl with the briefest of smiles, the kind that vanished as she picked up the next bite and stuffed it into her mouth.

Erin did the math maybe a hint faster than everyone else, but only because she was so keyed up to whatever subtle mischief Kathra was up to. She smiled at her commander as she caught on to what Kathra had caught and everyone missed.

Even a courier running like hell couldn't have managed to drop a major warship like that on top of the tribal squadron. Those things were slow.

The valence drive was the most wonderful thing in the galaxy, but speed was inversely proportional to mass. Septagons were the size of small cities, and weighed as much, so they waddled through hyperspace. That was the trade-off that the tribe made with the ClanStars, which were much smaller and faster, but couldn't mount Gravity Inducer Fields, many of which were almost the size of a ClanStar themselves.

At least the tense reserve around Erin and her two sidekicks was starting to melt. Sisters made eye contact now, offering silent apologies for the earlier, unspoken accusations. Those had stung, but she hadn't been able to refute them, even unvoiced.

The Sept had found them, in Wylanne no less. Had sent a sector warship after them, although it had just been enough to chase them off.

With a wicked grin she mostly suppressed, Erin wondered just how many ships it might take to actually threaten the Mbaysey. Septagons carried patrol craft: bigger, slower, heavier versions of the Spectres she and her sisters flew. Bigger and better guns. Slower to maneuver, attack, or cross valence space to pursue an opponent.

Two Septagons, perhaps. Maybe three? What would piracy be like in empty sectors, if Commander Omezi managed to draw that much tonnage into her wake? Maybe the tribe could take up piracy as a profitable vocation at that point? Lead the Sept ships around by the nose, never quite catching up.

Slowly, the sound around them returned to something approaching normal. Voices only a little strained, striving to act like nothing had happened. Words had never actually been exchanged. The kind that might have to be settled in a ring with gloves on. At the same time, fault lines had emerged, and Erin knew that she and Kathra would have to work twice as hard to bind the comitatus back into a tighter whole.

But one facet lingered unanswered. Erin wondered how quickly the other women would pick up on it. Kathra had cleared her, Joane, and Iruoma from the accusation that they had been sloppy or had betrayed the rest. But the Sept had still managed to find them.

That suggested that there was a spy somewhere, somehow leaking information to the lords of the Sept. Not the cook, because he had gone through a full inspection when he arrived, including the standard vaccination for men that covered any diseases he might pick up or bring, as well as functionally sterilizing him for the better part of a year, just in case one of the others felt the bizarre need to fornicate with such a creature.

Technically, it wasn't bestiality, but Erin didn't see much difference, at that.

So the cook was clean. Kathra was their Commander and heir to the tribal history. Erin knew she was completely loyal to the boss, as well as the dream of the Mbaysey. That just left everybody else.

Who was the spy?

8

Dinner had gone over like a pocket supernova, but Kathra was not displeased with herself. She had heard that naupati's words. Like the others, she recognized the significance of them.

The Sept had finally come looking for her. Specifically. For Kathra Omezi. And the Mbaysey as well, but her.

The Sept Empire had long memories, going back to her mother, the irrepressible Yagazie, and the Mbaysey first demanding their freedom and rights, after nearly a century of semi-slavery under Sept law. Freedom had allowed them to be ignored long enough to build up their strength. To build the ClanStars as trading ships. To carve out a spot among all the other merchant races and classes.

Until daughter Kathra had convinced them to leave Tazo behind and simply walk away from the Sept entirely. To only interact with the old empire of men when they needed to trade for those things they could not produce themselves. Skills that they needed to learn, by hiring in experts.

To skate into the endless darkness and leave planets themselves behind.

Kathra looked around her office and studied it, as if the whole of the galaxy would be changing so much shortly that it would no longer be something she could remember, if she didn't stop and memorize the details now.

She had always expected her eventual pregnancy to be the trigger, but she had not yet gone to the refrigerator to pick out her daughter's father. Apparently, the Sept were tired of waiting.

A knock at the closed hatch brought her head up with a smile.

Right on time.

Kathra keyed a switch to slide it open, and Daniel entered.

He surprised her by carrying a large flask and two cups as he entered and stood between the two chairs on the other side of her desk.

The apparent gravity in here was not as strong, because she was on the inner deck. Just under half a gee. Being on the middle deck would be eighty percent, while the outer deck was kept at one hundred fifteen percent standard gravity, to keep muscles strong and reflexes sharp.

It was much more comfortable sitting on her ass on this deck, when she had to do paperwork. Also, easier to get to engineering, located in zero gee inside the rotating shell, if she was here and there was an emergency.

"Sit," she ordered the man, wondering if he planned to drink with her.

Daniel took the chair on the right and put everything on the desk between them. Quickly, he opened the flask and poured two equal amounts, grabbing one glass and sipping.

"Sweet tea," he said simply.

Kathra let the scowl die before it reached her face. They did indeed share that one quirk, and he was apparently trying to make things appear calm and relaxed.

For an outsider, he had learned quickly in a single week. Or a lifetime of training in a kitchen had served him well.

Kathra took a sip and contemplated this chef.

"We did not finish our tours," she said after a moment.

"I have reviewed the logs that Ugonna left me," Daniel said between sips. "It would be nice to have more chickens generating eggs on a daily basis, but I understand that only the Ihejirika ClanStar deals in excess chickens to trade with the others, while the Okafor have a small herd of miniature cattle that each produce about two liters of milk per day. I plan to shift towards serving more milk directly by using it in white sauces and roux, while serving less bread and making more pasta. It stores dry for longer periods of time, and allows me to put calories and protein into the comitatus in a variety of ways."

"A French-specialist chef disdaining bread?" Kathra asked with the faintest hint of irony in her voice.

"You haven't have freshwater crab Rangoon, or Vietnamese spring rolls, I suspect," he smiled back at her. "And I like lasagna, if I can manage to find me someone to make specialty cheeses."

"There will be other problems, first," Kathra replied, pulling the conversation back to why she had ordered him to attend her.

"Yes, but I intend to hide in my kitchen while you and yours sort all of that out," he said simply. "If they didn't follow me to Renneth and then here, which I couldn't tell you one way or the other, then I have no part to play."

"And if they did?" she asked.

Daniel shrugged.

"You hired me," he said. "Of all the offers I got, yours was the only one even remotely interesting. I presume the recruiters you went through are either people you trust, or that's probably the easiest way for the Sept bureaucrats to follow me to Renneth. From there, I'm not sure how they would track you to wherever we ended up. Or wherever we are now. Unless someone has found a magical new way to track a ship making a jump."

"That cannot be done," Kathra confirmed. "But an observer watching a ship go into jump can make a good estimate where it will come out."

"I wasn't flying," he said with a serious face.

"And I've looked at the logs from Erin's flight," Kathra nodded. "All three of them short-jumped several times when leaving Renneth, so nobody could have followed them directly."

"There you have it," he said. "I will return to my kitchen then?"

"You are not concerned that some of the comitatus will suspect you of being a spy anyway?"

"Until one of them actually stabs me with a knife, they do not even rise to the level of threat of some of my former coworkers," he said, eyes suddenly darker than they had been.

Kathra just studied the man, one eyebrow raised in surprise.

"Kitchens are not always convivial places, Commander," he announced in a simple voice. "At least, not until you reach well-run ones. I have been stabbed or slashed several times, requiring stitches or glue to close up, on top of all the times I have been punched, shoved, or burned. The warriors around you do not intimidate me, for all that any one of them could bounce me off the walls and appliances until they got bored or I broke. I am here to cook. If you have other requirements, Commander, I will attempt to meet them as best I can, or perhaps find myself unemployed and standing bereft on a platform again."

"Again?"

"It will not be the first," he said in a flatter voice. "I do not expect it to be the last, either. Now, what should I prepare for dinner that would remind your killers that they are friends and comrades, rather than wherever they ended up at lunch today?"

"Something exotic," Kathra decided. "Spicy and new, to remind them that this is a grand adventure."

She watched his eyes grow distant within, seeking something.

How could she tell any of them that she had hired this man for two such radically unrelated reasons? First, because she had simply grown bored and listless with Ugonna's pedestrian cooking. They all had. Stew was not a treat, the fortieth or sixtieth time you had it, regardless of how the cook might play around with ingredients.

They had already come round to understanding what a new cook could do, especially a great one challenged to keep outdoing himself.

But second, and far more important to Kathra, was to remind everyone that while the Mbaysey were a tribe of outsiders, they could not grow insular as a result. Fresh blood would be needed on a regular basis. Fresh ideas, just like they regularly had to trade the excess metal ingots *ForgeStar* produced for grains grown on the surfaces of planets they never visited.

Her war with the Sept would not be fought with guns. She would lose quickly and be erased from history if she sought to challenge that mighty empire on a level footing. But she could win by providing an alternative to the planetary-based thinking that made so many others grow stale.

Kathra could have invested in an autochef capable of taking any manner of input chemicals and ingredients and spitting out meals that were good enough to satisfy your nutritional needs.

Those machines had no soul whatsoever, which was why much of the Sept relied on them. They had lost their own dreams, and were losing whatever elements of identity they had once possessed. The Mbaysey had managed to retain that element for this long.

Kathra Omezi, Commander of the tribe, was looking for something far greater.

PART II

COMMANDER

9

———

Daniel had even reached the point now, after four months aboard *WinterStar*, that he was willing to admit that he really had gotten lackluster and predictable, back on Genarde. That was the downside of being awarded the prestigious Golden Diamond. Once you had one, your menu was almost permanently locked in at that point.

Every meal had to meet the standards of the magazine, or more specifically, the critic that had snuck in that night and awarded you rock star status. No option to experiment now with a new menu, as tourists and locals would flock to your counter because you had established a *thing*. They wanted *that* thing, and no other thing would do to replace it.

Daniel wondered if any of the others like him had ever had such a quiet crisis of conscience. He supposed so. More than once, a top chef had suddenly closed down their restaurant for reasons never adequately explained. Daniel had always assumed a combination of burnout and poor sales, except, upon reflection, all of those places had been popular and well-regarded. Famous and successful.

It had taken Angel and her new boyfriend to show him

how unhappy he had gotten as an artist. The business side had been fantastic, and dreary. Daniel supposed he owed her an apology for all the things he had said, even if only in his mind, and probably for all the insults and invective Lucrèce and the staff had most certainly fired off at the woman and the rumors likely started.

She hadn't broken him. She had merely gotten him angry enough to realize how much he hated cooking such a limited menu. Such a limiting one. How *Seasonal* had come to represent something almost as predictable as asking the autochef for dinner or calling for delivery. How that Golden Diamond, so proudly displayed, was a chain affixed to his ankle like he was a criminal.

He didn't do *Seasonal* aboard *WinterStar*. Couldn't. He was back to the bistro days. Whatever was available and fresh, often with no more than a few days warning from the various vegetable growers, and only a few days to use something at its peak, else it had to be made into sauces and pestos that could be frozen for later use.

Every day an adventure in randomness. Except that his entire customer base came in for almost every meal, and he never served more than forty people at any one time.

And, thank the very gods above, they didn't all like the same thing. Breakfast was not continental nor English, to follow the two main, classical threads that had come into space with humanity. He had to find a way to satisfy frequently three or even four different sets of requests and dislikes, each of three meals per day. And the various groupings of the warrior women changed, based on what he did to feed them. Even better, not all of them wanted breakfast, so much as perhaps leftovers from last night stashed in the cooler and reheated, or an early lunch because they might be on a different personal clock from the rest of the staff.

He was running a boarding house. Almost a bed and breakfast, when he thought about it, smiling with the mental breakthrough.

Daniel could not remember having ever been as happy in his adult life. Even opening either of his restaurants had been more about the stress of making money back for his investors and building his name, than about actually enjoying himself.

Weird.

He also did not cook for the three hundred or so crew that made up the rest of *WinterStar*. The two populations were divided into comitatus and support, and even something so fundamental as the kitchens were divided into two, distinct groups.

The commander did hold a weekly lottery that gave five people from the Support staff the chance to dine with the comitatus, but she otherwise kept her warriors isolated enough to add…what? Prestige? Mystery? Something.

He didn't know. And didn't care. He was slowly learning the rest of the crew, faces that he really never saw otherwise, since his cabin was close to the kitchen and the gymnasium he used was one reserved for the comitatus. Eventually, all of *WinterStar*'s crew would come through once, and he would have notes enough that he could work with the staff kitchen to do something.

At least he had finally had a chance to meet Ndidi Zikora, the young woman cook from the other kitchen that he would have groomed to take over his spot eventually, were he the commander here. She was junior to her peers in that kitchen, like Ugonna, but in another league for her culinary skills. Ndidi would have been able to find funding to open her own bistro on Genarde, were she planet-bound. Perhaps been good enough to earn her own star in another two decades, when she reached his age.

For now, he was content sharing his recipes with her,

retiring to his cabin at night and translating twenty years of professional kitchen work down onto paper. He was too young to be retiring, but this felt more like training the next generation of cooks, and he had plenty of experience on both sides of that equation.

Before him was lunch. Handmade corn tortillas filled with shredded chicken in a tomato and corn salsa, the former fresh and the latter from cans traded from a recent TradeStation run that had swapped iron and exotic metals for corn and rice, the main grain exports from Viltri. The planet also did beef, but Commander Omezi had taken him seriously on the benefits of chickens, so she had concentrated there instead, only bringing aboard a few tonnes of ground beef for mixing into things, rather than steaks.

Daniel could get many eggs out of a chicken, plus an eventual meal from the meat and another from bone broth. Nobody seemed to mind stew now, but it also wasn't as mundane as had been before. Today's tortillas had been wrapped around shredded chicken and refried beans, doused in a spicy white sauce made from dried habanero peppers, and baked in casserole dishes.

Daniel watched with pride as the comitatus filtered in. Each plate got three to six stuffed rolls, each about the size of one of the taller women's long fingers, and a side of Spanish rice, almost the color of blood because one of the ClanStars had delivered such a bounty of tomatoes and onions last week and he didn't feel like canning sauce until tomorrow.

He planted himself off to one side as the women made their way to the two communal tables and built up a low roar of noise and laughter. Many smiled and a few made gestures he hoped were salutes in his direction.

It was good.

Commander Omezi and Erin Uduik came in together, deep in some discussion that only slowed down as they filled their plates and went to a corner. He counted heads and every woman was present. Daniel took a sip of sweet tea and considered the amount of rice in the main trough. He had a smaller one stashed in the warmer, behind him in the kitchen, against hungry warriors coming back for seconds, but it could also be stashed for something useful tomorrow, depending on his whims.

Silence fell.

It came so abruptly that Daniel was afraid he had gone deaf.

His attention spun back to the room in front of him, and he had the shock of his life.

Almost as one entity, the women rose, meals half eaten and utensils placed silently on the table. Slowly, they shuffled out of the room in perfect lockstep, these women who never did anything as one.

"Hello?" he called, but got no answer.

Not even a nod. Nothing.

Spectre Sixteen was closest to him, so he stepped towards her. Stina Carte, one of the few *Anglos* on the ship, and the only one in the comitatus, her skin a burnished gold so light it reminded him of the snows back on Genarde that nearly burned the eyes to look at some days.

Daniel stepped in front of the woman, trying to get her attention, but those green eyes were focused past him. She didn't even glance down at him, or shove him to the side like Daniel had expected most of the warriors would do. Instead, she slipped to one side and was past him so quickly that all he could do was grab a wrist, expecting a punch or an elbow for his pain.

"Carte, what's going on?" he almost yelled as she used her stronger muscles to drag him forward in spite of setting his feet.

She wriggled like a fish and slipped away from him, but

moved no faster than a mild walk. Daniel jogged after her, following the eerily silent group into the corridor outside, where they walked along single file in no greater order than how they had emerged from the mess hall.

He made his way up the line to where the commander walked. A snap of his fingers in front of that woman's face did nothing more than trigger a blink. He grabbed her wrist, as he had done with Spectre Sixteen, and found out just how strong the woman was when she absently bounced him off a steel wall without even glancing his direction.

Daniel cursed as he shook his head. Rather than get bounced again, he stepped close to the commander and just walked along, studying her.

He made more sound on the deck than the rest of these twenty-three women combined. Spectre Fourteen, Elyl Wardams, was the smallest woman in the comitatus, barely over one hundred fifty centimeters. She was still stronger than Daniel, but he stepped close and kind of sidled sideways to stay in front of her. Wardams was *Spanic*, in skin tone, redder than him in skin and perhaps in hair as well.

Those dark, brown eyes that didn't focus on anything seemed to glow with a strange, inner light, but nothing he could do got any sort of intelligent response out of her, or any of the rest.

He followed the comitatus to a corner, and saw them merge into another line made up of the staff side of the crew, mixing and mingling without any commentary or even sounds. He followed, trying to move silently, unaware of what was going on.

A quiet voice in the back of his head whispered. That was the one that had watched too many horror movies as a child, and offered several for comparison now. It did not make Daniel feel any better when he could not refute the images standing up side by side with the scene before him. Especially as the crowd made their way down a stairwell to where all the Spectre fighter ships and SkyCamels were generally parked on the outer dock.

For a moment, he began to panic at the thought that all of these silent women were about to board the shuttles and fly away, leaving him alone on a haunted starship. Then he heard the sound coming up from below, something remarkably like an airlock hatch opening.

It was the first thing he had heard since the commander and her comitatus fell deathly silent.

But if the whole crew was entranced, who was down there?

And how had they done it?

10

———

Daniel had let himself fall to the very back of the line of women, most of them at least as tall as him and many much bigger. It provided for a strange sort of cover as he willed his feet to move more silently than he ever had before.

Something was happening. Something dreadful.

Down the stairs they had marched, to the outer deck, the one at slightly over one gee of gravity, where the spinning hull looked like a top from the outside.

The Spectre ships were loaded into individual launch tubes after maintenance was completed. The spin of the ship would add that much extra push to get them clear of the ship when they ignited their thrusters, and it freed up a repair deck that ran all the way around the ship's waist.

The commander and what appeared to be her entire ship crew were walking to gather in the large space, facing an airlock where a SkyCamel could land and be drawn inside for unloading.

What had happened to everyone? And why had he been missed?

Daniel moved down a side corridor rather than enter the

space with the women, wishing again that he had a weapon of some sort, even for just the cold comfort it would bring him. Not that he was anywhere near as dangerous as most of the women in the next room, but still.

He should have grabbed a knife.

Daniel made a mental note to find a good Sakimaru knife, the kind sushi chefs used, and keep it in a pocket in the future. Not as good as a butcher knife, but far easier to conceal, and he was almost good as these women would be with it, if he pretended he was boning out a chicken, rather than a man.

The silence was eerie, broken only by the quiet hum of the life support systems pushing air around. Daniel sidestepped a small row of tiny blueberry trees in large pots along the hallway and worked his way towards the bow. The next batch of berries would be ready in about a week, glancing at them.

He was just about to return to his kitchen for the biggest chopper he could find when he heard a voice.

A man's voice. Alone?

Daniel had been the only male aboard the entire ship this morning. Who in the seven hells was this? And how had someone snuck up on the paranoid warrior comitatus of Commander Omezi?

And what had he done to them?

That was the question that left Daniel cold. Frigid and brittle, like any movement he might make would cause him to shatter into sand and dust.

"At last I have found you," the man boomed in a voice that sounded like six people speaking in perfect harmony with a reverb system running behind them.

Daniel froze, like a mouse hearing the owl's striking call.

"You have led me such a merry chase, Commander," the man's voice continued. "System after system, tracking your signals and exhaust, bouncing around the rim of the fools in the Sept Empire like a hunting dog on a short leash."

Wait. You aren't from the Sept?

Who's out there?

What?

Daniel had never left the confines of the enormous Sept Empire until he boarded *WinterStar*. Intellectually, he knew that the political structure centered on the human homeworld was tiny compared to the rest of the known galaxy, but even that part was small. What was a thousand stars, compared to the billions surrounding them?

Daniel pretended to be the kind of mouse he was always hunting in the cupboards as he moved to an open hatch. Turning to face the wall, he pressed himself up against it and slid sideways like molasses pouring on a cold day, hoping that whoever this man was, he was facing the long axis of the room, and that the one or six of them were facing away from him.

One man.

Man?

Maybe.

Bipedal with bilateral symmetry. Arms. Legs. Trunk. Head. Tall boots and heavy gloves in white, while the rest of the clothing was an ugly, neon lime color. No hair on an oversized, bald head with skin that reminded Daniel of a pair of ostrich skin boots one of his cooks had liked to wear everywhere.

The proportions on the man were all wrong, to Daniel's eyes, with legs too long and a head too big for the torso and arms. For the briefest moment, Daniel had to suppress a snicker, as his mind considered the creature to be what you might get if a T-Rex was transformed into a human shape, with those stubby arms competing with an oversized face for silliness.

But he held his silence.

There was only the one person. The creature was facing away.

The crew and the comitatus were facing in such a way that someone might have seen him, if they had mind to do so. Those women's eyes really were glowing now, a golden white utterly at odds with the dark brown eyes of most of them. Those who had been born Mbaysey.

"I have long considered what I might do with an entire vessel of women," the man boomed out in a snarl that left Daniel cold with rage. "And an entire fleet."

Yes, he knew what fantasies most men would have in this situation. Doubly so if the beast was somehow mind-controlling them. Most teenage boys went through and past that phase at some point. Usually about the time they turned thirteen. But those tones reminded Daniel of his own silly and stupid fantasies. And where they had taken him.

The left hand of evil.

With that sort of power you could just shut her mind down while you ravaged her body. Or leave her awake as a passive witness, trapped in her flesh and unable to fight back. When that got boring, that sort of power would probably make it possible to make her participate with an appearance of willingness.

And if you were really a rapist, perhaps make her enjoy it. Become dependent on it.

Daniel saw everything through a red haze as he slid back out of sight. He could still hear the lurid suggestions the beast was making, but it all faded back into a dull roar as Daniel looked around for something he could use as a weapon. There probably wasn't sufficient time to go back up to his kitchen and get the knives he would have preferred.

There. Fire extinguisher. Standard issue on every starship and vehicle repair bay in the Empire. Six in his kitchens, both here and back on Genarde. Compressed foaming agent capable of snuffing out anything merely burning, like hot grease or bread some idiot has forgotten about in the oven. Metal tube in the traditional red older than space flight.

Daniel growled at the tiny voice in his head asking questions. The one that had watched too many horror movies as a child.

Now was not the time. In the background, someone was working his way to the many things he might do with an entire harem of strong, beautiful women at his command.

At his command?

Daniel removed the device from the carrier on the wall and pulled the simple pin holding the trigger grip open. He turned and slid to the edge of the doorway to spy.

Commander Omezi was just finishing stripping nude as the beast watched. Her face was utterly slack with disinterest, telling Daniel that the man was indeed mind-controlling all these women somehow.

"You," the invader pointed at Erin next. "And you."

Iruoma joined *Spectre Two* in removing clothing without a pause or a squawk. There was little noise, so Daniel moved slowly, staring at the back of the beast's head as he stealthfully entered the landing bay. If he could somehow mentally assault the bastard from here, he would have, but the daggers he stared seemed to all fall short.

Seeing three of the amazing warriors nude did nothing to help Daniel's concentration, but this was something none of those women would have ever volunteered, unless someone had a gun pointed at them.

He couldn't see anything in either of the invader's hands, so Daniel wasn't sure how the monster was doing whatever it was. There appeared to be that glow, only because something seemed to be reflecting from flat surfaces, something the same hue as the light emerging from the eyes of the crew.

Daniel gauged his distance and hoped he was close enough. He would only get one chance to do this. He shifted a hair to his left, hoping that the creature had the same sort of right-hand dominance that was common in humans.

Anything for an edge, as he was about to do the second stupidest thing he had ever done. Opening his first bistro still took that cake.

"You next," the man with the short arms pointed at Areen Ojukwu, *Spectre Three*. Alone among the comitatus, Areen had cornrow braids in her hair that went clear down to her shoulders. Daniel had never figured out how she managed to keep them all in a flight helmet, but if they didn't have proper space suits, it probably didn't matter as much. Her skin reminded Daniel of an old, copper Half-Crown. Not the brighter red of a new coin, but an older one that had been out in the galaxy for a while and picked up some dirt and weathering. The kind you could clean up if you approached your task with enough patience and the right touch.

She was also one of the few willing to let a *Rabic* cook try occasionally.

Daniel figured that it was now or never.

"Hey, *connard*," he called in a quiet voice that still rang across the vast silence. "You missed one."

"What?" the monster bellowed in surprise and anger as he turned.

Both hands came up with some sort of frightening glow, but Daniel blasted him in the face with the fire extinguisher, moving patiently up and down from eyes to mouth, crossing the strange, vertical slits in between that were maybe nostrils.

Nobody likes a face full of fire suppressor.

The man doubled over, coughing and gasping, trying to wipe the foam away from his face so he could do something. Daniel had no idea what, and didn't care. If he could do that to all these stubborn women, the invader would have him for lunch, once he could breathe.

Whatever it was, the effect apparently required concentration. Daniel took four steps forward and reversed the grip on the metal tube as Commander Omezi and the others snapped out of their fugue.

"What?" the commander started to ask, but Daniel was focused elsewhere.

He got within reach of the *salaud* and hammered him on the side of the head with his fire extinguisher like he was chopping pork ribs with his favorite cleaver.

The first blow didn't drop the man, so Daniel hit him again. The sound rang out like the bong from a church bell calling a faithful. It was like working in an abattoir and learning to stun cattle. He had visited one, just to make sure he understood how meat was produced, but never actually held the mallet until today.

The third strike drove the invader to his knees. Daniel realized that the creature was no taller than he was now. He had only appeared bigger when he was glowing and monologuing.

Fourth shot broke something. Blood began to spurt. And brains, if they were really greenish pink. Daniel had better reach now. More torque.

The fifth shot crushed the top of the creature's head in and he fell, leaking pink and green fluid onto the deck.

Daniel stood over him, lungs working like bellows making steel. He would need a shower to get the gore out of his hair, but thankfully he was still wearing an apron that could be burned if necessary.

Maybe not even necessary. He might do it just so he never again had to think about what he had just done.

Just in case, Daniel went to one knee, working to stay

out of the pool of spreading blood. A hand on the neck could not find a pulse, if there had ever been one.

He glanced up and realized that he was surrounded by legs. Some of them were bare.

Commander Omezi was standing right in front of him. Utterly nude. Utterly beautiful.

Utterly carnivorous, if he had to classify the look that replaced the glow in her eyes.

"What just happened?" she asked in a cold, tight voice.

"I have no idea," Daniel said between gasps. "But this *branleur* was behind it, and he's dead now."

"How did we get here?" Erin demanded in a hotter voice. "And why are several of us naked?"

Daniel turned to her and let all of his anger loose.

"*Violeur*," he growled, standing so he could kick the rapidly-cooling corpse between them one more time as hard as he could, just for good measure.

"Huh?" she snarled.

"Rapist."

11

———

Kathra didn't have any personal hangups with nudity, but she had to work hard to keep from letting her rage take over now. Glancing right and left, Erin, Areen, and Iruoma were also nude, standing in the middle of the repair deck, surrounded by what looked like the entire crew.

"What happened?" she demanded of the cook that had apparently just saved her life, her command, and probably her entire tribe.

Daniel had a hard time concentrating. His eyes kept going down to the alien on the floor, and had to traverse her and several of her nude warriors in the process. She didn't have the slightest interest in the man, but she also knew that he was having a hard time focusing. Violence and nudity and whatever else.

"You were all eating lunch," the man finally said in a low voice, adding another kick to the corpse as he did.

The eyes came up and focused on hers. Probably the only way such a man could work. They were the weaker gender, after all.

"Everyone went completely silent while I watched," he

continued with a shrug. "You got up and walked out. I followed, but everyone else seemed bewitched and I could not do anything to distract any of you. Eventually, you all ended here, and I heard something, so I snuck to one side to watch."

Another shrug, but the eyes weren't seeing anything now. Erin suddenly thrust a bundle of clothes into her hands and broke the second spell that had fallen over her.

"Everyone to stations," Kathra yelled. "Prepare for battle, but do not launch *The Haunt*. Alert the ClanStars to remain ready to flee. Whatever hit us probably hit them as well."

She pulled a shirt on and that seemed to drag Daniel's mind back to the present with a wry smile. Single man, surrounded by hundreds of women, several of them naked. Every Sept boy's fantasy, perhaps? Around them, the room emptied quickly as crews ran for their stations.

"The *salaud* was in the process of forcing each of you to disrobe for his enjoyment," the cook spat the words out angrily. "You first. Then Erin and Iruoma. He had just selected Areen when I managed to sneak up behind him and empty the fire extinguisher into his mouth. Then I beat him to death with it, I think."

Kathra knelt beside the body and flipped it over with one hand, while the other held a knife poised to stab. Yes, the skull appeared crushed in at this point.

She had not appreciated that the man had that sort of rage inside him, but she supposed fire was what made him a chef in the first place.

The rest would be merely cooks.

The being was a species she had never encountered before. Bipedal, like so many of them. Rough skin that appeared to be scales over flesh, with dermal ridges on the parts of the skull that were still convex, as opposed to the concave parts.

The creature was dressed in a lime-green bodysuit with white boots, gauntlets, and belt. A gem the size of her palm rested at the base of his throat in a chrome and platinum setting and seemed to pulse with some inner fire. She was tempted to order the corpse spaced as is, but she needed to know how he had managed to sneak up on the squadron. How he had gotten aboard her ship.

What the hell he had done that had apparently captured the minds of all the women on this ship, and ignored the one male?

Daniel seemed to be in another realm when she stood again and looked at him. His eyes had gone hooded and face pulled dour and almost glowering. For a man that was generally just tolerated for his skills and occasionally despised for his gender, the man looked like he had taken the entire situation as a personal insult.

What had happened in his younger years that would inspire such a reaction? Kathra knew that he had run a good kitchen. She had agents who had quietly interviewed people who had worked for the man. Few had left the kitchen for anything other than chasing their own dreams, and all spoke of him in high tones.

Apparently he was a good person, in spite of his gender.

"Commander, we have signals from the other ClanStars," a voice echoed hollowly over the space. "Everyone is just waking up from whatever happened and…"

"And what?" Kathra demanded.

She could almost hear the woman gulp before she spoke again.

"And there is a ship off our bow, Commander," she said. It sounded like Kamharida, Spectre Four. "A really big one."

"How big?" Kathra felt her blood run cold suddenly, in spite of the pants and jacket she had managed to pull on.

"It's not a Septagon, but it looks comparable in size,

Commander," Kamharida finally said. "You need to get up here to see."

Daniel looked like a woman falling into shock. She grabbed him by the arm and gave him just enough of a rattle to focus his eyes on her again.

"How did he get in here?" she demanded of the only witness.

No, not only witness. There would be security footage she could watch, once she got the squadron out of the immediate danger.

If she could.

Daniel stopped in thought for a moment and then pointed.

"That airlock," he said.

Kathra nodded to Erin, now dressed, and the woman took off like a gazelle to check. Most of the comitatus had disappeared. If they weren't launching ships, there were other tasks to supervise: engineering, damage control, and bridge, for instance.

Kathra was fully dressed now and started to move, pulling a barely-resisting chef along with her.

"Iruoma, take the corpse to the medbay and guard it," she yelled over her shoulder.

Daniel put up no resistance once he figured out where she wanted him to go. The man needed to work out more if he was going to stay with the Mbaysey, but he didn't complain. Just put his head down and lurched along in her wake gasping.

Up to the inner deck, she had half a dozen warriors with her, all following the cook, as if they might need to pick him up when he fell or surrendered, dragging him along. Except he hadn't. Didn't now. Nearly ran into her until she caught him and stood him upright while they waited for a lock portal to the core to line up.

She thrust Daniel into the gap and followed. The two pieces of the ship rotated slow enough, relative to each other, that she could get the cook headed forward and out of the way while the rest of her warriors followed, half now and half waiting for the next portal.

They would be along shortly. She needed to be on the bridge.

Now.

12

———

Daniel had been up here on *WinterStar*'s bridge once. Just long enough to familiarize himself with the entire vessel, on the off-chance that the comitatus was at action stations aboard rather than in their ships, and he needed to deliver the commander dinner in the middle of combat. Or some other trouble.

Commander Omezi did all the zero gee work, so he just kept himself compact enough that she could do that. He ended up tucked into a corner nearby when they got there, with his feet hooked under an anchoring bar set here to keep landswomen like him out of the way of the professionals, with his one hand holding a bar to keep him still and on beam with the others.

Omezi was at the center of the room, seated in the main station, with four other women, staff side rather than comitatus, around her at their own stations. The rest of the warriors that had followed were staying out of the way, like he was, but doing a much better job at it.

He was a cook, not a zero gee acrobat.

"*Merde*," the commander muttered under her breath.

It took Daniel a second to realize she must have picked that word up from him. It wasn't like his kitchen was exactly safe for children, with hot surfaces and sharp knives, so nobody ever really paid attention to their language.

As long as you were quiet enough that the customers out front didn't hear anything they had never heard before.

He had expected a holographic display, but then remembered that the poverty of the Mbaysey was in the advanced electronics. They could grow fruits and vegetables. Several ClanStars specialized in mining asteroids and comets for raw materials, and *ForgeStar*, *IronStar*, and the two *WaterStars* processed things into useful goods that were swapped at TradeStations for advanced material.

The commander watched the scene on an antique-looking flat screen. He wasn't close enough or tall enough to see what was out there, and the blast shields were currently down.

"Open the shields," she ordered sharply.

Okay, spoke too soon.

Four flat sheets of metal, apparently several centimeters thick, slid out of the way.

Normally, the view out a porthole was deep space. Black and speckled with white dots. Occasionally, as at Wylanne, the Commander would move *WinterStar* close enough to a gas or ice giant planet that you had the most gorgeous views for a few days.

There was a thing out the front window.

Several voices joined his in a plethora of profanities.

He had seen the Septagon. Even studied it a little after they escaped, just because he was curious about a starship that could hold three hundred thousand people or more. That ship had been square lines and regular geometry.

The thing out there was almost close enough to dock,

had someone wanted to. It had an organic look to it that he didn't understand.

"What's it doing?" Commander Omezi called to her bridge crew.

"Nothing," one of the middle two said. "We've been reviewing the logs. It appeared almost on top of us before we had any scan signal. Then we were caught up in whatever happened, locked our stations down, and went out."

"Erin," the Commander had apparently opened an internal channel. "Did you find his ship?"

"There is nothing there, Kathra," the warrior replied in a voice packed full of doubt and nerves.

These women didn't do nerves. That was what made them comitatus.

"What do you mean, nothing?" the Commander snapped.

"There's nothing here," Erin said slowly. "I show that the lock cycled, but there is no record of a ship docking."

"Do you expect me to believe he just flew here?" the woman in charge demanded.

"Until you can explain it better, yes," but that was just Erin being twitchy.

Daniel had no better explanation than anybody else did.

But he did have curiosity. All good chefs did. You had to, in order to not grow stale and boorish, like those old men who had let life slip away from them.

Daniel moved along the rail and got close enough to the window to leave steam on the material as he looked out. It wasn't glass, but it acted close enough.

"*Merde*," he agreed, looking out at the invader's chariot.

If *WinterStar* was a giant, skinny top, spinning forever, and the Septagon a mass of solid geometry, then he would describe this as a turtle.

Daniel didn't serve sea turtle in his restaurant. Hadn't.

But he was familiar with it. This thing reminded him, looking.

An enormous oval shape, like a turtle that had two top shells, curved along a central spine, instead of a curved top and flat bottom. A head stuck out of one end, and six legs that looked vaguely like flippers from the corners and middle. It was even green, although a much darker hue than the color of the creature's costume. The tips of the broccoli's florets, perhaps, rather than the raw stalks.

"Tribal squadron, this is Commander Omezi," her voice drew Daniel's head back around to where the boss was seated like a war goddess. "All ships but *WinterStar* withdraw to the next Concursion. We will be along in a few days, or will send you a message."

That made sense. That *violeur* had been intent on capturing at least all of *WinterStar*'s crew. Perhaps the whole tribe.

Why the crew over there had done nothing since made no sense, but perhaps the invader had been out of touch with them and they were not aware that he was dead? The tribe needed to flee before those invaders over there could do anything to stop them, but the Commander would have to remain behind.

Daniel hadn't really signed on to die aboard a ship that the Sept apparently didn't like, but that turtle out there was nothing that had ever come from a Sept world.

Or any world Daniel could imagine.

Just how big was the galaxy? And who might be out there?

Humans had only been in space for about a thousand years. And even they had not explored much. A dozen other species had already been present, none of them as warlike as the Earthlings, but the Sept Empire was a recent thing, just in the last few centuries.

That had come from somewhere else.

"Is it armed?" the Commander asked her bridge crew.

"I have no idea, Commander," one of the women replied. "We have relied on passive scans only, because if we've all been hypnotized, we shouldn't be pinging her."

"If the tribe flees, they'll figure it out," Omezi said. "Ping him hard enough to tell. Prepare to jump if he does anything at all."

"Stand by."

Daniel found a rail to get a good grip on. *WinterStar* didn't have gravity inducers, so he would be subject to inertia if the ship started to move suddenly. The women around him would probably be fine with being tossed around in zero gee, but he didn't want to be bleeding. He already had enough blood on his apron and in his hair.

If that was blood.

Whatever the fluid was, he still needed a shower soon. He was beginning to stink, but now didn't seem like the time to remind these dangerous women that he was just a cook.

After all, he had just killed a man.

Tattooed psychopaths with knives, and all that.

The bridge beeped like an alarm clock that wasn't taking no for an answer this time. Everyone else tensed, so Daniel hoped that he wasn't about to join that other *branleur* in hell.

"Well?" Commander Omezi demanded.

"Uhm…" came the response.

Daniel did not have a warm and fuzzy feeling. It was like he had fallen through the glass instead of Alice, to be surrounded by doubt and rabbits. Not that he was any better, but these women were supposed to protect him.

Well, protect the tribe, but as long as he was hiding behind their kilts, they would protect him, too. He hoped.

"What?" the Commander followed up.

"The scan did not penetrate the hull of that thing at all, Commander," the woman said.

Daniel made a note to get all four of these women's names later. And figure out their favorite desserts. He had a feeling that he would want to bribe them occasionally, going forward.

"How is that possible?" Omezi said aloud. It sounded rhetorical, but there was nobody who could answer her anyway.

"No reaction from the turtle," one of the other women said.

Good, they saw the same thing he did, a massive, space-going sea turtle. More or less.

"No reaction?" Omezi repeated in disbelief. "How can they not notice?"

"ClanStars are jumping, Commander," the scan operator answered instead. "Space around us is now clear for maneuver."

ForgeStar, *IronStar*, and both *WaterStars* had gone quickly enough. Now there was just *WinterStar* and a gigantic Star Turtle contesting local space. Daniel didn't even know what system the tribal squadron had ended up in, too busy down in his kitchen to worry. Three meals per day for thirty to forty women, depending. Fruit and vegetables to can, jar, freeze dry, or just plain freeze.

A bistro that never even had a First Day off to close.

"Roll us on gyros to bring as many guns to bear as possible," the Commander ordered in a voice that sucked fifteen degrees of warmth out of the room.

WinterStar itself wasn't much larger than the head on that turtle, or one of the fins, and she was getting ready to fight it? Was this woman insane?

No. Not really. Desperate, perhaps. She had convinced the rest of her tribe to give up even a passing connection to the Sept Empire and flee into deep space. They were poor and free, which was apparently a good enough trade for these women.

Not one Daniel understood well enough to have made himself, but he was also a man, and the Sept were a highly patriarchal structure. He could see where all women were generally accorded second-class citizenship.

Plus, the Sept kept slaves. Occasionally *Spanic* and *Anglo*, but more likely *Africans* and *Asians*. Anyone that didn't fit the genotypal mold of the Persian Plateau that had forged the Seven Clans. Even the *Rabic* were accorded honorary citizenship with the Persians. Erin still had the mark of Grandma Ezinne permanently on her face, a barcode used to identify *property*, much like handhelds and personal transports.

Yes, they would fight and die before they surrendered their identity to an outsider. Their *agency*.

"Anything?" Omezi called as the turtle was suddenly lined up along a side of the ship, where presumably defensive turrets could all bear.

Daniel really didn't know how *WinterStar* was armed, either, come to think of it. The central cylinder rotated around the longer core, so perhaps there were guns at both ends and maybe spinning with the body. More questions to ask, although maybe he would let that one go unanswered.

They still didn't entirely trust him, so asking those sorts of questions might raise a red flag or six. A few of the comitatus and crew appeared to suspect him of being the spy that allowed the Septagon to find them several months ago.

If he was, it was because someone was tracking him secretly. He hadn't known that Kathra Omezi was apparently important enough for the Sept to hate. Hopefully he hadn't joined her on someone's shit list, because he had always intended to return to civilization at some point and start over with a new restaurant.

Hadn't he?

Daniel watched the other ship just hang in the darkness, almost looking like a dragon preparing to belch fire at them, but he couldn't remember what his actual plans for the future had been. Go home after a time. Open a bistro. Or maybe just a hot dog stand.

Wasn't that an even bigger challenge?

"Daniel, what do you see?" Omezi's voice suddenly broke him out of squirreling in on himself.

"What?" he fumbled around as he turned to face her, instead of the Star Turtle looming like doom over there.

"What is it that you see, when you look at the ship?" she asked in a slow, careful voice, rather like asking the five-year-old where the cookie in his hand had come from.

"A huge turtle," Daniel said, frantically trying to figure out what she was really asking.

Not that he had ever managed to understand any woman that well.

"And?" she prompted.

"Hanging in space watching us, except he hasn't moved at all," Daniel let the words spill out, hoping someone else could make better sense of them that he could. "Is there anybody over there?"

"Why wouldn't there be?" the woman who appeared to be in charge of the weapons asked.

"Erin said he didn't dock a ship," Daniel turned to look at the others, aware that he probably wasn't supposed to refer to these women by their nicknames, but Erinkansilemi Uduik was too much of a mouthful to pronounce correctly more than one time in three. Especially today. "Someone asked if he just flew over, but there was no suit. If I was going to attack the tribal squadron, I would have brought some crew with me, even if just to keep a stupid cook from ambushing me with a fire extinguisher and beating me to death when I was distracted."

Several someones chuckled.

"What if he had no crew?" Daniel offered.

"What?" Omezi actually, literally stood up to confront him. "A ship that big with no crew? Impossible."

"How the hell would I know what's possible?" Daniel demanded back at her, suddenly aware that he was the third smallest human on this bridge, and the least dangerous, even for having killed someone the most recently. "They haven't reacted to the squadron leaving, have they? Or *WinterStar* lining up to shoot at them. Is there anyone even over there?"

"Ife, open a radio channel and hail them," the Commander ordered, her eyes never leaving Daniel's.

He was plagued by images of hawks and mice. Or tigers and rabbits.

One of the women murmured into a microphone. Daniel held his breath. Others seemed to be doing the same.

"Well?" Omezi demanded.

"Nothing, commander," Ife said quietly. "Not even an automated acknowledgement."

"Has the ship moved at all, relative to us?" the Commander asked in a less violent voice.

Her eyes never left his.

"Negative," one of the other women said. "We are drifting towards its right flank now, but the ship remains facing the spot we were at before."

Kathra Omezi had never struck Daniel as a woman given to wild rolls of the dice. She had always been the careful planner, reacting calmly and intelligently to a situation, rather than emotionally.

Her next words nearly caused him to piss himself.

"Engage thrusters," she said in a hard voice, eyes still

locked on her cook. "Just enough to bring us alongside parallel and then stop. Flip us end for end when you do, so we are facing the same direction as the turtle."

Daniel gulped past a frog that had taken up residence in his mouth when he wasn't looking. There was a smile in her eyes now. He had seen some of his employees get that look when the stress had pushed them to the breaking point. When knives were coming out and you had to throw a bucket of cold water in someone's face to get their attention, right before the rest of the men tackled them and held them down long enough for sanity to return.

"You need to go take a quick shower and change," Commander Omezi smiled at him with lethal edges. "But make it quick."

"Why?"

"You're coming with us."

Somehow, he had known that was coming.

Merde.

13

RATHER THAN HANDLE the leaking corpse, Iruoma had wrapped it in a tarp and carried it over one shoulder inward to the medbay. There wasn't that much blood that had dripped on the deck behind her, but she ordered one of the mechanics to clean it instead of doing the job herself.

Kathra has specifically ordered her to guard the body. That meant not leaving it alone to take care of the mess she had left. Sorry about that.

Unwrapped and laid out in a bed, it was about the size of the cook. And probably weighed about the same.

Bright green and white clothing, where it had not been stained in blood, or whatever the grayish liquid was that was cooling and drying. The medical scanner did a thorough job on the corpse, but could find no match for species, so it wasn't one of the score or so that the Sept had encountered. Nor the trading clans.

Legs like a woman, longer in proportion to the torso than on a man. Short trunk and short arms. Strange, almost glowing gem at the base of the neck. Scales over skin, with a few places where they might have turned into the sorts of horny armor that lizards got.

Iruoma wasn't in the mood to check to see if the pupils were round or slitted. Or something equally weird. It was enough that the machine found no vital signs and was tracking the body as it returned to room temperature.

Someone else would get the privilege of performing an autopsy at some point.

"Iruoma," Kathra's voice came over the interior systems.

"Here," she replied.

"Still dead?" the boss asked, like perhaps there had been some doubt up on the bridge.

"Still dead," Iruoma confirmed. "Med scanner doesn't know what it is."

"Are there any radio signals emerging from the body?" Kathra asked in a strange tone.

"Repeat that," Iruoma said.

"Scan the corpse for communication signals," the Commander ordered.

"Uhm. Stand by."

Iruoma looked around for something that might work. This was a medbay, not a mechanic's shop. She called up the control board for the medical scanner built into the bed and it would do everything she didn't want, so she pulled open cabinets and drawers until she found something she had completely forgotten that they owned.

An electronic Scrutinizer that shouldn't have been left in medbay, so she supposed that someone had gotten hurt on some mission and in the rush to get them here, someone else had forgotten to put the thing back where it belonged. Iruoma checked the log, and made a note to yell at Areen at some point. The Scrutinizer had been in this drawer for almost two years now.

Still, it had enough charge to work today. She held it over the corpse and let the machine work its magic.

Body covered in keratin-like scales. More inside, so it was rather more like a shark or a ray. Light bones, almost birdish. Originally evolved from a quadruped lizard of some sort was the scientific, wild-ass guess from the machine.

Age unknown, with a lot of question marks.

"Weird," she muttered to herself.

"What's that?" Kathra was still listening on the open channel.

"Uhm…" Iruoma pushed a few options and let the device work. "The gem on the chest is a power source of some sort, but banked right now. No radio signals, but I'm reading strange amounts of entropy and decay in what should be a fresh corpse."

"Repeat that?"

"The Scrutinizer I found thinks this is a week-old corpse, Commander," Iruoma replied. "Not an hour dead."

"Recalibrate it."

"I did, Kathra," Iruoma snapped. "Same result."

"*Merde.*"

"*Oui,*" Iruoma fired back, just because she felt like being a shit. They had all started cursing in French because of Daniel Lémieux.

People on the bridge chuckled loud enough for the microphone to pick it up.

"Suggestions?" Iruoma continued.

"Keep a gun handy and stay put with it," Kathra said. "Keep scanning and see what other surprises it has."

"Where are you going?"

"Turtle hunting."

14

Because he had been the one that killed the thing, Kathra made it a point to bring the cook along. Something had kept him separate from the others when the invader had apparently taken over everybody else's minds. That much was obvious from the security tapes she had reviewed.

And Kathra made a note to remember the extra uses of a fire extinguisher in a fight. There was dirty, and then there was *rude*. And she quite approved of rude.

"*Haunt*, hold here," Kathra called as the ships circled the alien ship like a school of sharks.

Nothing had changed about the thing. It still resembled a Star Turtle, as Daniel had remarked. The bow was still pointed at exactly the spot that it had before, where *WinterStar* had been resting during the...

Could she call it an attack? Attempted kidnapping, perhaps? Something. Enough for a lethal response from the least dangerous person on her crew.

The Star Turtle lurked there in the darkness. If it had any weapon turrets aboard, none had emerged to track any of her hunters.

From here, the top and bottom were both slightly curved. Like half the curvature of the top had been stretched into the bottom, leaving the legs emerging from exactly the centerline, rather than along the bottom, like a sea-going reptile.

Kathra brought the nose of her craft around and triggered just enough thrust to push her aft relative to the thing. The ass end looked like a turtle as well. Flippers from where it would have had corners, were it rectangular. Stubby tail like a whip, trailing. No place where engine nozzles emerged from the carapace.

How in the nine hells did it get around without thrusters? Even the Septagon had engines on the aft facing. Seven of them across, of course.

Did this thing swim?

Worse, she had hoped that moving *The Haunt* around would allow the targeting computers to perhaps do a better job at scanning the interior of the creature than *WinterStar*'s eyes. But every scan reflected off the skin of the thing.

She could see the shape. Measure its dimensions in perfect detail, but nothing penetrated.

"Erin, tell me again about the airlock," Kathra called over the team line.

"I triple-checked the logs, Commander," her wingwoman said in a tired singsong. "There was nothing that docked and triggered the outer housing. He got in and pressed the inside panel to close the airlock, like we do when we're in a suit."

"He wasn't wearing a suit," Kathra said absently. "How did he get from here to there?"

"He flew," Daniel muttered low enough that the mic probably didn't pick it up. "But where was his suit after he arrived? Or is that the gem?"

"What was that?" Kathra cut the comm so she could have a private conversation with the lethal chef.

"How did he take control of all of your minds?" Daniel asked in a stern voice. "He was doing something, and it required concentration, because once I hit him, he lost it. Was it the gem? Iruoma said it seemed to be a power source of some sort, but banked. Was he controlling it? Was that how he did these things?"

Kathra opened the radio again and checked her transmission power.

"Iruoma," she said simply.

"Here, Commander."

"Take the Scrutinizer and scan the gem specifically," Kathra ordered. "How much power is there contained it in?"

"Stand by."

"*Merde!*" the woman continued a few moments later.

"Talk to me," Kathra said calmly.

"There appear to be two sources of…something, Kathra," Iruoma said in a voice suddenly much shakier than normal. "The gem itself is a massive sink of power, but there's a second something behind it, I think. Like the gem is resting on the platinum housing and a second one is contained in the metal somewhere. The gem contains much power, but is not doing anything. Whatever is behind it is much brighter on the scanners, but not emitting external signals I can detect."

"What's that even mean?" Daniel asked, apparently loud enough for the microphone to pick up."

"The signals are only visible if I almost touch the scanner on the thing," Iruoma said. "If I'm even forty centimeters away, they disappear."

"The gem and the frame are communicating?" Kathra asked.

"Maybe," Iruoma said. "Never seen anything like it."

"*Haunt*, return to the ship," Kathra decided. "There's

nothing more out here we can learn, and if it's not going to pick a fight, we won't either."

Kathra brought the nose of *Spectre One* around and began a burn. She was the farthest away of everyone right now, so she'd be the last one home, but they couldn't start without her.

Whatever it was they were doing next.

15

HE WAS GETTING BETTER at spaceflight. Daniel hadn't even felt queasy once on this flight. Granted, it had been a short jaunt, just out to circle the turtle once and then home, but he hoped he was getting the hang of flying in zero gravity.

After all of these shenanigans were done with, Kathra Omezi would either get rid of him quickly, or keep him around for a while.

Daniel wasn't sure which thought frightened him more.

They had landed. Always an interesting chore, where the Commander slid her ship up close against the hull on their left side, the ship's outer hull itself rotating away from them in such a way that a pilot had to hit her mark just right the first time, or either chase it around the trunk of the ship or wait for the dock to circle 'round again.

A quick burst of maneuvering thrusters and *Spectre One* fell into the docking cradle on her left side. A thump as two arms engaged and held the ship, and then a quick rotation on the nose axis so that down was down as the two entities became one. And he didn't even think he would vomit this time.

Daniel wondered why they didn't just dock with the cockpit looking up, and hadn't thought to ask one of the women. The Commander didn't seem like she wanted frivolous questions today.

One roll, from laying on your right side to sitting upright, like a really good drunk, and the Commander powered her ship down. Daniel waited until he heard her unbuckle things before he did the same. She was much faster and more experienced at this than he was, but there was precious little space aft of the cockpit. Just a small kitchenette and a bathroom, plus the ladder that would descend from the ceiling.

If he moved too quickly now, he'd be standing on her shoes while she tried to cook, always a recipe for disaster. Or at least an elbow in the ribs.

Instead, he knelt on his chair, facing rear and watched her climb out of sight before he went after her. Up the ladder and into the belly of *WinterStar*, or something. It always felt like emerging from the sewers, to go from the crowded dimness of a Spectre ship into the well-lit, curved hull of the flight deck.

They had only been out there for perhaps thirty minutes, so he didn't know if the mechanical crew would need to pull the ship inside where they could work on it, or just leave it there for now. Or maybe they would move it over to one of the flight tubes for quick launch while he was working inside.

Hopefully, he could go back to his kitchen now that they were back. Lunch was getting cold and sticking to pans if nobody from the other kitchen had been tasked with doing the cleanup that should have been mostly his responsibility.

"Come with me," the Commander said as he emerged into the light like a groundhog looking for his shadow.

Six more weeks of something, that much was sure.

Daniel fell into her wake, along with several other women from other Spectres, and climbed two decks to end up in medbay.

"Ew," the noise came out of his mouth as soon as he stepped across the threshold.

"Tell me about it," Iruoma nodded with just as sour a look on her face. "Got the fans turned up full blast, too. What did you do to him?"

"Beat the *salaud* to death," Daniel said as a wall of rotting something filled his nostrils.

In the kitchen, that smell was something that had gone so utterly rancid that you burned the box it came in and hosed yourself off with ammonia.

What the hell had happened?

The creature looked like somebody had attached a vacuum pump to a beachball and deflated it. Skin wrinkled into the sorts of folds you got when you stayed in the tub to finish the book instead of doing the reasonable thing and going to bed.

And the smell…

Daniel was a chef. He was used to strange smells, but death on this scale wasn't one of them. Fortunately, several of the women behind him were doing even worse.

Only Iruoma and the Commander looked phlegmatic at this point. But they would.

"Talk to me," Omezi drew herself up to her incredible height and pulled Daniel right up next to her.

Nothing like looking a woman in the shoulder.

Iruoma pulled out a small box. Maybe thirty centimeters tall, twenty wide, and about as thick as a pack of cigarettes. He could see a screen on the top and a bunch of antennae and stuff sticking out the bottom. She pushed a button and the machine happily beeped to itself for a moment.

The screen changed, but he was at a bad angle to read what was on it.

"How is that possible?" the Commander asked.

"You tell me," Iruoma answered. "The curves have just about followed the projections over the last hour, so whatever is happening is predictable."

Daniel found both women staring at him. All the women stared at him, including the handful out in the hallway where the air was presumably not as foul.

"What?"

Iruoma showed him the screen. He spent several seconds just figuring out what it was telling him, as he had never used something like this. Way more complicated than the devices he had used in his kitchen to judge the internal doneness of a Beef Wellington or a Steak Tartar.

"Does this say he's been dead for two months?" Daniel looked up at Iruoma in total confusion.

"It does," she smiled grimly. "And that's about what a corpse smells like in a closed system, if it doesn't dry out over that time."

Huh.

He turned to the corpse. They apparently expected him to have an expert opinion on an alien species nobody had ever encountered before. Presumably on the basis that Daniel had been the one who killed it.

Didn't that mean it was someone else's job to clean it and cook it? Wasn't that how it was supposed to work?

Kathra Omezi didn't look like a woman in need of a moment of levity, so he kept the joke to himself.

Dead. That much was obvious. Daniel hadn't gotten a good look at the face before. Two eyes, nose slits, mouth. Mostly normal-ish. Holes on the sides that looked like ears without the ears. Scales everywhere.

He had never had to skin a snake before cooking it, so

Daniel reached out and plucked a scale just to see what happened. It came away well enough.

Waxy. Not rough like fingernails. More fishlike, maybe.

He had lots of experience with dead fish.

Skull smushed in. Brains leaked out. Blood mostly dried. Body room temperature.

"What did you say?" Daniel asked, turning back to the Commander.

"Nobody said anything." She looked at him with almost a crossness to her eyes.

"I could have sworn…" Daniel let himself fall silent to listen. "There."

"Nothing," Omezi's scowl had deepened.

"Hey, I got something," Iruoma was peering at the scanner device in her hands. "Normally I only got that frequency when I'm standing where you are, but something blipped the system louder this time."

Daniel was an entire step backwards before his brain engaged. He bumped both women lightly with his shoulder blades as he did.

"What are you doing?" the Commander asked.

"Standing over here," he said simply. "She couldn't pick up a signal unless she was right on top of it. Then she could, clear over here, when I got too close. Ergo, don't get too close."

"Step over there again, Daniel," the Commander said in a quiet voice that seemed to promise untoward pain if he didn't.

He studied her eyes, weighing a black eye and a concussion against whatever the dead guy wanted to do to him. Even dead.

He wasn't going to win this round. Not with her. Never with her.

Daniel took a deep breath and kind of sidled closer to the bed with the dead guy on it.

"Anything?" the Commander asked behind him.

"Nothing," Iruoma said.

"Do it again, Daniel," Omezi ordered.

"Do what again?"

"Whatever it was you did before," she snapped.

What had he done before?

Studied the dead guy. Held his breath shallow and breathed through his mouth so he didn't have to smell it as much. Plucked a scale off the jawline to see what it was.

Touch?

Merde.

Touching the months-old corpse causes it to do something?

Daniel glanced back, but Commander Omezi was apparently reading his mind, because she had drawn her pistol and was holding it tight against her side, in case she needed to shoot something in close quarters.

Hopefully, a zombie and not a chef.

Daniel nodded and gulped. Twitchy fingers reached out and just poked the neck of the thing this time. He didn't trust that his nerves were up to actually doing fine work right now, and he didn't have a knife to get a larger piece of skin to work with.

"There," Iruoma said. "It spiked again."

Yes. It had. He had heard it.

Like someone had opened the door to a loud room for a second, letting a previously-silent space fill with one echo of noise.

Because Omezi had a gun in her hand, Daniel went to his left, clear to the bottom of the bed so she could shoot the zombie, and not the chef. At least not accidentally.

Silence now.

"Touch it again," Iruoma said.

"Absolutely not, madam," Daniel dug in his heels. "You do it."

"Daniel?" Commander Omezi had her attention focused on him, but not the gun.

Not yet, anyway.

Her voice was softer this time. Inquisitive.

"I heard it," he offered.

There didn't appear to be a vocabulary to encompass the sound.

"Heard what?" she asked, gun rock steady and pointed at his heart.

He would have done the same, so Daniel didn't begrudge her that. Hell, he might have already fired by now, but that was why she was *The Commander*, and he was just her personal chef.

Daniel licked his lips and searched for a word.

"A cocktail party in another room," he finally said, about the time the two women were starting to fidget.

"What?"

"The noise," he tried to explain.

It was like explaining blue to a woman born blind.

"What noise?"

"When I touched him, I heard something like a group of voices in another room," Daniel said. "Voices, but the words weren't clear. White noise, but people speaking."

"And?"

"And you touch it now," he could feel the edge of hysteria wake up and look around.

Kathra Omezi fixed him with that hunter's stare for long enough that he did begin to twitch. Not bad, but not good.

Oh, so not good.

This might be what a heart attack felt like. Good thing he was in the medbay and could fall into one of the other three beds. As long as he didn't mind sleeping with a zombie.

Maybe he'd just stagger back to his kitchen and pass out there. Anything to get away from that smell.

And those sounds.

Kathra Omezi was *The Commander* of the Mbaysey. Bad-ass warrior and leader.

Daniel watched doubt creep into her eyes.

Not much, but that panicked him even worse than the thought of zombies did.

His breathing got shallow and coarse.

"Okay," she said, nodding towards him in acknowledgement that they had all just found one of his absolute borders.

Everybody needed to know how far down the path they could go when dealing with zombies, right?

He watched her step into the spot he had been standing before. Saw her left hand come up, the one without the gun in it, and poke the dead guy on the chin with her weapon all set to make him more dead if he moved.

"Anything?" she asked.

"Nothing, Kathra," Iruoma said.

She turned back to him with cold, black eyes.

"Daniel, I need you to touch it one more time, just to be sure," she coaxed, staring down at him like a squirrel gone rabid. "Then you can leave. I have a theory."

Oh, lovely. Now we're going to be scientific, woman?

But he didn't say that aloud. Tried not to even think it too hard, afraid she might hear the voices in his head, like he had apparently heard the dead guy's.

Still, the worst she could do right now was shoot him. Was that a better outcome than the sound?

Toss up.

Daniel tried to get his heart rate back down to only insane. It didn't want to cooperate, either.

His hands wouldn't stop shaking. Neither would his eyes, but he could blink fast enough and they sort of behaved.

She stepped back as he continued around the bottom of the bed and ended up across the dead guy from all the women.

That was how it felt right now. This impossible moat of a dead guy separating him from the place that had been a happy life five minutes ago.

Daniel tried to breathe. Tried to pretend that nothing was wrong. That the dead guy with the crushed-in skull wasn't going to open his eyes and smile if Daniel touched him again. Wasn't going to suddenly sit up and do whatever dead rapists with mind control rays did when the Devil decided he didn't want the competition and sent them back from hell to walk the lands of the living.

Daniel stared at the other cold, black eye staring back at him. The one attached to twelve centimeters of barrel and a small particle beam emitter that was capable of knocking him clear over the bed behind him and tumbling his silly ass up against the far wall like a fire hose might.

Dead breath. Death Before Dishonor, or whatever these warrior women told themselves when things got too **REAL**.

He reached out a shaking hand and waved it at the corpse.

Nothing bit him.

More breathing. Less shaking.

You mastered chef school, you nitwit. You can do something so simple as poking a corpse, damn you.

He reached out a finger. Prodded the thing's cheek with it.

Listened to the voices suddenly erupt in his head:

screaming, ranting, laughing, telling sea stories and dirty jokes.

Somebody screamed. Probably him, but he couldn't be sure.

Darkness claimed him mercifully.

16

—————

Rather than leave him in medbay, which was probably the smartest option, Kathra had carried the chef back to his own cabin personally, once they were sure he was still alive, apparently functioning, and had merely passed out.

She and Areen had stayed with the male.

The look on his face, right there at the end, had been comparable to what she might have expected had she handed him a butcher's knife and ordered him to cut off his other hand.

His scream had been what she might have heard had he actually done it.

Iruoma had send Areen after another Scrutinizer with a snide commentary about not losing this one, and remained behind in medbay to watch the corpse of her piratical invader turn into a desiccated mummy. Erin was up on the bridge.

Kathra and Areen pulled chairs into the small sleeping quarters that she had assigned Daniel and waited, watching him from the side. The new Scrutinizer had been programmed to detect the energy the corpse had given off when Daniel had touched it, but Kathra could find no traces in the man now.

The corpse had stopped emitting anything as soon as Daniel collapsed to the deck.

Iruoma and Elyl were both armed and watching it. And each other, just in case, but her theory said they would be safe. For now, anyway, and that was all she could ask.

Tomorrow was always tomorrow's problem. Today was enough of a risk.

"Is he going to be okay?" Areen asked, flipping her dreads back out of the way with a nervous habit.

"I hope so," Kathra offered.

Areen was one of the few women in the crew that didn't mind the touch of a male occasionally, and Kathra knew they had been involved a time or two. She had not heard anything negative about the experience, so she hadn't intervened.

"Hope, Kathra?" Areen asked, eyes hooded and fierce.

"When he wakes, we will know more," the Commander said, as definitively as she could.

"I have never heard any creature make a sound like that," Areen murmured, more to herself than to her commander, it seemed.

"And I as well," Kathra said.

"Why did you make him do it?" Areen asked.

"Partly, to test a theory," Kathra replied simply. "Would he be woman enough to actually do it. But also to see if gender had anything to do with why he escaped the first time."

"Any doubts now?" Areen asked her with a harsh, sarcastic face.

"None," Kathra admitted. "Hopefully his mind survived."

"Survived?"

"You heard his description," Kathra fixed her gaze only

briefly on the warrior before returning to the chef. "Voices. The other Scrutinizer went almost off the scale when he touched it the third time. Nobody knows what it might have been, and the device more or less threw up its hands and walked away, but there was absolutely something there. My fear now is that we grounded something into Daniel's mind, like you touching a live wire accidentally."

"Oh," Areen's voice got small. "What if we killed him?"

"Then I own that, Areen," Kathra replied simply. "It was my decision and my order. Hopefully he'll forgive me for it instead of demanding that we end his contract and put him down on a TradeStation somewhere to get home on his own."

"Would he do that?" Areen tore her eyes off Kathra to study the unconscious man laying between them.

Kathra shrugged.

"Nothing in his contract required him to do what I ordered him to do, just as nothing demanded that he beat a pirate to death, Areen," Kathra said. "This male has shown unsuspected depths and talents, but I don't know if I pushed him too far. It was necessary, but it might have been too much."

"I hope he stays."

"And I," Kathra agreed. "I've known few enough women with his courage."

"Then let's not do that again, please?" Daniel groaned in a voice that sounded like the surface of an asteroid.

She looked closely and watched one eye open a slit and then slam shut again.

"Ow."

"Too bright?" Kathra asked.

"Yes," the chef replied in a quiet voice.

Kathra reached over and killed the overhead light, leaving only the normal night lights you needed inside a steel box in deep space. The room plummeted into near total darkness.

"Thank you," he whispered.

"How much did you hear?" Kathra asked.

"Just barely enough," he murmured. "God, my head hurts. What happened?"

"You tell me, Daniel," Kathra said. "I watched you touch the corpse. The readings went off the charts, and then you screamed and passed out. We brought you down to your cabin and Areen and I have been waiting for you to wake up."

"I was drowning," he said, voice still only barely above a whisper. "But instead of water it was sound. Voices everywhere. Hundreds of them. Maybe millions. Clawing at my mind, demanding I let them in. Then darkness."

"How are you now?" Kathra asked, aiming the Scrutinizer at the man and scanning him against the unconscious baseline.

Most readings similar. Heart rate elevating as she watched. Body temperature fluctuating.

"My head feels like someone used it to hammer nails into concrete," he said. "I'm cold. My eyes are incredibly sensitive to light. Is that thing still dead?"

"Last I checked, yes," Kathra said.

"Could you check again, please?"

Kathra nodded rather than argue. She would need him calm and cooperative right now, in spite of him being a mere man, the kind of creature prone to madness or whimsy.

"Iruoma, what's your status?" she opened a line to the medbay and asked.

"He's nearly dried out, from the scanner reading," the woman's voice came back quickly. "Smell has almost disappeared as well. How's Daniel?"

"Awake and complaining of a headache," Kathra shared a

smile with the chef. "I'll bring him up when he's ready to walk."

"Works for me."

Kathra heard the click of the line closing.

"Daniel?" she asked, sliding her chair back as he seemed ready to at least sit up.

She could always send Areen for a painkiller if he couldn't walk, just like Ndidi was already preparing to cook everyone dinner with him out of circulation.

She watched him take a deep breath and turn sideways off the bed, feet down and turning to sit upright like he was afraid his own head might fall off if he moved too quickly.

"Wow," he murmured.

"Too much?" Kathra asked.

"Head hurts. Stomach is reminding me we missed lunch. What time is it?" He looked around.

"Ndidi is cooking everyone dinner now," Kathra reassured him. "All you have to do is relax and recover."

"Oh," he said, snapping himself up onto unsteady feet as she rose, hands out to catch the man if he fell. "I think I can do that."

17

———————

Silence, mercifully.

Daniel had dreamt of cacophony. Endless waves of voices, most of them not even human. Hands reaching out and just on the verge of touching his skin but falling short.

Immense age. Millennia. Perhaps longer. That was what the creature was.

He stopped walking so suddenly that Areen had a hand on his shoulder and another on his hip, expecting him to pitch over face first onto the deck. He stared blankly up at her and blinked.

"Urid-Varg," he whispered.

Even over the sound of his heart pounding, Daniel heard Kathra Omezi draw her pistol. Probably centered on the back of his head.

That would make it all better, probably.

"What?" Areen asked, dropping contact and stepping back just far enough and to one side that his brains might splatter on her, but the beam would probably miss.

Assuming the Commander shot him center mass right now.

"That thing had a name," Daniel forced himself to stand perfectly still. "Urid-Varg."

"How do you know that, Daniel?" the Commander's voice was as cold as deep space.

He moved so slowly that they might think he was melting rather than turning, but today was already off the scales for weird, if he could manage to survive it.

It took him nearly two breaths to meet her eyes, intimately aware of the particle cannon in her hands.

"He's not dead, I think," Daniel whispered.

His eyes found a spot off to one side, as though he could see through all the intervening bulkheads to where the creature was dead.

"Not dead?" she demanded sharply.

He could also see her hand tightening on the grip of the thing that would kill him shortly. Maybe. Hopefully.

"There's more than one of them in there," he tried to explain. "Maybe all of them."

"All of who?" Areen asked.

Her voice sounded less likely to kill him than the Commander, so Daniel turned to her instead. They had been intimate twice, but that just meant that she knew where he was ticklish, not that she would protect him now.

But she might listen.

Daniel took a deep breath and searched all the languages he knew.

"It has mental powers," he said. "Had. This Urid-Varg. That was how he did what he did. But the bodies grew old, so he took new ones. I think. Rode them, like one does a horse or a skywyrm. Except he owned their minds as well as their bodies."

"Does he own you?" Kathra Omezi rasped.

"I don't think so," Daniel offered. "I got the impression

that being killed surprised him, so he wasn't ready for a new host."

"Host?" Omezi asked. "Like a parasite?"

"That's what he is. Was. Something," Daniel blinked too rapidly, but the air in here was making him faint. "A parasite. Sitting in his tower, watching each of his victims grow old and die until he takes a new one."

"How do you know this?" Omezi demanded harshly.

"I don't know," Daniel pleaded with her. "It's in my head, but he's not. At least I don't think he is. He almost woke up, but I passed out. Screaming, I think."

"Screaming," Areen agreed from off his right flank.

"And now?" Kathra Omezi asked.

"There are a thousand other men in that gem," Daniel said. "Beings. Minds. All the ones he has captured and ridden over the centuries."

He put a hand to his forehead, where it felt like Athena was trying to bash her way out with the pommel of a sword.

"I could really use a painkiller, or a drink," he said, unsure if he was going to his knees, or just collapsing.

One hand found a hallway wall and that seemed like a good idea. Cold transmitted itself up his arm. Kept the darkness at bay.

Daniel blinked. Blinked again. Finally registered where he was standing.

It was as though all emotions had been standing patiently behind a glass wall as thick as he was tall, as the wall slowly slid back and let them in.

"I know how to kill the *salaud*," he whispered, eyes lighting up. Maybe he was angry finally.

Kathra Omezi hadn't moved, a statue of Artemis carved in onyx. Except her bow was a pistol. And he was about to be turned into an ass. A real one, and not just the one he had been accused of being more than once.

Areen was behind him somewhere, probably lining him up for a long knife to the kidneys.

How the hell had they gotten here? And why me, you branleur? Enculer!

"Daniel?" Omezi asked as he got himself under control.

"He's in his tower, calling my name," he said quietly. "Demanding I come rescue him so he can ride me. Use me to reconquer a galaxy that has completely forgotten about him today."

"How do we stop him?" Kathra asked. "Kill him?"

Daniel drew a bottomless ocean of air into his lungs, trying to drive out the taint of brimstone.

"Iruoma needs to use a waldo or something," he said. "Nobody dares touch that gem except me. And I don't dare, either."

"Why not one of us?" Kathra asked.

"It's gendered," Daniel tried to explain. "Male. Tomcat. A female touching it would be…disrupted. Ended. Almost like he was, and almost as fast. Not even tongs will work."

"Maintenance robot?" Areen asked.

Daniel spun to face her, watching the woman step half a stride back as her hands came up defensively. Her blade was pointed at his right eyeball.

"Yes," he gasped, freezing in place. "That would work. Can you get one into the medbay, or do we need to very carefully drag him somewhere larger?"

"Why?" Omezi demanded.

"He's in his tower, but we can burn the moat bridge," Daniel found himself explaining.

The words barely made any more sense to him than they apparently did to the women, but he could see the entire thing in his head.

If he trusted his own mind right now.

Hopefully, none of the voices had managed to grab hold.

Or he could just ask the Commander to shoot him now. She would do that for him. Might not even realize what a favor it would be.

"Oh, I know," she smiled suddenly. "But I won't."

Daniel watched in shock as she holstered her pistol and stood straighter.

"Huh?" he asked.

"You're muttering out loud, Daniel," she replied. "One continuous monologue that is absolutely a chef from Genarde and not an alien creature."

"Oh."

Oh.

He remembered to breathe.

"I'm scared," he admitted.

He could do that. All of these women were warriors born and proven, and already considered *maleness* to be a much weaker gender. They wouldn't be insulted by male fragility.

"It's okay, Daniel," Kathra Omezi said. "We'll protect you. Let's get to the medbay and take a look at things."

Another breath. Less brimstone. Maybe more air. Less screaming in his head, like someone had loosened a band squeezing his eyeballs backwards into his brain.

He just had to put one foot in front of the other. Make his way to medbay and confront an undead, psychic vampire that had already decided Daniel Lémieux would be his next victim.

Piece of cake. Right?

18

———

Erin looked around the crowded medbay with a jaundiced eye. Daniel refused to even set foot inside the room, standing instead out in the corridor with the hatch locked open where he had a view. Areen had been ordered, by Daniel himself, to knock him unconscious if he started acting weird.

Nobody had a good definition of *weird*.

Erin really couldn't argue with any of them, though, after all she had heard.

Kathra and Iruoma were on the side of the bed closer to the hatch. Armed and keyed up for violence.

Erin was at the foot of the bed, out of the direct line of fire if violence happened, but close enough to the robot on her left to control it verbally and keep a close watch on everything. With a knife in her hand in case the dead thing on the bed in front of her stopped being dead.

They could have fit more of the comitatus in here, but this left everybody space to maneuver if things got strange. Stranger. Eight more of the women were out in the hallway, prepared for whatever Kathra thought might happen. Or

Daniel, but his explanations made even less sense that Kathra's.

At least Kathra's instructions were easy. Kill it if it moved. Take Daniel down alive.

If possible.

The maintenance robot was an upright bollard on treads, like an old-fashioned, four-sided column about a meter and a half tall. Magnets in the treads could be locked to hold it to the outside of the ship if they couldn't pull a Spectre into a bay for repair easily. A dozen arms of different sizes could be deployed out from the trunk to do anything from lifting a heavy piece of steel to soldering a pocket vox.

"System, come live," Erin commanded.

The bot lit up and rotated its head once clockwise to measure the room. The brains were in the trunk, so the head part was just a pair of oversized optical sensors with big, glass lenses like chameleon eyes, moving independently of each other.

"Ready," the bot's voice said in a calm, mechanical voice.

They had once considered reprogramming all the bots to sound like women, but it was easier to differentiate voices inside a repair space if they hadn't, so they didn't.

"Extend arm number four for grasping," Erin commanded.

Daniel had explained it all to her, but he was also on the soft edge of hysterical right now, so she was only doing it his way for now. She had other options handy.

One of the medium-sized arms came out, ending in a flat hand with four fingers arranged zygodactylly, like the feet of a bird facing each other two and two.

"Identify target," Erin continued. "Power source on the body in front of you, at the top of the torso. White light. Platinum setting."

"Target identified," the mechanical voice replied.

"Scan the target for attachments," Erin said.

A second hand deployed, telescoped up to nearly the ceiling, and then looked down. Erin was reminded of a scorpion's tale.

"Target embedded in organic frame," the bot said. "To a depth of seven-sixteenths."

Stupid machine had been stolen originally from some mechanics in the Uwalu system before Kathra had traded for it. Hadn't been worth the trouble to reprogram the stupid imperials back to standard metrics that the rest of the civilized galaxy used now.

Seven-sixteenths? So roughly eleven millimeters? Must have carved away bone at the top of the keel and replaced it with this thing.

Erin idly wondered if any of this tech was somehow organic, rather than mechano-electrical. Be a bitch to fix everything if that bastard had his own physics on top of everything else.

"Detect life signs," Erin ordered the dumb bot.

Might as well get it locked in now that the thing was deader than a white dwarf.

"No life signs detected," the bot responded. "Anomalous power source noted."

"Daniel?" Erin called across the space. "Tower, moat, village?"

"More or less," he called back in a shaky voice.

She suspected they were going to have to get the man drunk later, just so he could sleep. That, or hit him with enough drugs to drop a moose in its tracks.

"System, scan the gem and the setting as separate entities," Erin said aloud. "Confirm."

Or something. Daniel was having a hard time just standing still. Asking him to do orbital geometrics was probably more than he had in him today. And Kathra wanted it done now for reasons she hadn't explained.

Didn't have to. She was *The Commander*.

The gripper arm moved forward, over the creature's chest, and then turned on an elbow to point at the thing's head from just above his belly button. Assuming it had one.

The square, blunt fingertips had lights on the ends. And other things. Those came live.

"Confirmed," the bot said. "Setting contains the gem, but does not intrude into its volume."

Huh. Just like a regular gem, if you wanted a glowing, white diamond as far across as her palm and almost as thick as her hand. Set in platinum, but *ForgeStar* routinely found interesting metals to smelt down into bars as the tribal squadron mined the shattered remains of proto-planets in uninhabited systems. Platinum didn't impress Erin, except that with a little rhodium and some chrome, it would retain a mirror-polish for an *inordinately* long time.

"Daniel?" Erin called.

"It's not really a gem," he said with a shrug in his voice. "Or rather, expect a hardness rating of about sixteen and the ductility of good steel."

Was that even possible? But then, was any of this?

"System, use a wedge to separate the gem from the setting," Erin commanded the thing.

Another arm came out as the first gripper rotated over and above the stone. At least if the dead thing woke up now, he'd be more or less pinned in place by the bot's arms.

Long enough for one of comitatus to kill it.

The second arm ended in a powered wedge. Just the sort of tool you needed to pry open something that had gotten slammed shut too hard by a rough landing or wild-ass maneuvering to avoid someone flying the wrong way.

Erin glanced over at Iruoma and watched the other

woman's eyes dilate slightly with blush and look down, as they shared a rude memory.

Gripper hand took hold of the gem. It wasn't round, but maybe a square with enough facets to make it look round. She didn't do stones, so she wasn't up on all the nomenclature of the things. Didn't matter, either.

Get a good handle. Pull. Slip a jimmy in and twist slightly.

Sure enough. The second hand entered at the bottom and tapped itself right into the tiny gap where the stone was resting on the setting.

Erin listened to the hydraulics step up as the machine pushed. Or pulled. Tried to open its hand.

The gem started to glow internally.

"Daniel?" she called, feeling her hand drop onto a blade pommel automatically.

"This is why we needed the robot," he yelled back. "It would be inside your head right now issuing orders. Or maybe just killing you."

What a wonderful thought.

Erin checked her blade, held in a knife-fighter's grip in her right hand. Kathra had a pistol, in case she needed to knock the bastard across the room.

Erin didn't say anything to the robot. It would continue until it succeeded, or something broke. She didn't know how much pressure that would require, but she had seen this bot lift a corner of a Spectre off a landing skid to repair it.

It torqued at the gem as she watched, but nothing was happening.

No, that wasn't true.

Erin had the impression that the gem was somehow fighting back. Hopefully it wasn't the corpse deciding to not be dead anymore.

"System, scan the corpse for other power sources," Erin said on a whim.

She wasn't the least bit prepared for the response. Stupid bot had a beam splitter for marking things with a laser when humans needed to see where to work or weld. It came on now, painting the corpse.

The body was wearing a hoodless, green onesie, with a white stripe, about ten centimeters wide, that ran down his chest from the gem to his belt buckle. The belt was white. It connected to white stripes down the outsides of both legs. Both boots were white. Another white stripe went north from the gem and down the tops of both shoulders, along the outside of the arms to white gloves somewhere between what you wore to the opera and what you used when welding.

Everywhere that the creature had white, the robot's laser was painting pulses of light, like it was a circuit connecting everything. Looking closely, she couldn't tell if those parts were glowing all by themselves, or that was just the laser.

Any twitch over there and she would start hacking.

At least the rest of the crew was cursing under their breaths as well so she wasn't alone there.

Still, the bot should have succeeded by now. The damned thing was likely to break itself if she didn't intervene soon. But it was a bot. They'd just have it fix itself, or take it to one of the other ones for the work.

Something popped.

Erin saw a flash of light so bright she thought she was blind. A pulse of energy seemed to push her backwards like a wind on a planet was supposed to do.

She blinked furiously, wiping her free hand across eyes suddenly running with excess tears.

Damned corpse hadn't moved. But it had *changed*.

It had been deflated before. Now there was nothing but a

mummified skeleton. Skin that looked like leather left out in a desert for a century of sun. The bodysuit hung loosely where it had been taut before.

One hand slid to the side and a glove dropped off a mummified hand to fall loudly on the deck, nearly causing Erin to pee in her flight suit and start stabbing. At least it wouldn't go down her leg if she had.

The gem had separated from the platinum setting finally. The arm had moved about fifteen centimeters.

Erin smelled smoke. Looked over, saw flames licking at the housing of the maintenance robot.

"I've got open fire here," Erin called.

Stina leaned in and emptied the fire extinguisher already in her hands into the bot's housing, candy-coating it with sticky, white foam until it stopped.

"What the hell was that?" Kathra asked.

Erin agreed. She stepped around to make sure the bot was done and out, but she could smell the ozone in the air. HVAC systems detected it, too, and jumped to max draw again, like they had earlier when the thing was rotting.

Robot was dead. Erin wasn't even sure they could fix it, as parts looked like they had been spot welded by a drunk, flight-deck pixie. The most dangerous kind.

Looking at the corpse, it was beyond dead now. Mummy. Papery skin wrapped across ancient bones and pulled tight.

The gem had stopped glowing so hard, falling back to some more quiescent state she hoped meant that it was asleep. Or whatever magical diamonds did when they weren't trying to take over the galaxy.

"Daniel? You okay?" Erin called.

No answer.

She looked.

He was on his knees, holding his head, but Areen wasn't

kicking him, so he must have just collapsed. But he had been connected to it, when it did…whatever.

"Daniel?" Kathra looked back.

"He's dead," the feisty chef said after a few moments. "Really dead this time."

"As opposed to?" Erin asked, compelled maybe.

"All his victims are in that gem," Daniel looked up and locked eyes with her. "Screaming. He's inside the platinum part."

"How do you know this?"

"Did you miss the screaming part?" he snarled at her before he remembered where he was, who it was that was surrounding him and modulated his tone. "God, I need a glass of wine."

Areen helped the male to his unsteady feet like he was just another sister, holding him more or less upright with the help of the corridor wall.

Erin turned to Kathra.

"The bot's cooked," she said.

"Yes," Daniel said from outside. "That's why none of you could be touching it."

And then he fainted again.

19

"Hopefully, this doesn't turn into a habit," Kathra chuckled as they walked.

Areen was carrying the chef like a sleeping child. His eyes were open, but really not focusing on anything. They had run him through a med scan just long enough to confirm utter exhaustion and nothing deeper.

"What, you aren't expecting a giant space shark next, to come hunting the turtle?" Areen laughed.

The corridor wasn't wide enough for both of them, with Daniel's head and feet sticking out, so Kathra trailed by a half-step.

"Celestial octopus," Kathra suggested. "Nothing so mundane as a shark."

"Wait until you see what's on the turtle," Daniel muttered quietly.

"What's that, Daniel?" Kathra asked.

"Akami. Toro. Chu Toro. Harakami Otoro," Daniel said distinctly.

Sounded Japanese.

"Spacer, please?" she prompted.

"*WinterStar* is steel," Daniel said as they arrived at his chamber and Areen opened the hatch with an elbow.

"So?" Kathra was looking at him closely.

"That turtle is organic," he said in an utterly precise tone. "Ancient. And alive, in ways that I don't think I'll live long enough to ever explain."

"Controlled by this Urid-Varg?" Kathra asked. "Like he was trying to do to us?"

"Close enough," Daniel said. "Some of the oldest voices were awake at the end. I've seen a picture of that thing when it was barely larger than *WinterStar*. However long ago that was."

"So it's a pet?" Areen asked.

"It lacks any intelligence at all," Daniel said. "*Golem*, to use the old Hebrew term."

"If we killed its master, will it die?" Areen moved to the bed and rested Daniel on it carefully, still rumpled from before dinner and the evening's entertainment.

"We haven't killed him, Areen," Daniel said.

"But you said he was dead," Kathra pulled up her chair and sat.

Areen moved to the foot of the bed and sat there with one hand on Daniel's foot, probably to comfort him with touch.

He had already had a worse day than any Kathra could remember having in the last decade.

Daniel fixed her with a stare that didn't seem to focus on this side of the galaxy.

"Tower, moat, village," he muttered that refrain again, almost like the chorus to a song nobody really wanted to sing along with.

"Is the gem his tower?" Kathra asked.

"No," Daniel's eyes finally came back to the present. "The gem is the village. And the power source, I guess you'd call it.

He's somehow inscribed himself inside the platinum setting, like a very sophisticated computer program, except that it's alive enough that it would have eaten its way into my chest to set itself, like it did that thing back there."

"That's not Urid-Varg?" Kathra pressed.

"No," Daniel said. "Just his latest victim. A species he encountered at some point along his travels."

Daniel rooted around as she watched, pulling the blanket from under himself and curling up under it.

"God, I'm so cold," he whispered.

Kathra could see the male shivering, but she couldn't tell if it was nerves, adrenaline, or something else. Her own nerves were almost shot, and she'd just been a witness to all this for the most part. Daniel had been the player.

"Can someone grab me the spare blanket from the foot locker under the bed?" he asked in a small, tired voice.

Areen rose and pulled the box out in a single motion. It wasn't locked, so she flipped the lid and grabbed a quilt off the top.

Kathra wasn't sure how it had ended up clear down here, but it was one someone's grandmother had made special for someone else in some distant past. Still, she wouldn't begrudge him that. Not after today.

Areen spread it over Daniel and sat again.

"Better?" the woman asked.

"No, not really," Daniel said. "I'd go stand in the shower under the hottest setting right now, but I'm afraid I'd either drown, or pass out."

"Here," Areen said.

As Kathra watched, the other woman stripped off her holster first, and then her shirt and pants, standing proudly nude for a moment, almost challenging Kathra to have a verbal opinion before Areen slid under the covers with the male and climbed over him to put her back to the wall.

She wrapped long limbs around Daniel and held him. That seemed to help.

Kathra wasn't offended that Areen would lie with a male. Everyone had their own kinks and perversions. As long as nobody got hurt and everyone involved consented, it wasn't her job to police her comitatus.

All of those women were sworn to her anyway, life and soul.

"Thank you," Daniel whispered, glancing back.

His shivering didn't stop, but he sounded calmer.

WinterStar was always kept warm. He was the only male aboard, so he had learned to just wear lighter layers and deal with temperatures constantly in the low twenties. Kathra knew that the Sept kept their warships at eighteen degrees, but everyone aboard one of those monstrosities was wearing several layers of heavy wool, rather than the lighter linens and cotton that the tribal squadron imported for clothing.

"Daniel," Kathra said to get his eyes open again and focused on her. "What do we do with the gem and the corpse?"

"Ask me tomorrow," he whispered in such an exhausted tone that she wasn't surprised to find him asleep almost before the words were spoken.

Kathra looked at Areen with her Commander's eye.

"I'll have folks come in and check on you as the night passes," Kathra said. "Alert me if he does anything or has any issues greater than the nightmares I expect."

"Understood, Kathra," Areen said. "I don't expect him to move for the next eight hours."

"That would probably be for the best," Kathra said. "Ndidi will fix everyone breakfast, so don't let him get up. Tomorrow, we have to solve the turtle."

20

———

Erin sipped at the mug of cold-brewed coffee that Ndidi had just delivered to the Medbay. Only nineteen, the woman was probably going to inherit Daniel Lémieux's job, at least for a short period, but she was already impressing people.

Cold-brewed coffee on a warm, fragile night was just the thing Erin and the others needed now.

The comitatus called it Goldfish Brew. The homemade device was a metal frame about a meter and a half tall, with various glass bowls and pipes that let things drip and work their slow magic, but the way the light had diffracted through the top tank in a picture had made it look like there was a goldfish swimming in it, and nobody had ever let Ndidi live that image down.

But she made damned fine coffee.

Iruoma had gone to bed. Kathra and Areen had tucked the chef in and gone to bed themselves, expecting an early morning. Erin and Joane had volunteered to stay up all night, and all day tomorrow, to keep watch on things here.

The corpse had gone into a box. They would fire the *salaud* into space at some point soon, maybe by flying close

133

enough to a nearby star to make sure. Or tossing him into the depths of a gas giant. Those were more common, this far out.

All the clothing had gone into different crates. They had eventually cut the platinum setting out of the thing's chest with a rotary saw, taking a few centimeters of bone with it, just so they didn't have to touch anything. That got washed off and put into a storage container.

WinterStar wasn't a scientific exploration vessel, filled with hordes of boffins you could just set on a problem and get out of their way. Nobody had any idea how to explain some of what happened.

Erin was just happy that they were several systems away from any that the Sept claimed, and not scheduled to return to a TradeStation anywhere for at least another two months, give or take.

Assuming nothing even more strange compelled them.

"So is there anything anybody will tell me?" Ndidi asked as she leaned back, pitcher in one hand and a devilish grin on her face.

Like many of the support side, Ndidi kept her hair short and curly, maybe only as much as a two centimeters of poof around her skull. Unlike most of the comitatus, the young woman herself was short and rather stout, standing perhaps half a hand shorter than the chef, and probably weighing as much, most of it muscle.

Had Ndidi's reflexes and eyesight been as good as her mind, she probably would have been a candidate to join the comitatus someday, but she needed glasses for anything farther away than her hands, so she had turned her art to food.

Ugonna had been a perfectly adequate cook. Adequate being the key word. Kathra had demanded more for the women who shared her food and her risks, and had hired a chef with a Golden Diamond, even if he was male.

In another few years, Erin could see Ndidi giving the male a run for his money in a kitchen. She rather looked forward to that day, assuming Daniel stayed with them longer than the next TradeStation visit.

There was always that. Still, he had handled today at least as well as most of the comitatus had, so Erin wouldn't begrudge the male having had enough. She understood that feeling.

But Ndidi had asked a question. A good one, too.

"Tell you?" Erin asked the youngster, all of a decade behind her. "What's to tell? We got attacked by this *salaud*. Kathra's chef beat him to death. And then killed him a second time. I'm hoping we don't have to try a third."

"And the Star Turtle?" Ndidi's eyes were huge through those glass lenses, but they were large without them.

"That's next," Erin said.

"Are we keeping it?" the girl asked.

"That's Kathra's call, Ndidi," Erin laughed. "We're not even sure that there is anybody aboard it."

"But it's enormous," Ndidi gasped. "How could it be empty?"

"We'll see," Erin said with an elaborate shrug.

A sound at the hatch had Erin out of the chair where she was keeping watch and a pistol in her hand. Joane was up less than a blink later, moving to the left.

"Eep," Ndidi squeaked.

"Into the corner," Erin ordered the young woman with her free hand. "Stay quiet and out of the way."

Erinkansilemi Uduik was still the undisputed Second-in-Command of Kathra's comitatus. She could give those sorts of orders.

Ndidi didn't argue, but she was well trained. Not a

warrior, but not a slouch, either. She moved, putting the pitcher down on the deck in the exact corner of the storeroom to free up her hands if she needed to fight.

The sound at the door came again, and still made no sense. The three of them were in a little-used storage room, where Kathra had ordered the invader's body and gear to be stored. Either someone knew where they were and could open the door, or not.

Erin moved to one side, pistol still ready, and pushed the comm button.

"Who's there?" she demanded in a low voice.

"Erin, it's Areen," the other woman replied from the corridor outside. "I followed Daniel, but I can't get him to wake up. He's moaning and twitching, but seems to be sleep walking."

Daniel? What in hades name had happened to the chef now? Hadn't they killed the beast? Would they really have to do it a third time?

"What does he want?" Erin asked.

"To get in there," Areen said.

Daniel could be heard in the background, making noises and banging against the metal of the hatch, but not speaking or screaming.

She holstered her pistol and stepped close to a wall before triggering the door open.

There was a simple button you pushed, but apparently Daniel was too far gone, or the thing that had taken over his mind didn't remember that. Still, she was bigger and stronger, and had three other women handy.

They could take a single, male chef.

Daniel staggered into the room like he was having the best pub crawl ever.

Erin tackled the man to the deck and sat on him, face-down where the beast inside him couldn't get any leverage or claw at her. Ndidi and Joane closed. As did Areen.

Except Areen was completely nude.

Erin didn't even want to know. Last time she had seen Areen, the woman had been carrying the chef and walking out of the medbay with Kathra. But everybody knew Areen didn't consider it bestiality to lie with a man.

Except Daniel was fully clothed, down to his normal deck booties.

At least he had stopped thrashing after Erin bounced him off the deck. Smart men were like that.

"Daniel?" she asked quietly as he lay there.

All the women were poised for violence.

"Where am I?" the chef's voice came from an extremely distant place.

"Are you back?" she pressed.

"Yeah," he sighed. "I remember talking to Kathra and Areen, and being cold, and now a very cold deck. What happened?"

"You were sleep-walking, Daniel," Areen said. "I couldn't wake you up and didn't want to leave you so that I could get more help."

His head turned that way and Erin felt the flinch pass through his whole body.

"Why are you naked?" he asked in a much more nervous voice.

"I will explain it to you another time," the woman replied in a tight tone.

"Okay," he said. "I think I'm okay. Could someone wake the Commander up?"

"Already did," Erin heard Ndidi call from the hatchway.

"Thank you," Daniel said. "Who's on top of me?"

"I am," Erin replied, sliding her weight backwards off his

hips so that she could stand and step to a side before he could kick at her.

Not that she didn't trust the chef, but she wasn't sure who else might be in there with him right now.

Daniel moved slowly. Not carefully, like he was surrounded by armed warriors, but gently, as if tired and sore. When he was on his back, he just lay there for a moment, looking up at them.

"You okay?" Areen asked.

She watched him ogle the warrior's nudity for a moment, but he remained horizontal.

"I'm afraid to ever go to sleep again," she heard the man whisper.

Erin could understand that concept.

"You stay put and rest," Erin ordered him. "Kathra will be along shortly."

"Yes," Daniel said. "I have to kill that *violeur*. Or you do. Somebody. Soon."

It didn't make any sense to Erin, but she didn't think it made any more to Daniel, and he had to live with it.

Kathra and Iruoma arrived at almost the same instant, pounding down the corridor outside and only stopping to turn the corner.

Erin saw the Commander smile as she crouched down next to the chef.

"Finally discovered your place in life, groveling at the feet of every woman you meet?" she teased lightly.

Interestingly, that only got a half-smile from the man. He must be well down the path now.

"Maybe," Daniel finally said. "I'd like to get up, if you think it's safe."

Erin reached out a hand and pulled the chef to his feet. He was a little woozy, but held himself close and tight. It helped that every woman in the room was at least his size.

He turned to face the boxes that Erin had supervised storing on the various shelves along the side wall, without moving his feet at all.

"Big one is the body," Daniel said, pointing. "Gray box with the red paint splotch holds the suit he was wearing. Small box at the bottom of the top stack on the right is the gem. Round bin with the green lid holds Urid-Varg himself."

He turned back to them with eyes that looked a million years old.

"You can hear him," Kathra said.

It wasn't a question.

"I can," Daniel said. "*Salaud* had an insurance policy in place for all this, but never imagined that he would need to use it. Nobody had ever resisted him before."

"Why were you able to?" Kathra asked.

That brought the first smile to his face that Erin had seen all day.

"You," he laughed and gestured at the room. "The mighty and dangerous Kathra Omezi. Commander of the Mbaysey and her deadly comitatus. He never imagined you would actually have a male on your ship, so he didn't bother to look for one when he cast whatever spiderweb he was using to hunt. Since then, he's been trying to get me to replace his last host, and you all have saved me time and again. Now I want to kill him. Want you to kill him. I can't do it. In fact, you'll probably have to hurt me to stop me, when you go after him."

Erin didn't hesitate or ask. She slipped behind the man and wrapped her arms under his and up to his neck, where he couldn't do anything except maybe kick backwards at her shins. To stop that, she pressed down, putting her weight forward into his, so that if he lifted a foot, she'd be able to drive him face-first into the deck in such a way that he probably wouldn't break his neck.

If they were all lucky.

And she cared.

"Good," he said, unresisting. "I have to say this fast, so listen, and then ignore me later when I change my mind. You have to crush the platinum setting, and later melt it. If you do that he's…"

Erin felt the man suddenly stiffen for a moment. A growl escaped his lips, along with the sound of grinding teeth.

"Hurry," Daniel whispered.

It felt like two men fighting over one body as she kept him pinned and helpless.

Kathra moved, pulling the bin down to the deck at her feet and ripping the green lid off to fall somewhere behind her.

Erin had put the thing in there earlier, resting on a towel with several centimeters of breast bone still attached around the edges. The smell wasn't bad, because they had washed it, and it had already been a brittle mummy at that point.

Daniel tried to move forward. Or Urid-Varg. Whoever.

"No, you must not," a different voice emerged from the man's mouth now. Deeper. Louder. Desperate. "I will give you anything you wish, but you must not."

Kathra looked up at the chef for a haunting moment, like perhaps she was considering the offer from the undead creature that had stolen her cook.

"Such as?" Kathra asked in a voice like a puma waiting in a tree.

"Power," Urid-Varg offered, perhaps relaxing. "Wealth. Whatever the Mbaysey need to defeat the Sept, or conquer them. It shall be yours."

Urid-Varg might have been a mighty warrior, but he had still chosen a small human male as his vessel. Needs must when the devil drives, Erin supposed.

She felt the body tense.

Erin lifted Daniel bodily off the floor so suddenly the alien voice squawked in surprise. She shook him once or twice as he seemed to be about to do *something* that probably wasn't going to be friendly or even polite.

Kathra drew her particle beam pistol and fired several shots into the bucket as fast as the mechanism would cycle. Urid-Varg screamed in a bass so deep it was almost inaudible, except for where Erin felt it in the bones of her chest as it tapered off to nothingness.

He slumped in Erin's arms and relaxed.

"Did you get him?" Daniel asked quietly after a few moments.

"I did," Kathra said, looking down at the remains of the bin at her feet. "Is he dead?"

A particle cannon accelerated a packet of ionized plasma inside a magnetic pinch at a target, where it ruptured on impact, imparting heat and, more importantly, kinetic energy.

The bin had ruptured. Pieces of it had been shattered all over the floor, along with bits of bone, metal, and what looked like ceramics.

"Yeah," Daniel gasped in shock. "God, I haven't felt this good all day. It was like that shit was sitting on my head, tapping me with a hammer constantly."

Kathra holstered her pistol and nodded at Erin, apparently convinced that her chef was back. Certainly, he was a lot tougher than Erin had ever given the man credit for, and he had stood up to her more than once.

Maybe all men weren't such weak and easily-swayed creatures. Color didn't seem to factor in, as the *Anglos*, *Spanics*, *Rabics*, or Asian men she had known had all been wimpy little homemakers.

Or Sept soldiers intent on reclaiming the Mbaysey back into the Imperial fold if Kathra would let them.

Erin set Daniel down and let go of the grip on his neck, stepping back and to one side to look the man in the face.

His eyes had changed. There had been a cloud in there earlier, recognizable now only because it was gone.

He leaned back and pulled a huge breath into his lungs, like he hadn't been able to breathe for hours. Maybe he hadn't, she wasn't a good judge.

But he was good at fighting it off. Urid-Varg had apparently never run into someone stubborn enough to say no to him. It. Them. Whatever they were.

Her own head had cleared, so Erin was sure that the creature was dead. It had been trying to control them, but without the gem, he had just been an annoying gnat flying around. Perhaps his power was gendered, as Daniel had said earlier, so he couldn't ride a female. Not that any of these would have allowed it, but he wouldn't have known that.

Kathra Omezi and her comitatus. Even the Sept knew fear at that name.

Daniel turned in place, surrounded by all these warriors, and Erin was willing to include Ndidi in that group, as she had been standing close enough to help, but not get in the way.

He stopped when he was facing Areen.

"Are your clothes in my cabin, and I have no memory of it?" he asked diffidently.

Areen smiled and tilted her head at the man.

"Apparently, it just wasn't that good?" she teased him, comfortably nude and almost close enough to touch the man.

"I would love to rectify that oversight," Daniel shrugged. "But not now. Could someone give me a sleeping pill and set an alarm clock for spring?"

Kathra nodded at them and Areen took Daniel's arm in hers leading him presumably to medbay. Ndidi recovered her coffee and took off forward to handle breakfast for the warriors. Erin left Joane here just in case, while she followed Kathra up and forward to the bridge.

"Now what?" Erin asked as they crossed over into the central hull and floated finally without gravity.

Or listeners.

"Now we figure out if anybody can do anything with that damned turtle, with its master dead," Kathra murmured back.

"You think Daniel's up for it?" Erin asked.

It was obvious that the chef was going to have to be central to whatever they attempted.

"If I thought he would swear the oath, I'd add that man to my comitatus, Erin. Just to show the rest of you what tough really is," Kathra grinned.

Erin grinned back.

Who imagined a cook had *that* in him?

PART III

CONQUEROR

21

———

HE HOPED it was spring when he opened his eyes. That had been what Daniel had requested. He was in his bunk, in his cabin, just from the smells before he opened his eyes.

Daniel laid perfectly still under the covers and let his senses reach out. He didn't seem to be sharing the inside of his head with anyone, for the first time in… (was it days?). He was wearing a T-shirt and briefs, but nothing else. *WinterStar* was always warmer than he had ever kept his flat, but he had learned to sleep at this temperature. Instead of a heavy comforter and maybe a quilt, he usually just had a thin blanket and a shirt to sleep in, and that kept him warm enough to sleep.

The women of the comitatus controlled the thermostat on this ship.

Daniel was on his left side, facing the hatch. Someone had left the lights one setting above dark. Not enough to read by, but enough to see colors. He opened his eyes, looking on the floor or the chair for Areen's clothes.

They had indeed been there when she led him back to his cabin after…*that.*

Daniel knew that every man and a number of the women he had known would have been jealous, to see him with such a beautiful, athletic, naked woman on his arm like it was the most natural thing in the world, but he had had nothing at all left when they got back.

Chuck the pill into his mouth and swallow it dry. Strip off his pants and crawl back into bed while Areen watched. He couldn't hear her breathing behind him, so he reached one hand back tentatively, but he was indeed alone in his bunk.

Probably for the best.

Daniel took a deep breath and rolled onto his back. At some point, they would make him get out of bed. Or his bladder would. Ship-time said mid-morning when he finally turned to look at the clock.

Not spring, but also not early enough to fix breakfast for his charges. Ndidi could handle that for one more day. Or three. Maybe forever. Daniel wasn't sure how long he wanted to remain on this ship.

Or if he could actually leave.

Another deep breath. His body was awake now, warming up to the point that the blanket would have to go shortly.

And his bladder was going to win anyway. Daniel sighed and pivoted, putting his feet down on the deck and sitting upright like he was afraid his head would fall off.

Except it didn't hurt this morning. There was nobody trying to get in or out with an icepick. He had almost forgotten what that felt like.

Another sigh. It might have been better to wake up next to someone, although he was pretty sure he could never tell anyone that. Especially not these women, and Kathra kept him largely isolated from the staff-side of the crew.

He was certainly over Angel now, to the point he had to

stop and remember what she looked like. And who that Daniel Lémieux had been, once upon a time.

He wasn't even the same man that had first set foot on this deck so many months ago.

More sleep? Didn't sound rewarding. Wherever he had gone with the drugs in his system, they had washed out now and he was back to the land of the living.

Or the undead. But he was pretty sure that Urid-Varg was gone. Hopefully that *salaud* didn't have any other backups over on that turtle, waiting like trapdoor spiders for whoever came along. Because Daniel knew that Kathra Omezi was going over there next, and would probably be expecting her chef/assassin to join her.

Third sigh. Daniel stood up before it decided to become a habit. His cabin was actually a suite, tucked off from his kitchen but not directly connected, so he could come and go without having to participate in breakfast with everyone this morning. It also meant that he had his own bathroom without leaving. That was good.

He stripped and waddled carefully into the bathroom, unsure at what point he would come apart like a marionette with its strings cut. Morning ablutions and such took longer, but that was because he just stood still under the hottest water he could stand and let it wash as much of the last few days off as he could get without a wire brush.

That might be necessary later.

Out into his cabin and dressed, he looked around, as if seeing everything again for the first time. He had been a bachelor for so long that everything was put away or latched down. Spaceships were unforgiving places, as were kitchens, so you learned early to keep everything organized. Not necessarily spotless, but such that you could find anything in total darkness, and not have problems in gravity field failures.

Bon.

He approached the main hatch and just stood there for several seconds, staring at the inside of the thing like he could see through it. Or maybe it was a djinn who would come alive and explain everything to him. Perhaps what this silly shit needed right now was a good narrator to explain all the strange parts to latecomers. There were a lot of strange parts.

Yes, it was going to be that sort of a day.

Daniel reached out to key the hatch open. Nothing happened, but he wasn't particularly surprised.

He wouldn't trust him either, right now. Instead, he reached for the comm line to the one person he would have to convince. Of his sanity. His reliability. Whatever.

"Hello, Daniel," Kathra replied. "How are you feeling?"

22

WHEN THERE ARE no trained doctors within light-years, you learn to invest in the best medbots you can afford, and keep them up to date or replace them when something better comes along. Thus, Kathra knew almost to the minute when Daniel should awaken, based on the dosage Areen had given him.

She had slept. Eaten. Prepared.

The Star Turtle had not moved one bit, except as gravity and solar wind played on the hull. Spectre Twenty-One had gone and met up with the tribal squadron, updating them on all the news since they had fled. Kathra would send another messenger in twelve hours or so, once she knew where they were headed.

She had a responsibility to the entire tribe, and not just her warriors. While she had inherited tribal leadership as a result of being her mother's daughter, and her own fire, she could lose it again quickly enough if she was foolish.

Or unlucky. The Mbaysey had just come within however many minutes of perhaps being eradicated, but for the random luck of her chef, and his willingness to go above and beyond. But a good leader makes her own luck. And Kathra Omezi was in the business of manufacturing some today.

"Thinking about your chef?" Erin asked, seated across the desk from her and sipping some more of Ndidi's wonderful coffee.

The comitatus didn't really have a uniform, like the Sept militants they had escaped, but Kathra was responsible for dressing and equipping the women that had sworn their lives to her. Loose pants in cotton, usually a color that split the gap between gold and red. Almost the heart of a good fire. Pull-over shirts with three-quarter, raglan sleeves, fire on the torso and whatever color someone felt like wearing that day for the shoulders.

If they had to visit a TradeStation, or one of the ClanStars, a jacket might be added, depending on how cold those fools decided to keep their environment. Kathra kept *WinterStar* warm because that was how she liked it. And it wasn't like her warriors needed to train for planetary assaults. The whole tribe—every child, woman, and elder, including the poor males—couldn't take and hold a small TradeStation, to say nothing of a small town on the surface of a planet.

No, they lived their lives aboard the ships, and occasionally had to chase off pirates and fools. Cold weather gear was generally unnecessary, and they could always strip down to shorts and tank tops if they had to go someplace warm.

"My chef?" Kathra asked with an arched eyebrow. "Our chef, unless you were planning to retire from flying and take up weaving or something."

Erin laughed.

"I wouldn't have hired him," she said with a smile. "None of us would have. Male, *Rabic*, and cook? No. He was yours. And we would all be dead or enslaved again today without him, so nobody will argue with keeping hm. Will he stay?"

"That is the Four-Dragon-Question. Erin," Kathra replied absently.

The Mbaysey used Free World Guilders, rather than Sept Crowns in trade. The Free Worlds didn't like the Empire any more than Kathra did, so they had a currency system that used a system based on fours instead of tens, just to make conversions a complete pain in the ass. One Guilder, called a Sloth for the animal engraved on the front, exchanged with one Sept Crown at somewhere between two and a half to four Crowns to the Guilder, depending on the planet.

Kathra rather enjoyed watching Sept merchants having to count change.

Sloths, Eagles, Boars, Tigers, Snakes, Unicorns. At the top: Dragons, worth seven hundred and sixty-eight Guilders.

And I won't take Crowns from you at anything less than a fifteen percent margin.

"Four Dragons?" Erin chuckled.

"Maybe seven, just to watch that one fool on Renneth have to make change while grinding his teeth," Kathra grinned.

Erin joined her, a smile a kilometer wide.

One of these days, that man would learn that his gender-supremist views cost him all the good stuff. That Kathra traded with nicer folks, and only bought from him to burn all the Sept Crowns someone else had been forced to give them when they ran out of Guilders apologetically.

"Do we want him to stay?" Erin asked.

That was the question Kathra had no answer for.

Most males would suddenly suffer an onset of ego about now, given the situation, and how much Kathra and her crew owed him.

Their very lives.

She could see Daniel going down that path.

Kathra wouldn't kill him for it. She took her debts

seriously. But at the same time, she could easily fire the man, pay him off, and dump his sorry ass on the worst TradeStation she could find.

Mauta, maybe. Or F'Dashua, depending on how deep into Free Worlds space she wanted to go to make her point.

But she would be willing to bet Erin a Boar—eight guilders—that Daniel Lémieux was made of sterner stuff. Costing himself this job would mean he had to start over again, and he had finally relaxed enough around them to tell really good dirty jokes occasionally.

"I think it would benefit us all, including him, if he stayed on as my personal chef," Kathra sniffed, holding it as long as she could before she started snickering. "I don't see the rest of you demanding Ugonna coming back."

"No, you'd absolutely get an uprising on that, if you didn't promote Ndidi at this point," Erin pointed out. "Girl has earned her place, I think. At least her chance."

"I agree," Kathra said. "But we need to find out what our chef wants from life, now that he has been forced to step outside his kitchen for a while. He might retreat back to his oven and never emerge again."

"And the turtle?" Erin asked.

"I have several theories I wish to pursue, depending on how crazy and ambitious the man might be," Kathra said.

More was cut off by the buzzer on her desk chiming once. Kathra looked at the identifier and smiled to herself. She gestured Erin to remain silent and opened the line.

"Hello, Daniel," Kathra said with a smile in her voice. "How are you feeling?"

"Sufficient unto the day," he replied, obviously quoting some literary thing Kathra wasn't familiar with. Sept culture wasn't that high on her list. "I appear to be locked in my cabin, which was a good idea, but now I would like to entertain the idea of food, and whatever psychological torture you have in mind for me after that."

"Torture, Daniel?" she asked in a frosty tone.

"I remember your face from last night," he said with a laugh. "Whatever it is, I'm not going to like it, but I probably have no choice at this point, so I might as well eat and then get it over with. Else I might return soon and find that Ndidi has moved in with all her knives and favorite pots and I'll have to take up brewing instead or something for a living."

Erin mouthed the word expectantly as Kathra watched her.

Brewing?

What might a Golden Diamond chef know about making hootch? Not today's question, but certainly one to file.

"Are you safe to make it to the kitchen to eat?" Kathra asked.

She did allow more warmth into her tones. They had come to like this chef, even if he had been possessed at some point in the recent past.

"Twenty paces appears to be within my endurance, Commander," Daniel chuckled. "At least until I have some coffee in me. Will you join me there, or should I come up to your office when I'm done?"

"We'll be down," Kathra decided. "This entails the entire comitatus, so we might as well gather there, where there is sufficient space."

"Yes," he said glumly. "I was afraid you'd say that."

She heard the click as the line cut.

"Four Dragons," Erin reminded her.

"At the least," Kathra said.

She rose swiftly, checking that her blade and pistol were seated cleanly if she needed to get at either in a hurry.

"Gather up all the women," Kathra said. "I will meet you there."

"Where are you going?" Erin rose, confusion written on her face so deeply that the tattoo on her cheek almost disappeared into the wrinkles.

"To completely ruin Daniel's day," Kathra smiled grimly.

23

Daniel sipped his coffee, afraid that he would have to get up and refill it shortly and that was probably just too much to ask of him right now. Except that Ndidi came by with a carafe and silently topped him off.

The smile she gave him was so sad that Daniel almost just went back to bed right then. Except she meant well. They all did. And they were all here, carefully not watching him. Mostly.

Erin was seated across from him, sipping her own coffee more slowly, but she had probably been up for a while and already had some.

And not been previously possessed by an undead, planetary conqueror with an axe to grind and a need for an entire harem of beautiful, feisty women.

The rest of the comitatus was here, save only the Commander, so Daniel took his time consuming his porridge and coffee. Today wasn't likely to be getting any better as it wore on, and he had no enthusiasm to face it. Not that it would ask his opinion or anything.

The Commander entered and it was like a rock had been dropped into a still pond. Daniel was fascinated by the ripple of silence that the woman created. Noise fell to nothingness as she fixed those cold, hard eyes on him and approached.

There was space on his right and she took it, sliding onto the bench with him and resting her elbows on the table. She placed a small box on the surface, between her and Erin rather than close to him, so he continued to drink his coffee and reconsider joining a monastery.

"Do you know what's in the box, Daniel?" she asked quietly.

He looked. It was a small thing, perhaps a little thicker than the sort of box his custom dress shirts used to be delivered in, back when he did that sort of thing. Forty-five centimeters by twenty-five by ten, more or less. Plain, white cardboard stock, just like then.

Finding out would involve looking in. He didn't want to.

"No," Daniel finally said, retreating back into himself.

"Interesting," the Commander said.

Daniel realized how keyed up the woman was when he looked closer.

Oh lovely. Another day to possibly be beaten up by a beautiful woman. What an interesting lot in life to draw.

"Do I want to?" Daniel asked.

He was aware he was now the center of every pair of eyes in the room, including the ones half-hidden behind glasses as Ndidi had retreated to the serving table. That just put her closer to knives and a full carafe of coffee. The rest of the comitatus had blades and pistols.

"I want to test a theory," she said plainly. "And ask a favor of you."

Merde. They had gotten *there* in their relationship?

Daniel scraped the last of his porridge and set the bowl

and spoon down perhaps louder than was technically necessary, but the room was too damned quiet right now.

"I'm not going to like it, am I?" he turned his head far enough to look directly at her.

"Probably not," she agreed. "The risks are great, but the rewards even greater."

Fourth sigh. Maybe getting to be a habit after all.

"It's the turtle, isn't it?" he asked.

"We'd like to board it today, yes," Omezi said in a quiet voice that somehow still included the other twenty-some women. "I'm not sure how or where, and don't think it will just let us."

Daniel had to agree. Urid-Varg hadn't been paranoid enough, but he also hadn't been stupid, from what Daniel knew.

"And you think it will let me in?" he nodded to himself.

"I do," she nodded back.

"Why?"

"Because you'll be impersonating him," she said.

Daniel hadn't realized how quickly he had stood up until half the women he could see suddenly had weapons in hands. About half of *those* were pointed at him. Kathra Omezi wasn't one of them, but she could punch him easy enough from where she sat.

Daniel mumbled an apology and managed to sit back down without tangling himself in the bench or pitching over backwards. He looked at the box she had brought with her.

He couldn't smell what was inside it, but that hardly mattered now. He took a drink and sat his coffee mug down before a very deep breath as he waited for someone to just shoot him this morning.

But he couldn't even get that much out of these women.

Next sigh.

Merde.

He reached out a hand and pulled the box in front of him, wanting to just rest his forehead against it for a few moments while he prayed, but he hadn't actually set foot in a church for anything but weddings or funerals in decades, and today did not feel like the day to make up that deficit.

God, if she was listening, would probably be too busy laughing at him right now to help, anyway.

Daniel opened the box by sliding the top from the bottom, just like when his tailor delivered a new shirt. Lime green and white. Worse, the stone was sitting atop the pile of carefully folded cloth.

It was never dark, but it was as dark as he'd ever seen it, barely glowing.

His hand didn't want to move until he yelled at the offending appendage silently for several seconds. Reached out like a hot stovetop and just hovered at the edge of pain.

He was aware that he wasn't the only one that had stopped breathing. Deep breath, but not a sigh. Maybe an improvement.

He picked up the white gem and held it between thumb and two fingers like he could see light through it, instead of the souls of however many thousands of Urid-Varg's victims.

Touching it, he could feel something. Perhaps the combined wails of agony, or something equally constructive.

There were too many guns and fists pointed at him right now for his equilibrium, but he couldn't argue with the women. Not one damned bit.

Instead, he set the gem down in his porridge bowl so it wouldn't be tempted to sneak off when he wasn't looking.

Or something.

It was instructive, watching the room relax as the gem tinkled loudly against the metal.

The rest of the box held the haberdasheral remains of

Urid-Varg's costume. Gloves on top, those went to his left, in front of Areen. Boots, above the gloves closer to Erin, like the beginning of a moat protecting him from whatever stupidity was brewing next. Belt, dead center above his bowl. Tunic with ragged hole in the chest, where the box had been before. Pants below that where Kathra Omezi's bowl would have gone.

Empty box. Empty-headed fool holding a box.

Daniel looked around for a place to rest it, but Ndidi materialized beside him and it vanished from his hands.

Whatever count of sigh we were up to now.

Daniel had dated a true fashionista a few before Angel, so he had managed to pick up some interesting bits of technical knowledge. Those folk were at least as nerdy as cooks, once you got them going on a topic. Maybe worse.

He grabbed the tunic and turned it inside out to look at the seams. Those were always the marks of a professional, or a bloody amateur, but he doubted the conqueror had qualified that poorly.

Sure enough. Frenched seams from the feel. Except they weren't actually stitched. Glued, perhaps, except it felt more like a weld. Close enough to magic as to be indistinguishable right now.

The white stripes weren't cloth. At least not as he understood it. A little pixie in his ear suggested living copper as a superconductor, but Daniel *R E A L L Y* didn't want to consider how he might even know that.

The chest should have been frayed where someone took a rotary saw to it, but they might have been using an industrial cutting laser from the smoothness of the cut.

That same pixie muttered something about organic living copper growing fixed.

Daniel looked at the ceiling, to see if God Herself was behind these shenanigans, but She didn't answer. And it would probably be rude to ask if there was any bourbon he could add to his coffee right now.

Commander Omezi would want him sharp and focused, not passed out drunk in his cabin having even better nightmares than before.

Maybe tomorrow.

A hand descended on his arm.

"Breathe," the Commander ordered him in a quiet voice.

He had stopped. Forgotten, perhaps. Maybe unconsciously willing himself to just die, right here on the deck, rather than go back to that place.

She wasn't going to allow his cowardice to thwart her. That much was obvious from the look in the woman's eyes. And the others nearby, if just the slightest bit less brutal about it.

Deep breath. More sigh.

Okay, let's start small.

Daniel put the tunic back and picked up one of the gloves. Heavier than a woman would wear to the opera, and shorter. Lighter than that one artist had used when she was welding statuary. Entire thing made of the same material as the white stripe. Too flexible to be steel as a fighting gauntlet, but it had that feel.

Daniel turned to stare briefly at Kathra Omezi. She nodded, as if she could read his interior commentary.

Hopefully, he wasn't muttering out loud right now, but he really didn't care. They wanted something from him. And he was the only one that could do it.

The grumble might have been audible on purpose.

Daniel pulled it onto his left hand and waited.

Somehow, he wasn't shocked when it turned into a perfect fit, after a moment he could only describe as *flowing into shape.* Screaming like someone who has just discovered a large spider walking across their chest when they awakened might have adequately described the flash of something in his chest, but he managed to not make a noise. Not twitch any more than necessary.

Not do *something*.

Looking up, he could see almost forever up the barrel of Erin's pistol. And into the depths of her eyes.

He nodded. She nodded back.

Right hand reached slowly, deliberately into the bowl and took hold of the gem. Lifting it into clear sight, it was glowing harder now. As he suspected.

As he feared.

Living copper, huh?

Daniel rested the gem on the back of his left hand, felt the two flow together.

The glove started glowing about as bright as the gem had earlier. The gem could be used to read by, if he had a Quran handy and wanted to fall back into something more soothing than whatever Kathra Omezi had for him.

Daniel held his open hand up for everyone to see, turning it both ways.

Still, he couldn't entice anyone to just shoot him. Not without doing something stupid and actively suicidal right now.

He considered it. Withdrew consideration.

The damned thing had alit on his curiosity now. *Merde.* He was going to do this, wasn't he, just to see where it took him?

Daniel didn't have anything like a cookbook for the damnable tool. Commander Omezi had killed it for him. Still, he had seen that *violeur* using it.

He reached out with his mind and pushed at the gem, ignoring the voices he could suddenly hear when he did that.

All those trapped souls. Could he free them, eventually?

The glove's light was a torch now, filling the room and

causing the women around him to squint and mutter various profanities, mostly at him, he supposed.

Like frosting, Daniel told the glove to cover his hand with…force? Energy? Whatever?

He lowered his hand and rested it on the table in front of him, except he wasn't touching it. There was a soap bubble perhaps a centimeter deep between him and the metal surface. He banged his hand lightly a few times, just to be sure, but he wasn't imagining things.

Or he was still trapped in that other dream, waiting for Areen to wake him from a nightmare. There was always that.

Another sigh.

He turned to the Commander, feeling so bleak as to be transparent. At least she nodded sympathetically.

"I'm never going to get to cook again, am I?" he asked her.

"If this works, you can do whatever you want to afterward, Daniel," she reassured him.

If that was any reassurance.

He didn't want to be a god. Or whatever the Conqueror had been. He didn't know a language that could describe the bits of Urid-Varg he had picked up along the way.

The immense age of the mind that had touched him. Tried to ride him. Wanted to own him.

The Sept didn't technically allow anything like slavery anymore, but criminal trafficking still happened. Especially in sex. The Mbaysey had their own stories, passed down from mothers to daughters from before they had had enough. Daniel suddenly had a vision of himself hunting the traffickers down and eliminating them in the most painful way he could imagine.

He drew a breath in for once. Held it. Let the oxygen purify something inside like a blast furnace hitting hot iron.

Now the dangerous part.

He reached out his right hand and took hold of the gem. It was firmly embedded somehow in the glove, and perhaps his bones, but he was able to pry it free with nothing more than a quick pop.

The gem went dim. The glove returned to wherever dark place gloves go when you take them off and stuff them into a pocket when you arrive, as he removed it and put it back with the other.

"But for a hat," he murmured. "We'd all be dead right now."

"A hat?" Erin spoke up.

The gun hadn't wavered.

"A *taqiyah*," Daniel offered. "It goes under the *keffiyeh* to cover the head, like a Jewish *kippah*. Had he been wearing one, I probably wouldn't have been able to hurt him. Poof. We're all gone."

"You'll need one?" Omezi asked.

Daniel shrugged.

"You planning to invade another tribal squadron and take them all as your personal harem?" he asked, finally feeling some of the weight slide off his shoulders. "Be wary of the chefs."

That got enough of a chuckle that Daniel decided he might survive the morning.

Might even want to survive the morning.

Maybe.

He rose, slowly enough that nobody would shoot him accidentally, now that he decided he actually wanted to live through this.

Stepping carefully backwards over the bench so he didn't fall over and crack his skull, AGAIN, he pulled his shirt over his head and rested it where he had been sitting. Booties next as a couple of the women whistled sarcastically. Pants on top of the shirt until he was standing there in nothing but his briefs.

"What are you doing?" Omezi asked him.

"The stupidest thing I have ever even considered, Commander."

24

Erin had to give the man credit. He had watched her draw the pistol and aim it at his face, just to sort of keep him off track, and the chef hadn't even blinked.

She could see why Kathra considered him tough enough to join the comitatus. Not many of the others would have been that solid, surrounded by that much promised-but-unspoken violence.

Now he was mostly naked, standing in front of all the women. One hundred and sixty-eight centimeters tall. Maybe sixty-eight kilograms. Erin was bigger. So were all but three of the rest. Pale skin that reminded her of beef stew for a color. Dark brown hair starting to gray above the ears but still dark on the chest.

The man had hardly any muscle tone to speak of. Wiry, but skinny. Sure hands, though. She had watched him cook, early on, just to get a feel for the man's mind.

You could learn a tremendous amount about someone by letting them get into their own comfort zone and run with it. Daniel Lémieux didn't put a foot or a hand wrong in the kitchen. She suspected that they might have blindfolded the man and challenged him to make cookies, and still eaten them.

He wasn't there today. Erin could see his shakiness. Oh, he controlled it quite well. Anybody but her and Kathra would have probably missed it. Any maybe Areen, if he had truly spent enough time fornicating with the man to learn his naked body.

That deep breath. In and out, before he moved, like he had to plan each step, and then convince his limbs to actually carry out his instructions. The way his hands still had the slightest wobble as he reached out and picked up the pants that she had stripped off the dead mummy.

After a moment, he put them back down and picked up the shirt instead, pulling it over his head and tilting his nose down far enough to look at the gap she had torn in the center. It was much smaller than it had been, but Kathra had warned her that was expected, so Erin didn't shoot the man right now.

A breath rattled around that narrow chest before it finally found an escape. Both hands flexed into fists and relaxed twice.

The eyes looked up and met hers.

Urid-Varg, or whatever it was, wasn't there today. All she could see was a lifetime of pain and bad decisions welling up as they stared at one another.

Like: *How did I get here? And who did I offend to cause that?*

She couldn't help him with theological concerns. The daughters of slaves rarely believed in a benevolent deity.

The shirt hung strange. Daniel had a longer torso, and a far smaller gut than the other creature did. And his arms were long enough that the shirt fit him like her own three-quarter raglan sleeves, but that was accidental.

"Erin," he said to her quietly, "this shirt will adjust itself to fit me when I stick the gem into the middle of my chest. Please don't shoot me unless you really mean it."

Okay, that was an interesting request. And probably necessary. Kathra had warned her that she might have to take Daniel down, right up to the point where nobody might be able to stop him.

Ndidi was prepared to hit him in the face with a carafe of hot coffee, but anyone holding a fire extinguisher right now would just warn the man what they had prepared.

She watched him step close enough to pick the gem up again and study it for several long seconds before he turned it curved-side-out and rested it against his breastbone like it might bite.

Erin could see the terror in his eyes that it might embed itself right now and conquer him. And still he did it.

Fierce.

And the shirt *flowed*. Erin didn't have a better word to describe what happened. The gap around the gem disappeared, but Daniel didn't start screaming in pain, and his soul was still there at the back of those brown eyes. Sleeves extended. Gut got sucked in. It even showed off the lats and deltoids that weren't immediately obvious, until you considered how much lateral strength a chef needed to have to lift pans and move them with utter precision.

Still, she might have shot him without the warning. Or one of the others. Everyone was that keyed up right now.

Daniel seemed a little more calm now. He truly had feared losing his soul to the gem, hadn't he?

He reached out and snagged the pants, sitting down with his back to everyone so he didn't pitch face first when he put them on and stood back up. Again, the material flowed, shortening in the legs, expanding in the thighs, and shrinking to fit the chef's much smaller waist.

Daniel stood perfectly still for a moment, facing them. It

wasn't death she saw in his eyes. Well, not their death. His own, perhaps.

Dreams dying quickly as fate took you by the collar and shook.

"Commander, I won't be flying over to the other ship on your Spectre," Daniel said with infinite sadness in his voice.

"Why not?" Kathra had turned sideways, straddling the bench, to watch her chef come to grips with eternity, or whatever that damned gem promised the man to get him to take it up.

Daniel gulped once. A second time. Sucked a breath deep into his chest and held it hostage for several seconds.

"Urid-Varg flew over here under his own power," the chef said in a clear, bright voice that reminded her of the edge of her blade, just after she had sharpened it. "That's how I'll go back."

The barrage of sound that erupted around Erin was shock made solid. Denunciation. Anger. Fear. And a few other things.

She and Kathra had already guessed that part, since there had been no shuttle that docked with *WinterStar*. The suit was a portable spaceship, in ways nobody understood.

At least not yet.

"How was he going to get all of us over there?" Erin suddenly perked up.

She lowered the pistol, and after a moment, holstered it. They were past the part of stopping Daniel. And she had enough friends handy to kill him if they needed to.

And if he could be killed.

He shrugged with his head tilted to one side. Probably as good an answer as any other.

"Dunno," he said. "I'm assuming some sort of airlock, but I won't know until we get there."

Kathra handed Daniel the boots next, subtly pushing

him to keep moving forward when Erin could see just how much Daniel wanted to stop now, give it all up, and run back to his kitchen.

She didn't think she had ever met a male who would refuse to accept that level of power. Especially not one that had had two successful restaurants. That was the definition of power, because all decisions had to be yours, at the end of the day.

But he had also had enough. Sold the restaurant to his *Sous Chef* for whatever cash the man had in his wallet that night, according to the legend that had built up. Walked completely away without once looking back, even when people were trying to find him to throw money at the man.

Again, he turned his back on everyone and sat on the bench, close enough that Kathra could punch him or kiss him. Bent over and pulled a boot on, then the other.

He stood, facing them. Closed his eyes in true pain, as if he had just crossed some Rubicon in his mind.

And then he started floating. Not much, but his feet were high enough in the air now that he might look Kathra in the eyes if she stood.

If the last noise to explode had been fear, this one was wonder. Had they all come to claim Daniel Lémieux as one of their own? The only male ever in the comitatus?

In her head, Erin had given it even odds that someone would have shot him by now. So apparently nobody was that concerned.

Daniel landed like a cat. Fixed his eyed on her like someone was driving a knife into one of his kidneys with exquisite patience, and accepted the gloves Kathra was holding out. Pulled them on like he was going out into a blizzard, like they saw on one of their favorite entertainment vids about the team of scientists at the south pole of some forbidden planet.

He just stood there for several more seconds, staring down at his hands. Front. Back. Fists. Flat.

Without bringing his head up, Daniel's eyes found hers again and he pointed at a spot midway between his navel and that gem. Maybe centered just below bone, over his diaphragm.

"Erin, could you shoot me right there, please?" he asked in a quiet tone. "Just once. Areen and Commander Omezi, you might want to step back a little first."

Erin glanced over at Kathra as the woman rose and put space between herself and her chef. Areen did the same.

Erin pulled her pistol and centered it on the man. The gem was almost pulsing, and she could see the faint candy-coating of whatever he had done with his hand earlier, but this was over his entire body.

She hadn't put the safety on earlier, just in case she had needed to quick fire, so she lined him up and caressed the firing stud once. There was a hypersonic crack as the pistol fired, and the recoil drove it smoothly back into her shoulders and hips, like a perfect shot always did.

The bolt had nailed him exactly square and detonated, like it was supposed to. Daniel stumbled back a half-step and stood upright again.

"Well, apparently not," he muttered, looking down before he looked her in the eyes again. "Thank you. Once was enough."

Once should have slammed him backwards into the bulkhead behind him like he had been kicked by a large equine. He should be scorched across the center of his chest about the size that he would need a round dinner plate to cover it. Internal rupture. External bleeding.

Probable death, at this range and that location. Fairly quickly, too.

But Daniel Lémieux was no longer vulnerable to particle

bolt fire. Erin watched him blink rapidly several times as he processed that information.

Most males would effect a massive bravado right now, to be handed that level of power. That was one of the reasons that so few males were birthed by the Mbaysey. Just enough to maintain a wide vitality to the sperm bank, and to have some play toys for those women open-minded enough to consider something so barbaric.

Daniel wasn't most men. Erin wondered how much of his current temperament was a result of being a chef, and how much had driven him into the field in the first place.

He stepped forward with a tiny shrug, almost imperceptible, and sat down again in his spot. After a moment, he picked up his coffee mug, emptied it, and looked over Erin's shoulder.

"Ndidi, if you aren't going to hit me with it, could I get some more coffee, please?" he asked in a voice still finding its footing. "And some bourbon, if we have any handy?"

25

Kathra had offered to let him rest for a while, but Daniel had politely refused, whispering to her that if he didn't do it now, he might never work up the courage again. She could respect that. This entire day had been a calculated risk, the man's ruthless drive against his psychological fragility.

Now she was sitting in *Spectre One*, hanging midway between the *WinterStar* and the Turtle. Originally, she had intended to keep more of the comitatus behind, but they had given her a look that promised all manner of rebellion if they weren't allowed to be here with her, so she had twenty other ships handy.

What they might do, she wasn't sure. The craft were all armed, but that was sufficient for pirates and fools, not conquerors, as Daniel had proclaimed the creature he was usurping today.

"*Spectre One*, this is Daniel," the voice came over the radio sounding tinny.

They had made up a headset for him to wear. It didn't

have a lot of power or range, but it let her talk to the man, as he was truly intent on walking in space. Nobody understood how, but it had apparently been done, so Daniel was adamant that he would figure it out himself.

"Go ahead, Daniel," Kathra replied, wondering if she should go ahead and assign him his own flight number, like the rest of her comitatus had, so that he understood that he belonged.

Perhaps when they got back, and she was sure he still existed as a person, rather than having been hijacked by Urid-Varg over on the ship. Or getting himself killed in the meantime.

Silence.

"Daniel?" Kathra repeated.

"Working up the courage," he said. "Sealing up the airlock now and opening the outer door. Here goes nothing."

Kathra heard the beeping over the radio fade as the air was drawn out of the chamber.

"How are you doing, Daniel?" she asked carefully.

"I think if I peed myself right now, the suit would just absorb it," her chef replied with a slight chuckle. "We may find out soon."

"Keep talking," she ordered him. "If something goes wrong at your end, we might not know until your frozen corpse floated by."

"Thank you for that lovely image, Commander," his voice took on an extra layer of tartness. "I shall endeavor to remember it next time I'm making a dessert of some sort, where frozen spaceman might be an appropriate theme. When's your birthday again?"

Kathra heard several of her crew snorting over lines that they had left open. At least everyone was approaching this with an open mind.

She didn't think it appropriate to remind these women that their fates might come down to the decisions of one man. They might not appreciate her humor.

"Not for several more months," Kathra replied when the line got quiet again. "You can torture Erin first."

"Oh, thank you, Kathra," her best friend came over the line.

More laughter.

"The outer door is opening now," Daniel said. "And I'm not exploding, so we'll perhaps count this as a win. I can see darkness and distant stars through the hatch as it retracts inward. Dead silence around me, without any air to carry anything but the sound of my heartbeat."

She heard him swallow once, the mic being close enough to his throat for those sounds.

"And now, the stupid male is walking out into space, wearing a living gem as a spacesuit and pretending he's not going to lose his bladder as he turns and looks backwards at *WinterStar*, hanging still behind him and rotating," Daniel continued.

On her scanner boards, Kathra saw a new dot emerge from the stern of her flagship and begin to move in this direction. The space between the two ships was roughly a kilometer or so at the moment. Enough for all the Spectres to be in between, at relative rest and facing in all directions, with scanners pinging madly and guns ready for whatever trouble might emerge.

Kathra's greatest fear over the last few days had been another, damned Septagon finding her, even clear out here. She was well beyond even systems with Sept colonies being established, and well around the curve of their border from the heart of the Free Worlds. Most of this sector was empty of anything but prospectors, and perhaps religious minorities that had fled the reach of Imperial Earth at some point in the distant past. How long those folks remained free was a matter of speculation.

Kathra and her mother had both understood that being on a planet made you vulnerable to conquest. The tribal squadron could just fly away from the Sept, or any others. It kept the population extremely small, but modern medicine allowed her to maintain eighty-five percent of the adults as females.

"And now, the craziness begins," Daniel's voice brought her back from flights of fancy. "I am…uhm…telling the suit to fly over there. I think. Somebody be ready to catch me?"

"I have you, Daniel," Erin came over the line. "We'll chase you down if something goes wrong, and I'm in a suit so I can vent my ship to let you inside."

"Thank you," he said succinctly.

On the scanner, a blue-shift appeared as he started to move. It wasn't much, but the very recognition that Daniel Lémieux could move in space without a suit or a ship was dangerous enough.

Any other man…

"Commander, I must share an image with you," Daniel said quietly. "In my mind, in somebody else's memories, all four of the forward fins are landing platforms. The rear two are…I can't call them engines, because I really don't understand it, but they make it fly."

"Someone else's memories, Daniel?" Kathra asked.

"They're all in here, Commander," he said with a jerky, jittery voice. "Urid-Varg controlled them, but he's gone now. I don't want to enslave them, but some of them are willing to…talk, I suppose is as good a word as any other. They are trying to share memories with me. If you hear me talk in the present tense about those other men, that's what happened. Erin won't necessarily have to shoot me."

"Necessarily," Erin clarified with a chuckle.

"Necessarily," Daniel agreed. "She might do it because it becomes necessary later, but I can't help that. I am going to try to land on the right, forward fin. Is the correct term starboard?"

"Starboard One," Kathra said, classifying it for everyone listening.

"Yes. Very good," Daniel said. "Could you join me, please? I could really use some company."

Yes. She supposed he might. Nothing would prepare anyone for what he was doing. But nobody else on *WinterStar* could have done it. He was the first man to serve aboard her flagship in several years.

"Coming alongside, Daniel," she replied, manipulating her thrusters and gyros to bring her nose around and then start pushing her on an intercept course.

The Star Turtle was huge. Septagon-sized, without the gap in the bottom. Nearly two and a half kilometers wide across just the shell. Several times that from tip of the snout to the end of that tail, stuck out just like a real sea turtle's. As she approached, that fin looked large enough that the entire Haunt could have landed on the outside with space to spare.

Daniel hung in space beside her, glowing enough that she could see him with her naked eye, perhaps fifty meters away. The rest of *The Haunt* hung around the two of them protectively.

"I always wanted to do this," he said mischievously. "Open sesame."

Kathra recognized the term from ancient, Terran literature that had apparently infected almost all cultures eventually. The Tales of the Thousand and One Nights.

In front of her, the fin seemed to split open horizontally, the top retracting from the bottom to open a wide, slit mouth that ran over four hundred meters, from where the fin emerged to the hinge near the tip.

Curses and joy filled the radio as the others saw the same thing.

Daniel turned towards her across the space, like he wanted to make sure she was still there.

"I'm supposed to go in there," he said. "You'll come with me?"

She could hear the fear in his voice. That perhaps she and her people would blast off on their valence drives instead as soon as he was out of sight and he would be left alone with his fears and Urid-Varg's ghosts.

"Of course," Kathra reassured him. "Lead the way."

He moved quickly, with so little mass to accelerate. Kathra followed at a more sedate pace, knowing she would have to decelerate at the other end when she wanted to land.

Inside he came down onto what looked like a firm deck. She would have said metal, but it was too green for anything she had ever seen, much like the rest of the giant ship.

Still, Kathra flew into that maw and maneuvered herself adroitly. The deck here was deep enough for six of her Spectres to be lined up nose to tail, and perhaps thirty ships wide. And this was just one of four landing bays?

"Anyone else coming?" Daniel asked.

Kathra considered it briefly.

"Erin, Areen, Joane, join us," she called out. "Kamharida and Iruoma set up a watch cycle and rotate half the team back to *WinterStar* for now, but keep people in the sky at all times."

A chorus of assents as people began to move.

Kathra began to shut down her engines and power system, but she kept an eye on Daniel, standing in the middle of the deck, alternately watching her, the approaching

Spectres, and the place at the body where there appeared to be an enormous airlock.

What would they find inside?

Or who?

26

HE HAD ALWAYS WANTED to fly. Every twelve year old boy had that dream. Just step out a door and disappear into the sky, escaping all the mundane problems on the ground, but Daniel had never really let those flights of fancy dictate things to him.

Both his parents had taught him to find joy in cooking, rather than just relying on an autochef and a freezer for everything. *Certainement*, it was easier. Just stock up on premade food and keep it handy, but it lacked soul. Lacked joy.

Daniel had been born for the kitchen. Once he discovered that, everything else was easy. And it was all predictable. Ordered. Precise. So many cups and tablespoons of ingredient. Mixed just so. Baked for an exact number of minutes and you have a meal.

It might not be the greatest meal, but that came later. When you could look at the ingredients and adjust things on the fly to fit whatever your body desired today. Or peek into the oven and decide to leave something for just a few extra minutes to get it perfect, in spite of the time on the recipe.

When a recipe became merely a suggestion, a roadmap filled with all manner of possible tourist stops you could take along the way.

There was nothing, however, that had prepared him for this.

The deck was solid under his feet. He had flown here in mortal fear that it would be like landing on the soft innards of a true turtle, something wet and yielding when he walked.

Squishy.

He watched the other three ships join the Commander, powering down and waiting.

"I'm going to close the garage door now," Daniel said with as little trepidation as he could manage. "There will be atmosphere after I do. No, I don't know how."

He turned to the ship, staring down the long axis of the fin and tried to calm his breathing. It wasn't something so simple as pushing a button and letting gears grind. He didn't have words for it.

Perhaps need, and the gem translated it. Amplified it? Let him talk to the thing that was the Star Turtle.

It wasn't alive. Exactly. Wasn't an animal that could be trained, like a smart canine. But it wasn't cold metal, like *WinterStar*, either.

Daniel didn't even have the vocabulary to express some concept that seemed to somehow split the difference between creature and machine. Cyborg referred to those people like Erin that had replaced some organic part with something mechanical, perhaps wired to the brain, although he had never asked her if hers was simply metal, or if she had electronics in it.

Not his place to bother her. Then or now.

This thing was both at the same time, rather than two parts connected.

And not a problem he needed to solve today either. He hoped.

Daniel focused his mind on the turtle's and somehow told it to close the bay door.

There was gravity in here. He hadn't processed that until just now, but once inside the bay, down had become down. Something similar to gravity inducers, he supposed.

Lights came on. Or were already on, and became brighter. Bioluminescent strips in the ceiling, because they glowed like ten million fireflies behind a thin sheet of film, rather than the stark, white, electronic illumination he was used to.

The roof came down. One of the women cursed absently on the radio in his ear as it did, but she was just saying the thing aloud that he didn't have the courage to express.

The deck jarred. Not bad. Not even an earthquake. Perhaps as much as the wake of another boat passing under your own keel as it went by.

The lights went to full. Air flooded the chamber. Daniel knew it would be sufficient for him to walk around without the energy shield that had been protecting him until now, and for the Commander and her comitatus to exit their own ships safely. Well, Erin already could, but she had been prepared to save his life if he needed her.

Just as she had been prepared to end it.

Was that the definition of true friendship?

"It's safe now, Commander," Daniel said after a bit.

Again, he didn't know how he knew it, but he did. Was his mind extending to encompass the ship as well? It didn't have an ego of any sort. Had Urid-Varg supplied that?

So much nobody knew, and Daniel would be fine not ever having the chance to ask that *salaud*.

Commander Omezi emerged from her ship first. The Spectres were capable of landing on the surface of a

TradeStation or Planet, but rarely did, so the docking hatch was at the top of a ladder up from the deck inside. She climbed up into the light, walked across the left wing of her ship, and climbed down a series of notches in the side of the hull that Daniel had been unaware of until now.

He felt better, just knowing she was here. Kathra Omezi wouldn't be able to do much of anything, but she could make the decisions he couldn't.

The other women emerged in quick order. Erin still retained her deep-space suit, but had removed the helmet and hung it from her hip opposite the pistol she wore on the outside of her thigh.

Daniel hoped it would be unnecessary.

Hoped.

Quickly, he found himself at the bottom of a bowl, looking up at the women in front of him. He was used to that with men, being only one hundred sixty-eight centimeters tall. It had taken some getting used to when most of the women he saw on a daily basis were taller as well.

And warriors, while he was just a cook.

"Ready?" the Commander asked simply.

"No," Daniel replied. "But that can't be allowed to stop me now."

He took a deep breath as he turned and began walking towards the thing his mind interpreted as an airlock. It wasn't, not as he or anyone else understood the concept, but again, that was going to describe so much of what was coming, wasn't it?

He had seen a particular plant once. The major part of it was a funnel, like he might use to pour vanilla from the large bottle in the pantry into the small vial he used when cooking. Wide at the top and narrow at the bottom. What had struck him at the time was a bit of leaf, if he could call it that, that would be triggered when an insect entered the tube to get to the nectar at the bottom.

Bees were apparently favored, as the plant ignored them. Anything else crawling around got trapped inside when that leaf closed and locked, for lack of a better term to describe it. A cork going into a bottle, so that the ants could not escape when the plant emitted digestive juices and killed them.

The outer hatch to the airlock looked just like that leaf as he walked up to it.

It did not help his sanity that the doorway was large enough that the Commander could have flown her little fighter craft in here. And the other three women probably could have joined her in theirs, if everyone was careful in their piloting.

Someone could have held a petite concert in here, with the outer hatch closed to hold in air and sound.

Daniel entered the mouth of the galaxy's largest carnivorous pitcher plant and held his breath.

There was a smell in here after he remembered to release his shield. That just made everything worse. He hadn't smelled anything except his own sweat before.

He considered asking the women what they smelled, but terror took hold of his tongue and rendered him mute. Instead, he swallowed past the frog in his throat and focused his mind on the ship around him.

"Everyone ready?" he did manage to squeak.

They were, so he told the flower to trap them inside.

Airlocks make noise. Mostly as a reminder to people that really heavy equipment was moving around and they need to be out of the way. But also because death pressure was usually waiting just around the corner from you.

This one moved silently, uncurling from a side like a flower petal rather than pivoting on a heavy-duty hinge.

Daniel watched in patient awe as he was sealed in with

the others, and then they moved down toward the narrow end of the concert hall. The room seemed to have the slightest incline, but maybe just enough to roll marbles, or cause water to drain, rather than any sort of slope that made walking difficult.

The inner hatch to the thing he had to call an airlock was the same as the outer, but this one was only thirty meters wide, rather than the sixty or so of the outer one. It responded to the need he tried to communicate, and opened into another warehouse.

"*Merde!*" he nearly shouted as the hatch cleared.

The woman around him reacted in a similar manner.

After a moment of staggering forward, his brain caught up. Flight deck. Airlock. Storage. The things around him were more than a dozen space craft of one type or another, parked rather haphazardly.

Like one might do if being mind-controlled and brought here to serve a conqueror?

Daniel shivered uncontrollably for a moment, but a hand on his shoulder seemed to break the spell. He turned and looked up at the Commander.

He couldn't say she understood, because the only people who really did were dead and trapped in the gem, but she had at least some level of empathy.

"Anybody recognize anything?" she asked the other three.

Daniel wandered forward with the women, but space ships had never been his thing, once he was eight and past those sorts of dreams. The four women moved like big cats stalking in the high grass.

Each remained in sight of the others, but they spread out and touched things in passing. He heard casual conversations, but they were talking in a technical language so dense that he only understood about one word in five.

They appeared to be pleased, from what Daniel could tell.

"Three other fins?" the Commander turned back to ask him.

It took a moment for the words to achieve coherence.

"Yes," he finally translated her. "This one was the primary. The creature was right-handed, if I understand my own memories, but there are probably smaller inventories at the other three ports. Is it important?"

"Salvage," Commander Omezi said. "Or perhaps that's not quite the right term. These are collectibles, Daniel. I've never seen anything like many of them, so we might be able to sell them to a museum or a collector, if we can find a way to sneak them to the right TradeStation."

"Sneak, Commander?"

Daniel felt his brow furrow. More.

"Nobody should ever learn about the Turtle, Daniel," she said distinctly. "But we might be able to sell off some of the things Urid-Varg has acquired in his time. That is, if you would like to."

"Me?" he was aghast.

"You," she said, boring in on him now. "This is legally all your property now, Daniel. By right of conquest, if nothing else. My comitatus couldn't have gotten in here to salvage anything without you doing all the work to date, so if you'll allow it, I'll find a way to sell some of this gear and split the profits with you."

"Oh," he said emptily.

Had there been anywhere to sit, he would have collapsed into it, just because standing was a bit much right now. But there was not, so he just sort of rocked back and forth and tried to process himself as a mighty space pirate.

It didn't sound any less silly the second time, either. Or the third.

"Is it worth anything?" Daniel finally asked, giving up on the other line of logic.

"I've never seen some of these design architectures, Daniel," she replied.

"That's bad?"

"That's good," she corrected him. "That means they are alien to some degree. Cultures the Sept and the Free Worlds are not necessarily trading with today. Where did he come from?"

"Huh? Oh. Uhm, inwards, sort of," Daniel tried to explain it. "Except he crossed a vast darkness. Twice, actually. Once a very, very long ago, and once more recently. Does that make any sense?"

"Galactic arms?" Erin asked, having snuck up on him from his blind side and nearly causing him to jump over one of these ships with a shout. "Sorry. You okay?"

Daniel tried to breathe in a normal manner, but his body wasn't having it, so he just huffed and puffed like a badly-tuned engine burning alcohol.

"Wound perhaps three shades too tight," Daniel finally turned to the woman and explained. "I'll be fine in a few years."

At least she grinned at him before turning her more-serious face to the Commander.

"That's my guess," Omezi said. "He was very old and very powerful, but probably just exploring the galaxy and capturing things that tickled his fancy as he went, rather than forging some sort of stellar empire, like the Sept."

"Oh, he did that, too," Daniel perked up. "They got angry and tossed the *salaud* out on his ass after a while."

Both women had fallen silent in a way that made Daniel extremely nervous.

"Is everything okay?" he asked carefully.

"When was that, Daniel?" Commander Omezi asked.

He struggled.

"Very old memories, Commander," he offered, closing his eyes and trying to make sense of the visions. "I can see the night sky, and it was his long enough to change over time. How long does that take?"

"Thousands of years," Erin spoke up. "Every star moves in relation to others, but the arms generally move in concert. It would take a very long time for them to change alignment."

"Oh," Daniel said, more at a loss for meaningful words than anything. "Then he left and began to wander, but his body finally got old, so he captured a new one and rode it."

"Vampire?" Erin asked in an off-hand voice.

"Something," the Commander agreed. "Daniel, can your radio communicator reach outside the ship?"

He thought about it for a moment. Listened to the voices in the back of his mind come to some sort of consensus. That part made him even more nervous.

"No," he shook his head. "The hull is too…something. Hold on. Let me try something."

He thought really hard at the ship around him. It was like being inside a blanket that was just thin enough to allow light through it. One of the lights got brighter, at least in his mind.

"Can anyone hear me?" Daniel asked in a conversational voice.

"Spectre Four here," Kamharida replied in a voice that seemed oddly modulated.

But then, the crystals he was using were organic in nature. And he had apparently turned into some strange sort of sorcerer along the way.

"Kam, this is Kathra, checking in," the Commander spoke now. "Everything is good here for now, so cycle everyone back aboard *WinterStar* and I'll reach out at some point with more news. There will probably be things we can salvage, even if we can't move the ship itself."

"Understood, Commander," Kamharida replied.

"Should I leave the line open?" Daniel asked her.

"Can you connect to *WinterStar*?"

"*Ife* here, Commander," Ifedimma was suddenly on the line, clear enough that she might have been standing next to them.

"Okay, Daniel, leave this line open for now," Commander Omezi said. "Ife, just record everything and monitor for now. We've found a bay full of old ships that we might want to fly over to *WinterStar* later, but we're going to explore a bit more first."

"Very good, Commander," the woman said.

Daniel reached out with his mind and made sure the light remained on. Or something.

He still didn't even have the start of a working vocabulary. It was almost like promoting the dishwasher to prep cook and having to patiently explain everything to him three times.

You had to be prepared to do it three times, because they wouldn't understand anything the first time. Then they would get most of it only partly right. After three, they either had it reasonably down, or didn't have a future in the kitchen anyway, and it was best to let them go quickly.

He felt like he should just go back to washing dishes right now, but that wouldn't help the Commander. She had a plan, it seemed. And access to valuable things, now.

Daniel shook his head carefully, afraid it might fall off, and followed her as the women headed deeper into the guts of a Star Turtle.

Always, the fear that the *salaud* was waiting for him, just around a corner.

27

Just monumentally, freaking weird.

Erin couldn't nail down the right profanities that covered this craziness, even adding Daniel's French to the mix.

Past the flight deck, they had wandered ancient, empty hallways, stopping to look into side chambers occasionally. The chef was so twitchy that Erin had quietly warned the other two women to keep the horseplay to a dead minimum, so as to not give the little male a heart attack.

They still needed him, even if just to get back out of this ship later.

But if they could loot even a fraction of the stuff they had seen…

At one point Daniel had led them through a forest. Arboretum was probably a better, technical term, but she had never seen an indoor one with hundred-meter-tall ceilings, nor one that covered sixty or eighty hectares, with hills, ponds, streams, and even birds flying around.

He had assured them that there were no predators larger than housecats, so Erin hadn't felt the need to walk around with a pistol in her hand. She could always quickdraw even faster than Kathra in an emergency.

The weird part about all the trees was how few of them she recognized, but how many were bearing fruit right now. It was as if you had the perfect conditions, the perfect climate, and the perfect soil, across hundreds of trees.

Wouldn't feed even a ClanStar, but Erin could see harvesting this place regularly for fresh fruit to trade with the other ships. And Creator knew what else there might be.

Enough salvage to build more ships? Expand the tribal squadron finally? Escape the Sept for good, or at least push them back?

Erin had let flights of fanciful avarice consume her briefly as she trailed the group.

That had turned out to be a wise choice, because the next stop had been a hall of trophy skulls, embedded into the walls like an ancient catacomb. Each stripped of flesh as if left for the ants for a year, and then polished and sealed in.

Daniel had started out almost proud, explaining that they represented all the people that Urid-Varg had ridden as mounts, stored here as memories.

About midway down the hall, the chef had choked on his voice and fallen silent.

The skull had looked like an Upynth, maybe. Minus the cute little unicorn horn in the forehead, and with a longer snout and bigger eyes. Definitely equine in nature, rather than the simian ancestry of humans.

Turned out there were six of them, where the conqueror had previously only retained one example of each.

"Z'lud," Daniel said in a very quiet voice. "The second empire. Briefly."

He had fallen silent, apparently trapped in internal memories so intense she thought she heard sniffles coming from the man. But he was a male.

After that, they passed deeper. Through other trophy halls filled with things she could only barely identify, and those few were obviously weapons of some sort, which followed a universal physics. One room held land vehicles so ancient they still rolled on wheels, with about half pulled by various animals, to hear the chef try to explain it, and the others powered by a variety of internal engines representing technology of some level.

Again, places so weird, and so apparently distant, that they might never have heard of humanity itself, to say nothing of the Sept Empire or the Free Worlds.

Eventually, the group found the bridge.

Daniel was utterly white by then, so faded from his normal dirt-brown that he looked like someone had drained all the blood from an animated corpse. In response to Kathra's question, all he would say was that they were in the turtle's head.

The space was the same green as the rest. Not metal, but perhaps an organic plastic with similar properties. It wasn't large, but felt that way with a high vault to the ceiling above and nothing at all in here except a chair Erin could only classify as a throne, surrounded on all sides by empty space.

The throne itself faced a blank wall, rather than being up on a platform where the king could be seen and worshipped by his followers. Assuming he had any.

Urid-Varg had lived as solitary an existence as possible on this ship. They had seen a chamber where he could sleep, with a small bathroom attached. A place where he could prepare food.

Nothing else.

No libraries. No salons. Just an endless stream of forests and trophy rooms, without any dust or insects anywhere.

"Are we in one of the eye sockets?" Joane asked as she looked around the room.

Daniel had frozen just inside the door.

"*Non*," he muttered. "Those are weapons. Just as the maw is designed to bite asteroids and comets for raw materials."

"Weapons, Daniel?" Kathra asked as Erin moved closer.

"*Oui*," he said, perhaps a shade louder. "Powerful beams. Urid-Varg feared nobody."

Erin shared a quick glance with Kathra.

Enough to chase off a Septagon? Damage one, perhaps?

Those beasts were the largest ships Erin had ever even heard of in space. At least until the Star Turtle appeared.

What could they do to push the Sept Empire back, the next time one of those naupati decide to throw his weight around? That many Ram Cannons on a Septagon were enough to destroy *WinterStar*, to say nothing of the Axial Megacannon that was the basis of Sept power.

"Daniel, is this really the bridge?" Areen asked. Looking around.

"It is," he said glumly, eyes locked on that throne sitting in the middle of the room.

Looked uncomfortable as a place to sit for more than two minutes. Mostly square, as if carved out of a block of that green hull plating with a laser, but without any thought to human shape.

Of course, the creature Daniel had killed hadn't been human. Nor had any of the other skulls he had shown them, embedded securely in the walls of that other trophy room.

"How does it work?" Kathra asked.

Daniel looked like he was on the verge of tears right now, but as he had said earlier, if he didn't do everything now, he might never find the courage again.

"He liked to sit here," Daniel had moved a few steps closer to the throne and pointed at it now. "He would commune, I suppose you would call it, with the turtle, and could see in all directions, almost as if he was the turtle, in ways I cannot understand. Like so much else."

"Blank walls?" Areen asked, stepping close enough to the man that Erin figured he might be able to feel the warmth of her body.

Perverts.

The chef looked around for a second, but he wasn't actually seeing anything. That much was clear when she looked in his eyes as they passed.

"Need is will," he muttered. "Hear me."

Erin felt her hand stray ever so slightly to the butt of her pistol, but Daniel had turned away from her to look at the wall where the throne faced. He didn't sit, but the wall did something.

It wasn't like the shields on *WinterStar*'s bridge retracting. These walls seemed to fluoresce briefly, and then turn transparent. Erin could see stars and darkness out there.

That almost felt like home out there.

"*WinterStar*, this is Daniel," he said in a bleak voice. "The turtle is going to move now, but that's me. Please do not be concerned."

Kathra caught her eye now. As did Areen and Joane. Could he really control all this power? What then?

"Understood, Daniel," Ife replied. "Standing by and scanning."

"Thank you."

He turned to Kathra with a pained face and hollow eyes. The muscles on his jaw stood out from where he was clenching them enough to probably give himself a headache in a few hours.

Kathra nodded once at the man.

It felt wrong to Erin. No, just bizarre. The male had all the power in this situation, but none of the will. Oh, he was a stubborn, opinionated shit at times, but they all were. He was frozen by indecision.

Daniel was afraid. Of them?

Perhaps of himself as well?

What might someone do, when suddenly granted the power of a god?

She watched and listened as he took an immense breath for such a small body, and then closed his eyes.

"*Putain*," Joane muttered under her breath.

She had moved to look out the portal into space.

Erin watched aghast as *WinterStar* came into view, spinning quietly out there in the darkness like a child's top as the turtle turned. They didn't come all the way around, where the beak and the eyes might be lined up with the flagship, but enough that everyone on the bridge could see the vessel.

She even saw the quick flinch that passed through Kathra's frame, but only because she had moved around to the back of the room already.

Yes, what could they do with Daniel as an ally?

And how did they keep their hold on him?

28

———

BECAUSE IT WAS STILL TECHNICALLY his kitchen, Daniel had turned the lights down in here. Everything on the Star Turtle had been extra bright to the point that his eyes and head hurt.

But he was home now.

Maybe.

Back on *WinterStar*, at least.

He focused his entire attention on the bowl in front of him on the counter and stirred with a wooden spoon. The rolled dough had risen, so now he just needed to finish mixing up the sugar, melted butter, and cinnamon to spread over the half of the dough awaiting him on the counter.

"Is there anything I can do to help?" Ndidi asked quietly.

Daniel felt angry eyes lock onto the young woman. She wasn't close enough to bite, and that was probably good right now.

"Sit down and shut up?" he offered in a dark voice. "Take notes."

He had returned to *WinterStar* and taken a shower. All that *salaud*'s clothing was still in his cabin, waiting for him like a plague vector, quiescent and lurking. Right now, he was wearing his old gray pants, an older blue T-shirt, and the black apron that would hopefully shield him from the rest of the day.

Yeast, water, scalded milk, sugar, shortening, salt, flour, and an egg. Together, they formed that most magical of things, a dinner roll. He had gone sweet with this batch, doubling the sugar because he was making cinnamon rolls instead.

The current mixture got slathered over the rolled out dough and sprinkled with raisins. Roll the sheet up and pinch the ends. Slice with the sharpest knife you have into three centimeter disks, lay flat on a baking sheet.

Ndidi had fallen so silent that he'd forgotten she was there for a moment, glancing up in surprise that she was watching him with an intensity perhaps a notch worse than Erin considering if she should draw and shoot the chef when he wasn't looking.

"Notes?" he asked.

"Long half cup white sugar. Quarter cup melted butter. Long teaspoon and a half of cinnamon. Third of a cup black raisins at the end, just before you roll and seal."

Merde, he had forgotten Ndidi had a near-eidetic memory. If the Mbaysey believed in the sorts of genetic engineering that some other renegades from the Sept did, they would have fixed her eyes when she was young, and the woman would probably have ended up challenging Erin for place in another few years.

Maybe Kathra Omezi needed to broaden the definition of her comitatus. Ndidi's brilliance was wasted, living in a kitchen.

Well, not wasted. Any more than Daniel was. But she would be a good leader at some point, if the Commander found a place for the young woman.

Daniel grunted and realized that he was taking all his self-hatred out on her and she had done nothing at all to deserve it. He handed her the spoon and stepped back from the counter.

"You do the other half," he said, trying to find a calmer voice.

Something that sounded closer to human.

"You sure?" she asked, holding the spoon but not moving.

As if it was a trap. Or a test. Almost the same thing, at least in Daniel's kitchen.

"This is my grandmother's variant on a recipe older than starflight," he said simply. "I need comfort food and comfort cooking right now. The women will not mind getting the leftovers after I have eaten two and you have had yours."

Ndidi smiled and nodded. Daniel expected her to grab a clean bowl, or wash this one, but she just grabbed measuring cups and went to work right into this one as he watched.

And judged.

"Should I replicate your batch perfectly?" she asked as she started to stir.

Yes, she probably could, having watched him do this thing.

"*Oui*," he replied. "Then you will have the proper baseline against which to make your own variant next time."

She nodded once and focused with an intensity that might have made the bowl glow with light had he been standing there. Her hands moved with a precision that only the best chefs and cooking robots ever achieved, so he let go the breath that had been trapped in his chest and tried to work on the knot between his shoulder blades.

Another tube of dough turned quickly into a layer of disks on the second baking sheet.

"Now what?" she asked, looking at him with penetrating eyes only mildly hidden behind those glass lenses.

"Now they rise for twenty minutes," Daniel said. "Then we will bake them. The stove is already set, so you will make a double batch of simple frosting, but only frost half of them."

"Which half?" her face grew serious.

"Half of each," Daniel's voice turned conspiratorial. "Then mix them up on serving plates and see if any of the women can tell the difference."

She snickered quietly as she moved this bowl to the sink and grabbed a new set of weapons.

Yes, it would not be his kitchen much longer, but these women would be in exceptional hands. Daniel didn't know what he would do next.

Cooking was a social thing. He could cause the Turtle to create a kitchen for him. Liberate a few pots and pans and utensils from *WinterStar* so he could cook. But if he was alone over there, he knew he would never rise to the level of *cuisine* without great effort.

Quickly, Daniel would fall into simple comfort foods. Gratin Dauphinois. Ratatouille. Onion soup. Ragout. Perhaps a Cheese soufflé.

Nothing of art.

And yet, he knew that the Commander would be counting on him to help her loot the Star Turtle. Perhaps to somehow add it permanently to the tribal squadron, providing the Mbaysey a guardian hound that not even the Sept could brush aside.

To do that, he would have to live aboard the turtle all the time, without a chance to return to *WinterStar* and cook for his favorite fans. His friends.

Solitude, at the moment when he had discovered that just perhaps he liked people, after all. Some of them, anyway.

He should have known that God would enjoy visiting Her black humor and wit upon a simple cook like him. What better way to keep a man humble, when he had perhaps come to believe the silly things that gastronomical journalists were wont to write about him?

"Daniel?" Ndidi suddenly broke his reverie.

"*Oui?*"

"I asked if we should consider moving the comitatus to live aboard the turtle," she apparently repeated. "So you could keep cooking for them? At least as much as Kathra allows you the time."

Hopefully, he hadn't been muttering out loud in front of Ndidi. Kitchens were normally noisy places, so his apparent habit would normally go unheard. Hopefully unremarked. Some probably even considered it a mark of his genius.

Morons.

He ran a hand down his face as if that would wipe away the dark things that wanted to cling to his flesh.

"We can ask, but would that mean you'd have to remain behind?" he focused more of his attention on the woman.

"On the contrary, *m'sieur*," she smiled serenely. "I'm sure she'll keep you going so hard that you barely get to cook one meal in five. She'll need me running the kitchen the rest of the time."

He laughed, and felt his shoulders finally come down. Yes, hopefully the Commander would listen to this dangerously-brilliant young woman. He couldn't call her a child, for all that he was about old enough to be her father.

She was not his equal in the arts of cuisine, but that was just a matter of time, not talent. He hadn't known his ass from a hole in the ground when he'd first started.

No, she was certainly his peer. The youngest he had ever known, but that just made her a *Commis Chef,* learning everything at once, even as she was also *Chef de Tournant,* filling in at all stations as she learned those few things still outside her grasp to become *Sous Chef* when he was around, and *Chef de Cuisine* when he was not.

He supposed he still had a few things to teach the youngster, at least until they opened a restaurant on a planet or TradeStation together and she had to learn the interesting bits of running a successful *bistro*. The business side.

Here, at least, Ndidi knew what fish were coming, what meat was next in the freezer, and what vegetables she could call upon on short notice. She would need a few years in Nice or perhaps Brest, up north in Brittany, to become truly a master, negotiating with farmers and fishermen who could just tell her to piss up a rope if they wanted, something yet out of the reach of the leaders of the ClanStars providing Kathra Omezi her food.

"*Bon*," he said simply, holding out a hand for her to shake, in the ancient manner. "Let us go see what mischief the Commander has in mind next."

29

––––––

After so many years of being in charge of her own destiny, Kathra knew that the unease in the pit of her stomach would take some time to get used to. If they went deep into the Free Worlds and found the right person, she could sell much of Urid-Varg's trophies off and perhaps have enough cash to build several more ClanStars, or replace *WinterStar* with something larger and more dangerous.

The important question at that point would be Daniel. Would he stay with them, if he accidentally turned into a god? At a minimum, the turtle could probably annihilate any patrol forces that came looking for them, especially as Kathra would shift most of the tribal squadron deeper into uncolonized space and away from Sept bases, just so nobody discovered her new weapon.

Nobody could know who would win the first battle between Daniel and a Septagon, but Kathra did not really desire to kill three hundred thousand people in order to find out, at least not without a really good reason. Even the Mbaysey's history with the Sept Empire did not rise to that level.

Or shouldn't.

They had not all been slaves, when her mother managed to challenge their status in the courts and somehow win. An oppressed minority, perhaps, relegated to a small reservation on Tazo, where poverty forced many of them to make horrible choices to survive.

From there, Yagazie Omezi had led them into space. Had reshaped the tribe into a tribal squadron before her assassination by the Sept. Most of the men of the tribe had left long ago, recruited into military service, colonization efforts, or something worse, leaving the women behind. Which had probably been the Sept's stupidest mistake.

The women had adapted.

As they continued to do today.

Kathra sat comfortably against an enormous tree and looked around the orchard as Daniel and Ndidi cataloged plants into weird groups. Edible, medicinal, industrial, neutral, toxic. Growing season and storage, drawing on his deep memories, or nightmares, depending. Closest approximation for taste. Eligibility for fermentation.

That latter suggested that he was planning to remain with them for a while. Not many men were welcome.

Yagazie had taken her newly-won freedom and traded nearly everything the tribe had for a space ship. A small one. Poor. Old. Too useless to even have gravity inducers, relying on spin instead.

But enough to trade. The women of the tribe had always been experts at the bargain. That one ship grew into a second. A third. A ClanStar. Another. Eventually, a whole squadron, allowing them to one day simply fly away from the Sept and live truly free.

At least until the assassins found Yagazie Omezi and Kathra became leader in her mother's place.

"Daniel," she called and drew the two closer.

Erin and Areen appeared from wherever they had been napping and joined the conversation, such as it were.

Daniel and Ndidi were roughly of a size, which was always strange to look at. Her glasses kept her from flying a Spectre, but her brains were good enough. Idly, Kathra wondered if they should have considered doing something for the woman earlier, as they had gone into the Free Worlds to fit Erin with that replacement leg that let her remain a pilot.

Water under the bridge, if she understood the saying correctly, but Kathra reconsidered her second chef.

"Should we begin planting some of the better-suited fruits and vegetables on the other ships?" Kathra asked. "Much of what we grow is not particularly suited to space, but will work in the various hydroponics rooms. Can we improve things?"

"I was just explaining that to Ndidi," Daniel replied diffidently. "Most of the fruits are just complex sugars and useful trace minerals. I am not sure about soil needs, so I don't know how they might interact with our plants."

"My proposal was to begin a garden here, Commander," Ndidi spoke up. "Kitchen spices. Annual and perennial vegetables. Begin planting larger things like blueberry and pear trees to see what will be safe. We will need your permission to make such changes."

Kathra considered Ndidi's words. Technically, they only needed her nod if Daniel still considered himself part of the Mbaysey. This would be his ship. Everyone else would be his guests and nothing more, because she didn't think anybody could do so much as open the big bay doors to escape without Daniel.

Unless she brought in some other male and took the power away from her chef.

They were not anywhere near that at present. Kathra

Omezi didn't know a male in her squadron with the requisite toughness to take on that role. Certainly not one she would trust afterwards.

Worse come to absolute worst, the tribal squadron could hopefully flee from Daniel instead, if he developed a megalomania that threatened them. There was a whole galaxy out there to hide in. She was already doing that to the Sept.

"If you are bringing plantings here to grow, you have my permission," Kathra said. "From there, we should probably build a whole new hydroponic facility on *WinterStar*, Erin. Isolated completely from the water and probably airlocked in with positive pressure until we know it's safe."

Her Second in Command nodded, always watching with hawk's eyes over that barcode inherited from Grandma Ezinne.

Kathra rose from where she had been resting and looked down at the group. Possibly her innermost circle right now, depending on how you wished to classify those things, and Ndidi was handling herself well enough to be admitted on a trial basis. She considered her words carefully.

"Should we consider basing half *The Haunt* here and half on *WinterStar*?" she asked, looking at the various faces for reactions.

Ndidi and Daniel had made a compelling argument to move everyone here, but that put all of her power in his hands. His control. Any male, when Urid-Varg might yet find a way to sneak back from whatever hell Kathra had condemned him to.

Splitting the force, even in rotation, caused the group to become two, unless someone moved each direction every day, rotating in and out on an eleven-day cycle. Certainly a change in doing things, but not a wise one.

Dare they risk it?

Erin's face had turned sour, ever so slightly, but she had

the same opinion. The same arguments. The comitatus was Kathra's, but putting the Spectres and their pilots here separated them also from the mechanics and crew on *WinterStar*. Broke that subtle, personal connection that kept everyone flying as a team.

On the other side, Daniel would be alone. She could see that cold reality gnawing at him. The fear in his eyes, of facing all those ghosts contained in these halls. And perhaps the conqueror himself, hiding around a corner with a pipe.

Alone.

Areen surprised her by speaking up now. Normally, the woman spoke last, having allowed the others their say, but perhaps the silence meant that all words had already been spoken.

"No," Areen said simply. "The risks and rewards are not balanced. Better to keep a shuttle intact to run crew over here when needed, and keep everyone on *WinterStar*. Including Daniel. He can board the turtle quickly if he needs to, but should stay with people in a safer environment."

Kathra suspected that Areen had ulterior motives, all things considered, but her logic was sound. And about where Kathra had landed, after weighing all the options. If they were careful, nobody could sneak up on the tribal squadron or follow them home from a TradeStation.

The greatest risk would be approaching the Free Worlds to trade many or most of the antique shuttles off for cash.

Daniel might have been reading her mind. Or had learned how she thought. Or something equally interesting.

"Commander, when we do visit civilization, there is one unresolved mystery ongoing," he said quietly, glancing carefully around the group. "Urid-Varg had power. Mental abilities that the gem multiplied. Multiplies. I have not even attempted to see if I could read anyone's inner thoughts, but I can see each of you as a palette of colors, for lack of a better term, without much effort. All of you are loyal to the Commander or I would not speak, and capable of keeping secrets or I would not reveal myself now."

He paused and took a pair of heavy breaths as he studied his audience. Kathra nodded for him to continue.

"When I first joined you, there was some concern that I was a spy that had brought the Sept Empire down upon the tribal squadron," he said in a dark voice. "They knew who we were and where to find us. But the Commander pointed out that no Septagon could have caught up with us by following Erin. It is entirely possible that pure luck played a role, but there is still the risk that there is a spy in the tribal squadron somewhere. Someone who could get a message to the Sept about where to find us."

His eyes found Kathra's now, and locked on like Ram Cannons.

"We have something valuable enough now to perhaps bring the hyenas to the campfire," he said ominously. "How do we keep this secret?"

Kathra nodded. That same question kept her awake at night. The Star Turtle was not a simple treasure chest that could be looted and abandoned. It was not a derelict that would provide them some spare parts, or perhaps a new ship that could be repaired and added to the tribal squadron.

It was a game-changing thing.

How did she want to alter the rules of play?

30

─────

Ndidi had never expected to be allowed to sit at a table with the Commander as an equal, so she tried hard to keep calmness as her signature and competence as her watch word. Nervous sweat occasionally caused her glasses to slide down her nose a little, but she was used to automatically fixing them. The same thing happened in the kitchen regularly enough.

Daniel had cooked dinner. As she knew he would given any opportunity, but she was not offended. He was still capable of teaching her many things she did not know, and the Commander would soon keep him perhaps too busy to contribute.

He had taught her the subtle difference between *Sous Chef*, *Chef de Cuisine*, and *Executive Chef*. The one who ran the kitchen, the one who ran the restaurant, and in a large enough corporation, the one that ran multiple restaurants and rarely ever cooked, respectively. That latter was where he was eventually headed, at least until he reached another milestone in his recovery and decided he wanted to go and open his third restaurant one of these days.

She had gotten most of the other information about the man from Areen in tidbits and repeated stories, plus things Erin tossed off occasionally.

Tonight she found herself seated across from the Commander, between Erin and Iruoma. Daniel, Areen, and Kamharida were across the long table around Kathra.

"What do we know?" the Commander asked.

Ndidi knew perhaps the least, so she was content to sit and listen. It was already an honor for someone not in the comitatus to be here, someone other than Daniel, that is, so she needed to prove that she could keep secrets well enough that Kathra Omezi would come to rely on her someday.

"Nothing at all," Erin said, glancing at the hatch to make sure it was closed, as well as the door into the kitchen.

The group was too big to meet in the Commander's office, so they were here, in the hall where the comitatus ate and reveled.

"In fact," Erin continued, "we are not even sure that we do have a spy, per se. Merely poor timing and paranoia, perhaps."

"Perhaps," Commander Omezi nodded. "When we were poor and irrelevant, it was enough to simply flee deeper into the darkness. *Septagon Vorgash* was looking specifically for us. And a ship that slow knew where to find the tribal squadron when it went hunting."

"They had to know they couldn't catch us, though," Areen spoke up. "No Septagon can challenge even a ClanStar for speed. Our valence drives give us too much flexibility. We see him, we run. Simple as that."

Ndidi nodded at Areen's wisdom. It made perfect sense.

So why had they even tried, if all they could do was cause the infamous Kathra Omezi to laugh in their faces and flee? And why hadn't the Sept managed to chase the squadron across the seven systems they had crossed after that?

She must have made a sound, because suddenly everyone had fallen silent and was staring at her.

At least the Mbaysey couldn't blush as obviously as the lighter-skinned folk like Daniel.

"A thought, Ndidi?" the Commander asked.

"It was the first time the Sept has ever come against us with that much force, Commander, right?" Ndidi asked.

The Commander nodded with a calm, closed face.

"And we haven't been near a TradeStation since," Ndidi continued. "Or even a colonized system. So if there is a spy, they've had no opportunity to get a message out. Was that perhaps the first time the Sept had taken a prospective spy up on information given? Tested it to see if it had truth?"

Eyes around her got wide and then narrowed harshly as they all considered her words. Ndidi didn't have anywhere to go from there, so she closed her mouth. Until recently, she had been an assistant under Ugonna, learning the craft, not a warrior like the others.

Daniel was a warrior, in his own way. She could emulate that.

"And our next visit to a TradeStation is not for two months, if we keep to our regular schedule," the Commander said dryly. "Would there be one or perhaps even two Septagons waiting for us there, along with enough patrol forces to attack all the tribal squadron at once?"

"Why do they hate you that much, Commander?" Daniel asked, confusion etched deeply into the furrows around his eyes. "What have I missed?"

"I do not know, Daniel," Omezi replied. "We have been space-bound for nearly two decades now. In that time, patrol forces have chased us from time to time, but nobody has interfered with us trading at a Sept TradeStation."

"Should we go visit one early?" he asked. "Just to see what information might leak? You could always circle around and start spending more time around the Free Worlds, instead of the Empire."

Ndidi watched Kathra turn to Iruoma and Kamharida with the stern face Ndidi had learned meant *danger*.

"I must tell you two a secret," she said simply. "Something new and deadly to know, but you are the Inner Ring of the comitatus. If I cannot trust you, my troubles are so much deeper than any of us imagine, and we are probably doomed. Am I understood?"

Wow.

Both women nodded warily. Both were among the oldest who could still fly the Spectre in combat effectively, women who had served under Yagazie when they were young. This was a young woman's job, and both would end up probably grounded in another few years, as their reflexes were not as good as someone Ndidi's age. Old age and treachery can only work so long to overcome youth and skill.

"Daniel? Are we safe right now?" Kathra turned to the other chef.

He looked around once and scanned each of their faces. Ndidi couldn't feel anything, but she hadn't when the monster had taken them all the first time, either.

"You are, Commander," he whispered, blinking rapidly and scrunching his face up, like he was just feeling a migraine come on. His breath came short.

"Excellent," the Commander said, turning to the two women. "Daniel has the ability to detect lies, when he works at it. To know falsehood. Perhaps, if we are lucky, to find out if we really have a spy among us. Or if the dice just came up lucky for that naupati at some point."

She paused, and Ndidi realized that she had stopped breathing. So had the others. Such was the power of Kathra Omezi. The charisma to draw everyone into her orbit like gravity and hold them there.

"Ndidi will fix us breakfast in the morning," the Commander continued. "Daniel will assist, and then he will use his power on the entire comitatus, just to confirm my own belief that all of you are loyal. Starting at lunch, we will return to the old pattern of bringing in people from the crew, a few at each meal, so that Daniel can watch them as well, until I know if *WinterStar* is safe. Questions?"

"Can you do this thing at range, Daniel?" Areen asked patiently, watching the chef perhaps a shade closer than the rest.

After all, she had been intimate with the man, and none of the rest had, thank the gods.

"No," he muttered. "It is hard to do, hurts my head, and I must see someone to read them. Short of touring each ClanStar and holding a mass meeting, I'm not sure if I could be of much use."

"Anything else?" the Commander asked. "If not, then I will see you all in the morning. Daniel, Ndidi, could you remain behind for a moment? I have some kitchen questions for you two."

Ndidi planted her butt right back down on the bench and waited as the warriors departed, leaving the Commander alone with her *chefs*. The other kind of warrior, maybe.

The outer hatch closed.

Kathra Omezi smiled conspiratorially at Daniel.

"You don't really have to work that hard, and it does not pain you, does it?" she asked.

Ndidi hoped she kept her gasp quiet enough that the woman missed it. Hopefully.

"No," Daniel said. "But I hoped that if they thought it took great effort, they would not be so nervous around me in the future. And it gives you an extra tool, if we do have a spy feeding the Sept information."

"I agree," the Commander nodded, turning now in this

direction. "Ndidi, you will be working extremely closely with Daniel for the near future, so there need to be secrets that you are privy to, that not even the comitatus knows. At least not yet."

Ndidi gave up trying to breathe and hoped she didn't pass out as she nodded at her Commander.

"Ask your questions only of me, or him, until I tell you otherwise," Kathra Omezi instructed her. "Your other job will be to keep the man sane."

The Commander's whole face broke into a smile at that and she laughed once.

"At least as sane as the rest of us, perhaps," the Commander continued in a lighter voice. "None of this is actually rational, but I want him to feel safe and protected, as much as possible. He is as much one of us as you are, or the rest."

Ndidi turned to Daniel with a questioning look. He nodded just enough to recognize the situation and the need. The situation had perhaps raised him to the level of a god, a mad one, or at least a monster from most of the Mbaysey's worst nightmares, able to reach inside their minds and *change* things to suit his own desires.

The Commander was asking her to spy on him, but doing so in front of the man so he could understand that they were protecting themselves, and not trying to harm him or drive him away.

Areen could see to whatever physical needs the male might have. Ndidi wasn't nauseated at the idea, but neither was she attracted to the thought. Her job was to see to him emotional needs. To help him when he just needed to make cinnamon rolls, or some other comfort food.

To be his friend.

Urid-Varg had not had any friends, to hear the stories. Only slaves and victims, most likely.

Ndidi Zikora had to help Daniel. And protect him from himself.

If that was possible.

31

BREAKFAST. Always the most complicated meal of the day, because these twenty-something women seemed to delight in wanting a different *concept* of breakfast every day. Daniel suspected that it had something to do with Ugonna always serving the same two or three things, rather than getting outside herself and trying to *experiment*.

Breakfast burritos today. Ancient, *Spanic* comfort food. Eggs, cheese, peppers, onions, and a little pork ground up as sausage to stretch, wrapped in handmade flour tortillas. Chunky red sauce on the side. Eggs and vegetables for those that didn't like burritos. Cinnamon rolls and fresh fruit for the rest.

Nobody was getting oatmeal today. Daniel suspected that Ugonna would be desperately offended by the concept, but that woman was only a pedestrian cook to begin with, even after her long years learning the trade. Only her seniority in the kitchen had put her in charge of cooking for the comitatus. Kathra Omezi had specifically looked for someone like Daniel to replace her, relegating Ugonna back to cooking for the rest of the crew.

And without Urid-Varg intruding into their lives, he suspected that Ndidi would have taken over that role in time, and then replaced him when he finally moved on.

Would he have moved on? Daniel didn't have a good answer for that. Probably. Eventually. Being the lone male on the ship, surrounded by women who considered themselves superior to him in every meaningful way, would have driven him back to a planet at some point. Back to finding a few investors. Opening a bistro.

Starting over.

Probably changing his name so people didn't realize it was really him. His mother still called him *DQ*. Daniel Quentin. Maybe grown his hair long again and affect a beard?

Except that it was unnecessary now. He was part of the Mbaysey, although he still couldn't quite figure out how.

When was easy. Just slay a god and many people will change their opinion of you. However, not always for the better.

Daniel smiled grimly and studied the women as they ate.

Kathra Omezi. *The Commander.*

Erin. Areen. Iruoma. Kamharida. Joane. All of them the varied, dark tones of the African Diaspora, plus Elyl, who was *Spanic*, and Stina who was *Anglo*. There were none like him that were *Rabic*, but he suspected that was just luck and timing, as there were many of his genetic kin on the ClanStars, refugees happier to live free.

Only the sharpest warriors were invited to join the comitatus. Plus a pair of cooks, apparently. Daniel didn't know what that said about him and Ndidi. Or rather, didn't dare admit to himself.

That way lie madness.

So he concentrated on faces. Accepted the good-humored

ribbing that the women cast at him this morning, as if he were an honorary woman now. One of them.

Ndidi had held her own for cooking, ordering Daniel around peremptorily as though he was just a *Commis Chef* in her kitchen, or perhaps *Chef de Tournant*. It had been more than a decade since someone else was in charge of a kitchen around Daniel, and he smiled at the concept.

Yes, she was a warrior peer of the comitatus. The two of them needed to make sure the other women understood that. Gastronomical warfare, as it were.

"What's so funny?" Ndidi murmured as she walked by with a carafe of coffee in her hand.

"I will explain later," he chuckled. "Too complicated for here."

"Have you looked at them?" Ndidi paused and stood by his side for a moment.

Offering her own strength, if he needed it. It was such a strange feeling for him, but she was his peer as well.

"Doing so now," he replied, screwing up his face into a grimace he hoped looked convincing and rotating left to right. He had already lightly checked each woman as he served her, but Daniel knew he was putting on a performance today. Best to make it interesting.

He knew all these women. Not intimately in the technical sense of the word, but close enough. It had been his duty to feed them. To bring them joy in food, which was perhaps the highest calling a chef could strive against.

Intimacy of the soul, rather than the flesh.

Watching them now, he scanned them harder than perhaps necessary, but it had become a defensive mechanism he would need later. One might be a spy, an assassin set to kill him or the Commander. He needed to know their hearts.

Daniel nearly blinked in utter shock and lost all concentration when he scanned Yejide, Spectre Eleven.

Areen had overcome her own inclinations to occasionally explore her occasional bisexuality with Daniel. Most of the women considered the concept little better than bestiality, but he knew that and did not let their ideas bother him.

Yejide looked at him now with a sharp longing balanced tightly against her own upbringing, plus her relative shyness on the topic. There was also a note of deference to Areen, as if the other woman might have staked a claim around him and no others were allowed to cross.

Daniel could reach out with a hand and touch her. In his mind, each of these women were like the long control panels of a musical recording studio, or an atomic power plant. Hundreds of dials and gauges and knobs and switches, measuring every aspect of their minds and souls.

Yejide was trapped and unsure how to overcome herself. Desire at war with socialization.

It would be the work of a moment to adjust a few settings and free her. It was so wrong that he felt a burst of nausea threaten to overcome him.

The Left Hand of Evil.

"Daniel?" Ndidi whispered sharply.

He clung to her voice like a life preserver. Let it draw him back out of himself before he became the very thing he considered the most vile in the entire universe.

Urid-Varg.

He pulled a deep breath into himself and physically turned so that Ndidi was the only person he could see. She reached out a hand and placed it on his arm. He tried not to flinch as she did.

Touch grounded him as well. He blinked rapidly and tried to breathe.

"Are you okay?" she asked.

"I touched them all," he whispered in a guilty tone.

"Deeply. I have never done that before. You can learn unsettling things when you do that."

"Such as?" Ndidi turned now to face him, the rest of the room forgotten.

Daniel drew a sigh inward and considered. The Commander had instructed this woman to know his secrets that she could perhaps keep him as sane as was possible. And Kathra Omezi trusted her to do that.

"Yejide would like to sneak into her chef's cabin some evening to explore certain desires and feelings," he said quietly. "But she never will. Her upbringing will prevent her. And she will be unhappy as a result."

"Should you talk to her about it?" Ndidi asked carefully.

"The woman has never given any outward sign that I am aware of. Probably none that the rest of you would notice," Daniel said. "It would be a betrayal of the sanctity of her mind for me to even know these things. Worse, for the slightest moment, I considered adjusting her so that she might be less frightened of herself and more forward."

The way her eyes grew wide for a moment told him she understood. Feared him, just a little, perhaps. But that was the path of the mad god, so easy and seductive.

"Evil," Daniel continued.

Ndidi nodded shallowly. Watched him like a hawk as he just stood there and tried to become human again and not some foul beast from the pit.

"Can nobody help her?" Ndidi whispered back.

"Not until she decides to admit these things to herself, let alone one of the others," he grimaced. "I must live a complicated double life, even as I am trying to help the Commander and save the Mbaysey from the Sept. I will tell you and the Commander things that cannot get out, ever, Ndidi. That will be the only way I retain some shred of sanity."

"Understood," she squeezed his arm once and then seemed to settle as he watched. "You should go sit with Kathra and let her know everything is safe."

"And you?" he asked, not moving.

"We need to begin planning a lunch that will bring you peace, Daniel," Ndidi replied. "This will be a very hard road for you, and nobody else can assist."

He nodded, turning to find the Commander's concern written on her face.

She knew.

Not the details, but perhaps the weight he bore. But she was *The Commander*. He would expect her to be that many steps ahead of a simple cook when it came to games of power and death.

32

Kathra rubbed her eyes in frustration and considered the three people on the other side of her desk. The door was closed and nobody would open it now without an invitation.

And a damned good reason.

Erin sat to the right, facing her. Ndidi was in the middle. Daniel was on the left.

For a moment, Kathra considered the symbolic image of one chef protecting the other from the rest of the comitatus. Not entirely an inaccurate description.

"Nobody?" she asked again, just to make sure she had heard the report correctly.

"Correct, Commander," Daniel said simply. "All of the ship-side crew has now cycled through to eat with the comitatus at least once over the last month. I have scanned them all, touching most deeply enough to be sure."

She heard a catch in his breath and focused her attention on the man.

There were lines there that hadn't been present six months ago. The gray along his temples was far more pronounced than it had been, but she had never met the rest of his family to know if he was merely showing his age younger than most men, or if she was causing him to use himself up at an accelerated rate.

Nobody knew what the powers of the conqueror exacted as a cost, either.

"But?" Kathra asked after it was clear he was done talking.

"But I agree with the original assessment, Commander," he said. "My gut tells me that there is a spy, and we have somehow missed them."

"There are twenty-two ClanStars," Erin spoke up. "Average population around three hundred people each. Two *WaterStars*. *ForgeStar*. *IronStar*. *WinterStar*. Tribal population close enough to seventy-five hundred souls. How do we find one grain of sand on that beach, if we're not sure that it even exists."

"I do not know," Kathra replied. "But we do know that *WinterStar* is secure, so we just need to pay better attention to communications security when we approach the TradeStation over Carggi. *ForgeStar* is fully loaded with trade ingots and bars, so we'll park the Star Turtle a few systems away and move the tribal squadron close enough to put a full detachment of SkyCamels in space, along with *The Haunt*, just in case the Sept do put in an appearance, especially over a colony that far beyond their current boundaries. From there, my plan is to head out to the Free Worlds and find places we can sell used shuttle craft. At least the ones we don't want to keep, or know how to fix."

That got a smile from Erin. Several of the ships apparently required more limbs than a human had in order to control everything at once. All of them could be powered up and held air. Erin or one of the others, with Daniel watching, had moved them all out onto their various landing fins. Fifty-three strange craft, some of them reeking of boundless age and exotic cultures.

Whether anyone wanted a ship that they could perhaps not repair or maintain was an entirely different question, and why she would try to find a wealthy dilettante with a thing for exotic space craft to add to their collection.

"Will the turtle be safe, alone in space?" Ndidi asked a perceptive question.

"Without testing larger weapons than we have, I do not think someone could damage the ship," Daniel replied. "Notwithstanding the Ram Cannons or Axial Megacannon from a Septagon, which I simply do not know how to compare. If I am not there, nobody could board the ship without first doing so much damage to the hull as to render it destroyed anyway."

"Perhaps we should hide it better?" Erin spoke up.

"What would better look like?" Kathra asked.

"Daniel, how deep into a gas giant's atmosphere could the ship continue to hover?" the woman asked.

Kathra watched the man's eyes lose focus in a way she had come to associate with him asking the ghosts in the gem for their knowledge. What must it be like to have hundreds, or perhaps thousands of people on call, if you could get them to speak in harmony, rather than the dull cacophony he had described as their normal noise?

"Sufficient that you would have to be in close orbit," Daniel said. "Looking straight down with scanners making much noise."

"Could you park it there and then fly up to space to rendezvous with *WinterStar*?" Kathra asked, seeing where Erin was headed.

"*Oui*," he said. "Easy enough. Probably a very pretty

view, if I took a camera with me to capture the storms and clouds from inside them."

"Perhaps another time," Kathra smiled. "I want to run this much more like a combat operation than a tourist caravan."

"As you command," Daniel nodded to her, sobering.

She dismissed the three of them and focused instead on the list each of the ships had provided. With ships mining comets for water and organics, and *ForgeStar* turning asteroids into all the metals they needed for *IronStar* to turn into machinery components, the squadron was largely self-sufficient. The ClanStars produced a little surplus food, over feeding the five specialized ships, but with raw planetary systems to explore, the squadron routinely produced significant amounts of various refined ingots, usually iron and copper, but nearly all of the metals in some amount.

That became trade with various worlds, allowing them to purchase all the little things that the tribe needed, if they refused to be bound to a single planet.

It also became a point of risk, as they had to fly the squadron into a system in order to get everyone moved around. That gave the Sept a place to trap them, if they could.

The ships could flee, easy enough, but if they lost all that metal, it would be a season of poverty again, like when she was young.

Kathra smiled though, when she considered selling alien space ships to collectors. Could she really break the dependence on TradeStations? Perhaps buy or commission a FarmStar capable of feeding many more people? Or several more ClanStars, to give them place for a population boom to expand their numbers? Space was ruthlessly exploited now, but there was still an absolute number of tribal members that they could support.

What if they weren't limited anymore?

What if they could be free?

And if the Sept decided to complain, what if she decided to destroy a Septagon to make a point?

What could the future be like for a daughter she needed bear soon?

33

———

It was a moment of déjà vu for Erin, approaching Carggi TradeStation in SkyCamel Six. The planet below wasn't that much different from Renneth, at least seen from space. If she was leading six SkyCamels this time, rather than flying solo, and had the entire *Haunt* out there protecting her, that just measured the risks of this mission in much starker terms.

Daniel was riding along with her. The ancient term for such a person was *shotgun*, back when a coach had a person armed with such a weapon to keep bandits at bay. *The Haunt* would do that for her just fine, but she did appreciate having him present, along with whatever weird powers he might possess to do things to troublemakers.

Carggi was about as boring a station as they ever visited, but everyone was still keyed up. And Daniel could protect her and the other camel pilots in ways nobody else understood.

That helped.

"Six leading," she said into the radio. "Docking imminent."

"Spectre Two," Kathra replied by way of

acknowledgement, using the woman's usual callsign. The other five pilots were shuttle regulars, rather than comitatus, but they appreciated that she would be there when they hit the station, off schedule, off season, and loaded to the gills with metal and goods to trade.

Kathra was clearing the decks, metaphorically as well as literally, before that next adventure began.

Erin threaded the needle of the dock and let the station grab hold of the SkyCamel. She powered things down as the grav inducers took hold and unbuckled. Daniel was already standing and moving to the rear of the craft for the outer hatch to open.

He looked a little silly, with that lime and white outfit just visible at the edges of his regular clothing, though covered over with long pants and a long-sleeved shirt, but that just meant that nobody would notice him doing things. His gloves were rolled up and stuffed into a thigh pouch if he needed them, but she had her pistol and a knife. If the other five Camel pilots weren't currently comitatus, they were still veterans, having seen enough TradeStations and bar fights, so they could take care of themselves.

And the chef.

Her vox chirped with a signal from the station, acknowledging receipt of her manifest. Probably choked a little, when the system realized the tonnage she was hauling today. Enough to maybe depress the market for a while, but *WinterStar* wouldn't be this way again for some time, so others would just have to deal with market fluctuations instead.

Erin keyed open the hatch and let the station air in. Carggi always had a sweet/dry smell she had never been able to isolate. Cardamom and ginger maybe, now that Daniel had taught her a greater appreciation of such spices in her food.

She emerged first, with Daniel right behind her. Station had put them all together on a terminal, a deck below the usual cargo spaces, since they were delivering metal stock pure enough that it could go straight into the machine shops for processing. Outbound cargo for the return trip would need to be brought down a level, but that would still be easier, since that stuff weighed far less and the limits for the six camels would be space rather than tonnage.

Erin gathered up the other five pilots and waited for the rep of the StationMaster to arrive with receipts. Crews were already standing by with roller carts. The complicated dance of trade.

Rep today was a woman who looked *Spanic* at first glance. Same dark as Daniel, but redder. She was perhaps in her late thirties, an older woman compared to the pilots around her, about the same as age the one male.

Paperwork got signed. Receipts got exchanged. Life was good.

Daniel got a raised eyebrow from the woman, but he wasn't dressed like the rest of the crew, and Erin didn't volunteer anything. Daniel was a shit and leered openly at the woman, like he hadn't gotten laid in a year. Erin would have had to drink half a bottle of something hard before she would consider that woman, but she suspected Daniel had no more interest than she did.

Just wanted to act tough, or something. Out of character, if you knew him. Setting boundaries early, if you didn't.

"Bar," Erin said as the rep departed.

Part of the reason Erin had usually flown these missions in the past was the opportunity to have different food on a TradeStation while waiting for crews to unload and reload the camels. Being Kathra's Second-In-Command just meant that she could pull rank on the others, unless they wanted to fly a camel as well. Four of the five women with her had retired from combat flying to safer tasks, but they understood her logic and agreed with it.

Except that, upon consideration, she really didn't have to do that anymore. Daniel was a far better cook than Ugonna on his worst day, and willing to make exotic things, if he had the ingredients to match her hunger. Only thing he wasn't doing right now was making different kinds of beer from the grains that usually came off Ihejirika ClanStar in trade.

Still, she got to have adventures on a station while the others stayed home, even as little as those adventures usually were. You had to travel to one of the major Sept TradeStations before you were likely to get into a really good fight on the deck.

Not that she was looking forward to one. Honest.

Chinese Diaspora food today. Ancient recipes as reinterpreted by *Anglos* in the distant past and standardized into something the true ancients of the Chinese homeland would have been appalled to consider. Tea. A little whiskey. Finger food, because she had never bothered to learn how you were supposed to pick something up with two pieces of bamboo half as wide as her smallest finger.

Halfway through the munchies, Erin decided that Daniel did this better, too.

Oh, the sacrifices we make.

34

PERHAPS THE WEIRDEST thing about the scene, at least for Daniel, was that there were others in here who looked like him. *Rabics* from the central regions of the homeworld. *WinterStar* had mostly Africans, with a few *Spanics*. There were several people in here from the same ancient lands on Earth, including the family that owned the place. Lebanese in their case, to use the ancientest term, rather than Algerians, but close enough cousins, when you got down to it.

The food was industrial generic. The sort of thing you might find on any TradeStation or planet-side food court, where they would advertise with a tiger and a panda. Factory-made dim sum. Adequate for fuel. Good enough if you normally ate something different.

He could tell from the women around him that he would need to add a round of something similar to the menu more frequently when they got home. Their faces had fallen from anticipation to experience, and it was not that great, at least compared to the taste they had in their minds when they got up this morning.

Worse, he would have to have a chat with the Commander, and possibly Ndidi, to make sure these five women were in the rotation to eat with the comitatus, the next time he did this. He would likely never hear the end of it if they were left out of good dim sum, having to eat down in the main mess that day.

Something niggled at the back of his head as he grabbed a fresh bit of sweet and sour pork with his chopsticks. The sour looks he was getting from the six women were priceless, but chopsticks weren't a thing on *WinterStar*, so they had never learned the trick. Might have to fix that, too, when he got back. Not with bamboo, but it would be easy enough to have a machine shop do him up something in plastic.

And then get enough made for the main mess as well, since not everybody got to eat the good stuff, except about once a month.

The shock hit Daniel so hard that he dropped his pork right onto the table.

Erin started to grin, as a prelude to teasing him, when she saw the look on his face. Instead, her right hand dropped out of sight below the table top, where she was, no doubt, unlatching the strap that held her pistol in place and putting her hand on the pommel.

"What?" she whispered fiercely.

The other five women stopped laughed and chatting like a guillotine had dropped across the conversation.

Daniel blinked rapidly, letting his mind cycle as he stared at Erin blankly.

"When we went and interviewed everyone on *WinterStar*, we forgot someone," he said quietly. "It was my fault, because of the way we did it."

"Who?" Erin whispered back as the other women also seemed to be contemplating sudden, industrial-scales of violence in a fast food bar.

"Someone who normally talks to TradeStations anyway," Daniel said. "And could easily pass along messages when nobody would even notice."

"Oh, shit!" Erin sat bolt upright.

"And someone I suspect might have an axe to grind," Daniel continued. "I don't know the woman at all. Would she be that angry?"

"Who?" one of the other pilots asked. Daniel hadn't gotten all their names, yet, so he couldn't call her anything but SkyCamel Three, which didn't sound even remotely polite at this point.

"Is this a trap, Daniel?" Erin focused her brighter eyes on him and ignored the other women. "Are we about to be attacked here on the station, or are they waiting out in the darkness?"

She caught his glance at the other women and understood the significance.

"If you wish to keep flying with Kathra Omezi, you will take this secret to your graves," Erin said in a voice that had Daniel twitching, so say nothing of the five pilots. "Am I clear?"

One by one they nodded, barely daring to breathe.

Daniel put both hands on the table, framing his plate and the rogue sweet and sour pork. He closed his eyes and let his mind reach out.

Urid-Varg had been able to do this over distances that were frightening. Perhaps that was his vast depth of experience. Perhaps his native species had the power. Perhaps there had been something in the mounting that the Commander had destroyed.

Daniel didn't dare pursue that matter anymore than he had. God-like powers were bad enough. Mad Gods were not the sorts of people he wished to have as peers.

Still, now was the moment he needed to push to see just what he could do.

The dining hall around him was easy to see in his mind's gem. Mostly human, with a pair of Se'uh'pal back in a corner behind him. One hundred and twenty centimeters tall to the tops of their heads, with another thirty of what looked exactly like bunny ears above that. Round faces covered with a fine fur and big eyes. Merchant/traders. Apparently most of the species were, at least to some extent, but these two made a primary living at it.

Okay, good enough. Daniel reached out.

He had no idea who the Lords of a TradeStation like this might be, so he could not lock in on a person, like he could do with Erin, seated across from him. Instead, he let his subconscious mind sniff for something marked as *danger*. Strong emotions centered on Erin, or perhaps Kathra Omezi.

The station was a gray, foggy mist as he let his mind flow. People living normal lives. Occasional bits of triumph. Long stretches of anguish. Nothing jumped out.

No, that wasn't right. He tasted something. A flavor too bright for his Ratatouille, almost a sweetness instead of the normal earthy tones. Daniel had no other way to describe the casserole around him, but that at least made sense to him.

He focused on the flavor. Let it resolve itself into an image. A person. A mind.

Daniel growled deep in his throat and did the one thing he had sworn would be an evil too great.

He stepped into the man's mind and rode him, just like Urid-Varg had done.

Human. Male. Middle aged. Not a boss, but a senior-enough bureaucrat. Except he wasn't. Or rather, wasn't just.

Daniel peeled back the layers of the man's mind. Found two beings in there, one sheltered behind the other. He rifled the man's memories ruthlessly, turning over boxes and pulling drawers out of the wall to find what he wanted.

The man would probably be plagued by the most exquisite nightmares for a week after this, but Daniel really didn't have any sympathy for him at all.

The man was a Sept spy.

Deep cover. Hiding as another. Living a double life so precisely that even his wife did not know the truth. Not revealing himself in any way, except that he could send messages off to his true masters, without the StationMaster knowing any better.

Thus did the Sept keep their fingers intertwined with all of their children colonies, lest one think to break away and join the Free Worlds, costing all those banks that had funded the colony everything, and perhaps necessitating a forceful intervention.

Say, perhaps, a Septagon arriving overhead.

Daniel reread the message the man had sent. Memorized the words with mental abilities that were more the act of telling his ghosts and asking them to remind him later. They were allies. At least for now. Later might be a different story. But later he might be able to let them go to their graves properly as well.

Daniel opened his eyes and nearly fell over as he let go of the stress in his body. The woman on his left caught him with a hand and held him while he drew a breath.

"And?" Erin asked quietly.

"The station is not a trap," Daniel managed, reaching out a hand to grab his tea mug and empty the now-cool liquid into his mouth. He poured more and wrapped his hands around the mug to warm them, a cold not just metaphorical.

"But there is a trap?" Erin pressed.

"There is," Daniel said.

Quickly, he repeated the message that had been sent,

triggered when the ClanStars first arrived in system and began to communicate with the TradeStation for docking schedules and trade needs.

And an extra message, buried within the others.

"Does their spy know who ours is?" Erin's eyes became pools of dark death as he watched.

"No, but I recognize her vocabulary," Daniel nodded. "Her speech patterns."

"And it is indeed her?"

"It is," Daniel whispered, sipping some more tea.

"Who?" one of the others asked in a quiet snarl. "Who is the viper in our nest, betraying us to the white men?"

Daniel didn't take offense at the woman's rage. Her kind had been slaves and worse within the lifetimes of their still-living elders. He was close enough, ethnically, to be mistaken for one of the Farsi Overlords of the Sept, the Seven Clans, even if he had never been to Earth himself, and his ancestors were from nearly a quarter of the planet away.

He still looked like the oppressors.

Daniel instead looked a question at Erin, asking permission to share some small bit of the secrets with the others. She nodded and grabbed more food. Probably they would need a to-go container for the rest so they could pay and flee.

Most of the ClanStars were close by, conducting their own trade with the station for things they needed personally, while *WinterStar* handled the major work. Only the four support hips were not in the immediate vicinity: *ForgeStar*, *IronStar*, and the two *WaterStars*.

But trouble was coming.

Daniel turned to the other pilots and waited for each of them to nod back.

"Our spy is Ugonna."

35

IT WAS like waking from a midday nap, but Kathra wouldn't do something so amazingly stupid as that while flying. Not on escort duty with Erin and more than a dozen SkyCamels currently docked with Carggi Station.

The Haunt was maintaining a polite patrol around the tribal squadron. Just sitting out there, generally hovering in a complex pattern that let their scanners see in all directions, because Kathra's paranoia knew that someone meant them ill.

She shook her head to clear it and saw a message on her board where she normally tracked internal systems. Apparently, she had opened a note-taking program and overlay it.

What had she been meaning to jot down?

The words sent a spike of fear through her soul.

Commander Omezi, I must apologize to you now, and perhaps every time I ever see you again forever, for doing this. Erin insisted that the message be delivered, and done in strictest secrecy, so I had no choice. In order to do that, I had to locate your mind in space, take it over, much like my nemesis Urid-

Varg would have done, and write you a message using your own hands.

I'm more sorry that you can possibly imagine, but there was no other way we could find.

Carggi TradeStation is not a trap, but there is a spy here, and they have been in communication with a spy on WinterStar. One we missed.

Sitting at dinner, I realized that in the process of cycling the rest of the staff through the comitatus to eat with us, where they could be inspected, we missed someone, because she was always in charge of feeding the rest of the crew. The oversight is mine, I should have made a proper checklist to follow, instead of relying on a flawed system. Once that realization was confirmed by finding the spy on the station, I reached out to our traitor and confirmed it.

Ugonna has internalized a great rage at you for being, as she sees it, demoted from the prestigious job of cooking for your comitatus, to merely cooking for the junior varsity. Her words.

It was she that passed a message along at Renneth, as soon as the squadron arrived, giving the authorities time to indeed contact Septagon Vorgash and vector them down onto the squadron. That we fled immediately still proved to the Sept that she could be relied upon to provide more information for a future ambush.

Another message is making its way to the Lords of the Sept as we wait at Carggi. As before, I doubt that there are sufficient patrol forces nearby to threaten The Haunt and risk the SkyCamels, but Ugonna has told them of the gas giant at Azgon where we have hidden the turtle. She did not say what they would find, only that a great treasure awaited them there.

We are being watched by the spy here and his minions, so we must move with care, awaiting your orders. It is possible to communicate this way, as distasteful as I find it. If you tell Erin to check her message pack for an update, I can return here and read a message you have written on this board.

I wish there were other ways to do this. With your permission, I will work with Ndidi at a later date, in safer climes, to find something that is not evil itself, but the devil pursues us now and time is of the essence.

Your humble and chastened servant,

Daniel.

Kathra had already gone through the stages of rage and acceptance before she was halfway through the letter he had written her. The violation was so severe that thoughts of just killing the man outright were foremost, but he had to know that. Had feared it. Had told Ndidi how sickening it was that he had the power to do something like that, and had to fight the urges to fix the things around him, lest he become the conqueror he had defeated once.

She reread the message. It was an exquisite trap for her.

The ClanStars could simply vanish into the night without giving their former Sept Overlords any opportunity to pursue them meaningfully. Those fleets requires bases and forward supply stations to operate for any significant amount of time. The three hundred thousand people on a Septagon ate an enormous amount of food on a daily basis. Far more than their ship could grow on its own. There were deliveries on a near-constant basis. Food. Medicine. Even mundane things like new uniforms and replacement filters for air systems. One continuous stream of supply freighters.

But right now, she was half-way trapped at the station herself, awaiting her SkyCamels returning.

Perhaps on some future date, *The Haunt* needed to start attacking that Sept supply chain? Just damage the ability of the Septagons to control space, if they didn't dare get any great distance away from their supply stations?

Or maybe she and Daniel needed to figure out how to

capture a supply depot, loot what they needed, and destroy the rest?

She might be finally getting angry enough, if the Sept had decided to begin hunting the Mbaysey with that sort of commitment and energy.

Tomorrow.

Today, she needed to escape this trap and get to the Star Turtle before the Sept could destroy it. They couldn't capture it, unless they could somehow turn a gravity inducer field inside out and use it to pull the ship up from the atmosphere of the planet where it lay hidden, but the Sept could easily destroy it.

For the briefest moment, Kathra wondered if Daniel was setting them a trap, but if that was the case, he could have just remained silent and let *WinterStar* emerge from the jump right on top of a Septagon that was waiting. The massive Ram Cannons would be more than sufficient to terminally damage her flagship in those moments when they were blind to their surroundings, waiting for sensors to return to normal.

And then the Sept would be able to break her and the comitatus. Without that, the tribe would not survive.

She could either trust Daniel now, or never rely on the man again. It was as easy as that.

Kathra saved the message file and closed it up so she could see her boards again. Everything was running normally on her ship, at least for now.

She opened a different program and typed a message out for Erin, rather than calling her on the vox, as Daniel has suggested. Part of her didn't want that man inside her head, but he had already given her the pieces she needed, in order to save them all.

Erin,

Got your note about you being delayed longer than the other

SkyCamels. Make sure they're all accounted for when your team is ready to depart. Half The Haunt will return to WinterStar now and prep for our next mission. Good luck and see you shortly.

Kathra.

36

"No, I don't understand," Daniel shook his head and tried to understand what Erin was telling him.

Being in a public space where they had to keep things obscured from casual listeners did not help.

Erin nodded and thought about it for a second.

"There are twelve camels on station right now," she said. "Us and all those from ClanStars. Kathra wants us to make sure the others are all home and docked before we detach. Assuming she understood your message, she's going to go take care of her urgent problem right now, and then wants to be able to run like hell to get to our other destination."

"That's how that reads?" Daniel was skeptical, but he'd know the Commander for six months, and Erin had been raised almost from birth with the woman.

"It is," Erin reassured him. "I'm going to send a note to the StationMaster now and get an update on our departure windows, and then we're going to go window shopping as a group. Understood?"

Daniel nodded along with the other women. Safety in numbers. The spy would not likely want to reveal himself now, unless something exceptional were to happen, such as being able to capture Kathra Omezi herself on this deck, rather than chasing her across space again and again.

The Sept were playing an exquisitely long game here, so the group should be safe from the authorities as long as they did nothing to provoke those folks. Individual women, even bad-ass, ex-comitatus killers like these, could be surprised if they were alone, if a committed group of men wanted to cause trouble.

There was no group large enough that Daniel could not stop them. Today, that might involve hurting them, badly, in ways that were not explainable, unless Erin decided to start spreading stories that she was also a shamaness of some sort, capable of inflicting the evil eye hex on her victims.

That might be fun. Daniel made a note to mention it to her and the Commander later, after they had escaped the current trap.

When. Not if.

They paid for the mediocre food and set out to shop. A TradeStation was not a place that was served by normal trade shipments from industrial planets. You could bring up food and materials from the planet below, but the stock in trade was normally whatever oddities might have made their way across space in the back of a SkyCamel or a tramp freighter.

Once you got past the bodegas with a fixed inventory of goods, almost every store turned into a pawn shop of some sort eventually, filled with mysteries you could never solve, being reduced instead to making up wildly entertaining stories, however implausible they might be, to explain how something got *here*.

The women were warriors and pilots by training. They did not have any great, esoteric needs, at least none they were willing to admit to in public, so Erin let Daniel stop at one shop that seemed to call his name for reasons he could not even formulate, let alone articulate.

Junk. That was his impression when he stepped past the line in the deck where a hard hatch closed each night. Assuming they recognized night.

Daniel had never really spent much time on stations. Were they constant affairs, running in shifts, but never actually closing? Certainly the humans would need to sleep, but they didn't have the sun rising to reset their personal clocks, so they might remain on whatever schedule their ship ran, or just adjust to something here.

Yet another mystery to solve, if he truly was going to remain in space.

He wasn't sure that he had any other option at this point, with the Star Turtle. *Certainement*, he could give the power away at some point, but to whom? And he didn't dare just navigate the great beast up to a TradeStation like this and dock. If nothing else, the turtle was larger by overall volume.

And so utterly alien that it would bring adventurers and assholes who wanted to see it, steal it, or at a minimum hassle him to the point he had to do something to them to make them stop.

But the junk store called his name. Not like one of the voices in his gem, but just some triggered subconscious thing that said *walk in here and shop.*

So he did.

There had been a store between his restaurant on Genarde and the flat he rarely slept at, spending too much time sleeping in his office or at Angel's apartment. It had started out selling military surplus clothing and personal gear in some forgotten past, and then moved on to random, industrial junk. Not electronics, although the few times he had wandered in curiously, there had also been that sort of thing scattered about.

Surplus uniforms of a military cut and color, mostly the dark monochromes of the Sept, as if the owner got used things from retired military, or had a cousin who knew a dude who handled disposal from military depots. Thing had fallen off trucks with stunning regularity in that old neighborhood, to hear the stories bandied about.

The women behind him were occasionally poking and prodding things, but mostly seemed content to follow him into the deeper parts of the store. The owner was human. Or at least close enough to pass in the semi-darkness he seemed to prefer. Daniel glanced up to confirm that half the lights were just off, and that he hadn't wandered into a cave with a troll.

Books on a shelf drew his eye. Deciphering the spine on one, it appeared to be a thick, Sept Navy cookbook. They always seemed to have complicated manuals on doing everything, from cooking, to vehicle maintenance, to all the ways to kill a human with common, household goods.

Daniel ran his hand down the worn spine and pulled it off the shelf.

"Finally going to learn to cook, Daniel?" Marra teased from close behind him.

He suspected she occasionally regretted retiring from the comitatus to have her two daughters, if for no other reason than she didn't get to eat his food all that often. She did, however, know an astonishingly broad range of dirty jokes.

"Perhaps," he said with a wink back at her. "If they capture me someday, I can always work in their kitchen instead of the laundry."

That got a round of chuckles out of all the women. They were close enough to him now that he could smell the rich scent of the soap they washed their hair with. Somehow it split the difference between coconut and pine, in ways he had never figured out, since no ClanStar grew either.

Flipping it open, Daniel knew a moment of disappointment. The thing was a four-ring binder of the military style, straight on one post and seven centimeter loops for papers to be stacked.

None of it was in a language he understood. If it was a language.

From the heft, he had been expecting a complete inventory of everything a Sept naval cook should be expected to know, including starting the stove, cleaning it, and dismantling it for repair, as well as a thousand recipes. Useful, if only for the inspiration to go beyond the fifty or hundred dishes he normally cycled though.

"What in the world?" Erin murmured, leaning over his shoulder to peek.

"Something else, obviously," Daniel replied. "Not what I was expecting."

He looked closer. Not Latin characters. Nor *Rabic*. Vaguely similar to Chinese ideograms, but written left to right instead of vertically. And denser in their construction, with many characters having six brush strokes at a minimum, with one on the first page containing twenty-two.

Somebody muttered something, but Daniel didn't get even the gist.

"What did you say?" he turned to Erin.

"I didn't," she retorted. "None of us did. What did you think you heard?"

"Somebody said…" his voice trailed off absently.

Daniel closed his eyes and *looked* inside.

His ghosts were always just that. Vague shadows in half-light, half-shadow. Slightly-glowing eyes if he concentrated, but nothing more substantial than mist. One seemed to glow brighter. Daniel studied it.

Three eyes across the furry face, with the nose below that

stretched into a snout halfway between feline and canine for size.

You speak this tongue, Daniel focused on it.

The man nodded slowly. He had petite horns that swept back from his forehead and outward, rather like an ox.

Show me, Daniel commanded.

The characters seemed to change shape under Daniel's gaze, settling on Latin letters arranged in French. Not what Daniel had learned as a child, but what he was most likely to communicate in, when he wasn't speaking Spacer with these women.

"*Merde!*" he whispered, suddenly reading a K'bari history of space exploration. Published nearly two thousand humans years ago, if he understood the date conversion. About the time humans were discovering industrial metallurgy, on the way to exploring space for the first time.

"What?" Erin challenged him.

Daniel had closed the book and pulled it tight against his chest, understanding that there was nobody within several thousand light-years capable of even translating it.

If that.

What other strange prizes might lurk, if you had all these friends willing to help?

"Mine," Daniel whispered to her. "I can read it."

"How…?" she started, before correcting herself. "No, not here. I know how. Anything else here we should snag?"

Daniel turned and started to scan the shelves, but he needed both hands to do that.

"Hold this," he commanded Marra with as much intent sincerity as he could manage while his heard pounded.

She took it from him after a cross look from Erin, and Daniel pulled every other book down. Most of them were what they professed to be, being bound rather than ringed.

Mostly literature of one flavor or another, plus a shelf of repair manuals for starships Daniel had never heard of.

He did pull each of those and study them against the memory of all those shuttles he had inherited, but there were no matches.

But somewhere, someone had written such things. Now he knew to hit every TradeStation and look for them. At least he didn't have to carry physical pictures around that might arouse suspicions.

"Nothing," he finally admitted glumly.

At least until Marra handed him back the first book and Daniel felt a surge of wild excitement pass through his whole being.

Urid-Varg's victims had memories, but not annotated logs and star maps detailing the conqueror's journey through the galaxy. Daniel knew the creature had at least touched the K'bari species at some point. Daniel could find them. Or at least their legacy.

Daniel turned and staggered towards the front counter. Erin caught him by a shoulder before he pitched over. The price marked on the inner cover was three Guilders. Dinner for two at a regular restaurant, but not a fancy place. Eleven Sept Crowns, since Kathra had given him those coins to burn on this station.

He let Erin bicker the man down to two Sloths and a fifth, and called it good. Seven Sept Crowns. The merchant seemed like he wanted to dicker merely for the practice, to break up an otherwise empty day.

Daniel made his way out into the rest of the station with the tome in his hands.

Did a star-borne species ever go extinct? Daniel had memories of destroying planets. Or at least nightmares, but he wasn't trying to dig deep to determine right now.

If your world was destroyed, did your species go with it?

Losing Earth would not end humanity as a thing. They were on too many other worlds now. Plus spaceships.

The K'bari were probably still out there somewhere as well.

If he could find them.

37

At least they had escaped the Carggi system without the first of the many possible attacks Kathra had feared. Half of the SkyCamels had flown back to various ClanStars and docked, and then all the other ships besides *WinterStar* had moved at once, vanishing on cue on their valence drives into the darkness on the first of nine jumps to the eventual Concursion.

If anybody had been planning anything stupid, that should have ruined most of his plans, as she had changed the original destination. The other five camels and all *The Haunt* had been in space for the last flight home, once Kathra knew her schedule.

Nobody had tried their luck. And she had not been forced to rely on Daniel as an ugly surprise. Not yet, anyway. That day was coming.

Kathra Omezi had to determine how intent the Sept was on pressing her and the tribe before she bit back, but that day was indeed coming.

She hadn't really understand the coded messages from

Erin about a book Daniel had found, and thank the various gods of spacers that it wasn't critical enough that he had to explain it to her himself, using the only utterly secure method of communication they had right now. But it had made Daniel happy, and Erin confident in future adventures, and that was enough for now.

Even being a position to plan for a future was sometimes an iffy proposition.

Kathra was on the bridge of *WinterStar*, having docked first and gotten the ship into position to flee even before the camels docked.

But they had made it to jump safely.

Given the time-criticality, Obioma had plotted a course with only two stops to get to Azgon, rather than the more-leisurely path the tribal squadron would take to meet up with them in a week in a nearby system.

The Sept might find the rest, if Ugonna had given them enough information to crack codes, but Kathra had changed the original destination at the last minute before they leapt.

"We are away, Commander," Obioma confirmed as the stars went from dots to lines, when viewed out the open blast shields. They didn't do that on a screen, becoming merely rapidly-moving dots, but the human eye interpreted things strangely in jump. "Twenty-seven hours to first coordinates."

"Very good," Kathra replied, pushing herself off from a stanchion and heading towards the hatch aft and the elevator stack that would take her down to the ring. "Keep all of the cannons warm for now, just in case, and make sure everyone knows that we will come out of jump ready to flee or fight immediately."

"Understood, Kathra."

She didn't fidget as the elevator carried her down into increasing gravity, but Kathra knew she was too wound up right now.

Ugonna had been taken into custody without warning and put into a cell for the time being, but the woman needed to be dealt with, and everything needed to be resolved, now that *WinterStar* was away.

But the only way to do that involved asking Daniel to do even more evil than he already had.

At what point would her fragile, little, male chef break? She knew him to be tougher than most men. Almost a match for her comitatus in his own way. But they were well beyond *Commander* and *Chef* right now.

They might never return to that simpler, magical place.

Erin was waiting when the doors opened. Daniel was immediately behind her, with Areen and Kam as well. All of them looked harsh, although she doubted that the latter two knew why the situation had gotten so tense.

"Follow me," Kathra said simply, turning to her right and walking some of the excess energy off.

Uphill, around the ring, her feet making almost as much noise as Daniel's on the metal deck. *WinterStar* didn't have a proper jail, as the Sept would have expected. Kathra's ultimate sanction wasn't to imprison someone, or even have them killed.

No, if your crimes were sufficient, she would just leave you on a TradeStation somewhere and strike your name from the tribal rolls.

That wasn't an option with Ugonna. The woman knew too much. Too many secrets, even before Daniel and the Star Turtle entered their lives. Now, she could tell the Sept about Urid-Varg.

The Conqueror.

Kathra stopped at the place where they normally held classes for small groups. The door was locked from the outside, and the interior had been isolated easily enough.

Kathra nodded to Stina and Nkechi, who had been guarding the door, and they unlocked it.

Ugonna had been surprised when Kathra ordered her locked in there earlier. As Kathra entered now, at the head of a small force of her warriors, Ugonna stood up from the floor and her face took up a snarl.

"Come to kill me?" Ugonna sneered.

Kathra nodded to Kam, who closed the door and stood before it, just in case the older woman decided to somehow make a break for it. Perhaps throw herself into an escape pod, leap out of jump and back into the universe, hoping that she was close enough to a planet or ship to survive?

Those odds were still better than Kathra's anger.

"Do you have anything useful to say to give me pause?" Kathra asked.

Most of the room separated the seven on this side from the prisoner. Ugonna's eyes fell on Daniel. She spit on the floor between them.

"You chose a male," the woman snarled. "A *Rabic* one, at that, and not even a proper Mbaysey. An outsider. You are weak. The Sept will break you, and teach you that you will never measure up to Yagazie. Kill me, so I can be standing at the gates of hell to welcome you shortly."

Kathra nodded, a bit surprised at the rage bubbling off the woman, even now. It was more of a confession than she had been expecting, but the woman had to have known that she would be found out eventually.

Or perhaps she had already been planning to die with the rest of them, if a Septagon was waiting for *WinterStar* at Azgon.

Kathra considered her options. As Commander, she could just shoot Ugonna now, and let everyone know as much of the truth as they needed. But she needed to make an example of the woman, lest some future spy decide to try her luck.

"Daniel, I need your help," Kathra said, turning to face the tiny man, surrounded by so much taller women.

His eyes met hers from under hooded brows, like a recalcitrant teen called to discipline.

"How?" he whispered carefully.

"You have seen the truth," Kathra said. "Can you show the rest of us?"

Whatever he had been expecting, this was not it. She watched his face fall slack in surprise and fear. His eyes lost focus before they found hers again.

"Urid-Varg rode a victim," Kathra said simply. "You ride the gem. Is there a way you can carry us?"

Now the eyes were blinking too rapidly, shifting back and forth. According to Ndidi, he could occasionally speak with his ghosts, so perhaps she was watching him ask them something.

"I can try…" Daniel offered weakly.

"Do it!" Kathra commanded him in a stern voice.

She had no idea what to expect, but Daniel reached out and took her hand in his. She could feel his tension in the sudden coldness.

"All of you," he whispered, reaching out his other hand as she watched.

Kathra found herself looking at the room as if she was floating a whole deck above it with nothing in the way. The seven of them over here. Ugonna over there, growing rapidly more fearful, but not moving yet.

In her mind, she became Daniel in a way she could not describe, other than perhaps he was indeed carrying her and the others on his back. She could taste the flavor of his fear, swirling like fog around the pillars of duty and strength holding his mind upright.

Erin was there with her. Kam. Stina. Nkechi. Areen.

All of them standing on Daniel's shoulders as he carried them across a raging river in a storm.

Suddenly, she was aware of Ugonna as another layer of consciousness below them.

Kathra watched the rage and fear war with each other as they entered her mind. Already, the traitor was bracing herself to rush them. Perhaps to grab a gun from someone and kill before they finished her off. Perhaps to just knock them to one side and make it out the door.

Kathra reached out a mental hand and grabbed the woman.

"No!" she commanded in an angry tone.

Suddenly, Ugonna changed. Stopped fighting Daniel. Stopped anything.

The traitor stood perfectly still, eyes and mind unfocused and watching nothing.

Kathra hadn't meant to *change* the woman. Merely to order her.

But Urid-Varg had been able to change anyone he pleased with his powers.

Kathra could see where her hand had reached out and flipped a switch in Ugonna's mind.

How is this possible? Kathra asked the presence of Daniel that was all around her.

You are me, he replied in a calm, detached voice. *We must become one to do this thing. All of you are me.*

Kathra felt a gasp in her physical form. What could he learn about her secrets, if they were thus?

But he had already been inside her mind. Had used her to write a secret message from Erin.

That meant she was also in his mind.

Kathra did not wish to violate his privacy, but she would perhaps never gain an opportunity like this again.

She reached out.

Daniel did not fight her. If anything, he felt the man's mind guiding her towards some of the places she might not have found on her own. At least not initially.

She watched him as a man. As a person.

As a chef.

All of his identify lay open before her, spread out on a table top like a jigsaw puzzle, except she could see how each and every piece went together.

You understand, he said quietly in her mind.

She did.

Daniel was more at risk of her asking him to do too much evil, than he ever was of doing it on his own. Bright lines were apparent, with footprints in the snow walking right up to them in many places, and crossing only a time or two.

She felt him redden with embarrassment as she probed those places.

The Left Hand of Evil. She had not truly understood the implications before now, but she could see all the places where his power could take him in a moment of weakness or rage.

Turn a victim's mind off while he had her body.

Leave her awake and trapped in her flesh watching helplessly as a means of torture.

Cause her to participate in the act.

Make her enjoy it.

Bring her to *dependence* on it.

Truly, the potential was frightening.

You have another power, Daniel, she told him and watched the man's mind blink in surprise.

What? he asked.

Kathra smiled.

With but a touch, you could induce a woman to experience

the greatest orgasms she has ever imagined possible, my little Warrior-Chef, she teased him lightly. *Remember that, as well.*

The blink of surprise he pulsed back at her was tinged with newly-awakened possibility. And a depth of surprise greater than the man stood tall. Especially as the other women snickered and Areen managed to blush so hard she might start a fire.

Kathra smiled.

She turned her attention to Ugonna now. Ripped open the woman's mind for the others to see. Saw the jealousy. The anger. The betrayal of what Ugonna considered hers by fiat taken away from her.

That's not how comitatus works, traitor! Erin snarled across the mental gap. *You earn it. You earn the right to keep it.*

Kathra nodded with the words. She turned to each of her women's minds to make sure they carried this memory with them.

And the possibility that Daniel could be a power for good with a little help, and not just the Left Hand of Evil.

Daniel, I must do a thing, Kathra pulsed back at the man. *It may be your power, but it is my will, if you allow it.*

I serve, Commander, he grinned tightly and paused for a fierce moment. *And I cook.*

Kathra Omezi, Commander of the Mbaysey, reached out a hand and grabbed all of Ugonna's mind inside it.

She could do this thing, and it was her responsibility to own. The others were merely witnesses whose testimony would not be questioned.

She crushed Ugonna's ego in her hand and willed the woman to simply die.

Across the room, a body collapsed to the deck bonelessly.

Kathra let go of herself and Daniel as an entity and stepped back into her own body.

Seven of them fell into an awkward silence.

"Now what?" Daniel asked in a tiny voice.

"Now we must go rescue your turtle, Daniel," Kathra said. "Before the Sept take it."

38

———

NDIDI UNDERSTOOD that it was necessary for her to only be a helpful assistant today, rather than the person in charge. Daniel needed to cook this meal, as even in his own mind he saw it as a Last Supper kind of thing, reaching back to the old religions he had known as a child and still used to flavor his idioms when they weren't food related.

She could see the stress taking a toll on the man, even as his hands never made a false move. Spiced chicken in Spanish rice with refried beans covered in cheese. Drop biscuits with jam. Not quite the extremes of comfort food, but Ndidi knew that this was one of those easy-to-make meals that would bring him some level of solace and calm while everyone waited to find out if the Sept had made it there ahead of them with their trap.

Ndidi did make him eat when they put out the trays of food, dragging him by one hand to a spot at the middle table where the rest of the comitatus seemed to crystalize around him when he sat.

"I can handle things from here," Ndidi scolded him. "You refuel your strength for what's coming."

Daniel grumbled, but did not greatly resist her. Ndidi delivered more food than he probably needed, but that would keep him focused.

Kathra and her crew surrounded the man and seemed to just generate waves of warmth towards him. Ndidi didn't really have any other way to describe it.

She had heard the story from Kam, and it had made its way around the entire crew by now. Ugonna a spy and a traitor, executed by the Commander herself, but not before a message had gotten out to the Sept.

Thus the race to Azgon.

The comitatus couldn't do anything when they got there. Even a patrol force would probably be so large that *WinterStar* and *The Haunt* would be overwhelmed if they offered battle. If there was a Septagon, resistance would be so ineffectual that the Sept might not notice.

The only thing that Kathra could do at that point would be to flee, and perhaps lose the Star Turtle forever. The Sept could not use it, but Ndidi knew that they would not allow another to have it.

No, only Daniel could act. Kathra was the Commander, and one of the most dangerous people Ndidi knew, so she suspected some level of cunning planning had taken place, but they would not know what their options were until they arrived.

Ndidi kept coffee topped off and delivered more biscuits to whoever asked. She could see this turning into a permanent job shortly, if they were successful, or she might have to take over for the crew mess, with Ugonna gone.

Without the turtle, would Daniel stay? Or would its loss break him somehow?

Ndidi wasn't sure what it would take to bend the chef. He had shown himself to be the equal of any, save perhaps Kathra, with his will. So unlike a male.

But they were all in uncharted space now.

Kathra checked her handheld and looked up at the group.

"We will arrive in an hour," she announced in a calm, simple voice. "All Spectres will be ready to launch on emergency notice, but we will not do anything until we know who is there. If they open fire the instant they get a lock on us, *WinterStar* may be destroyed before we can escape. If battle erupts, you will launch and determine if you should remain or flee. If it is a trap, at least half of you need to make it to Concursion to let the rest of the tribal squadron know the outcome, especially if they need to select a new Commander. Questions?"

"Have we considered sneaky?" Daniel spoke up, asking her from across the table. "Instead of just attacking?"

Ndidi grinned at the look of confusion on the Commander's face.

Warrior-thinking.

Sometimes, a chef has to take whatever ingredients she has and spoof them into pretending to be something else, when a customer has a specific desire in mind and kitchen falls short. Daniel had taught her that trick. If you never tell them the truth, they might never know.

"Can we drop out early?" Daniel asked. "I don't understand how FTL works, so I have no idea what I'm talking about, but could we land clear out at the end of observation range first?"

"What good does it do us if they are already there?" Kathra asked. "They'll detect us and be alert when we do jump close. Here we would have some level of surprise."

Ndidi was at the end of the central table, filling coffee with one hand and watching both faces as they talked. Daniel's smile was the sort of evil thing that brought a bit of warmth to her soul.

"Do we have to jump close at all?" Daniel grinned. "Perhaps you just toss me out the airlock as you drive by and disappear? I might sneak by even a Septagon, if they are looking for big, metal warbirds and 'Stars."

Ndidi grinned with him. Misdirection.

Chef-thinking.

"He's right, you know," Erin spoke up to a chorus of assents from other women.

Kathra looked around and took the temperature of the room before nodding.

"If you are sure, Daniel," she replied.

"Sure?" Daniel asked. "Not at all. I might be even crazier than the rest of you. Probably am. Would it even work?"

"It might," the Commander said aloud. "And I like the idea, if you are willing to spend that much time alone, assuming trouble is waiting in ambush."

"It protects the Mbaysey," he said. "You can drop me off and immediately head to the Concursion from well outside the range anybody can hurt you. There you pick up the rest of the tribal squadron and flee, knowing that we've hopefully eliminated the spy that was telling the Sept where to find you. Eventually, I can catch up, assuming the Sept doesn't kill me in the process."

"Could you stop them?" Erin asked. "Reach out and do something to them?"

Ndidi watched him shrug with pained ignorance. That had been the one thing that the two of them had talked about when they were alone cooking. He could see the things Urid-Varg had been able to do, but Daniel didn't have the amplifiers that had been built into the jewelry when Urid-Varg poured his mind into it. Nor the native mental powers that the conqueror had apparently had or developed later.

"Against a dozen, *certainement*," Daniel nodded. "Against perhaps three hundred thousand? No. I presume the issue will fall somewhere in the middle, so maybe. What is the worst thing they could do, kill me?"

"They could capture you," one of the other women called out.

Daniel turned his head to lock eyes with Joane, who had apparently been the one who spoke.

"No, they could not," he said in a cold, dark voice that reminded Ndidi of the deep gap between stars and the hungry, angry things legend said to live there. "They could shoot me with one of those big guns, and probably kill me, but if they brought me aboard their ship, I would be in range to do things to them. *Terrible things.*"

Ndidi shivered at those words. Daniel had confided his nightmares to her, as Kathra had ordered. Except they both knew that many weren't nightmares.

They were memories of things the Conqueror had done to other people. Other planets.

Entire species.

More women shivered at Daniel's tone. Most of them had never heard a male with that level of angry cruelty in his voice. Males weren't like that, at least not around here. Ndidi had no doubts that in the Sept, some men rose to that level.

The naupati in command of a Septagon, for instance.

"I will make some changes, Daniel," Kathra said, rising from her empty plate. "We know the rough distance the Ram Cannon can hurt us, so we will try to land outside that. You will need to prepare for space."

The other women took that as a dismissal as well, and in short order Ndidi and Daniel were the only two in the room.

"You get ready," Ndidi said. "I can clean up."

"No," he said, moving to the basin where the women had left their plates and utensils and lifting it to carry into the back. "I'll start dishes while you pack food. It will take me all of five minutes to get dressed and meet the Commander at the rear airlock."

Ndidi nodded, understanding that spending the rest of the time waiting would just eat at his soul and take him to even darker places than he was now. He needed the company more than anything, especially as he was facing the need to walk right up to a Septagon, perhaps, and challenge them to single combat, all by himself.

So she got leftovers into bins and stowed in the refrigerator, where they would turn into snacks later, and alternatives to whatever she ended up making for dinner. Pasta in red sauce was the current plan, but she had a full cabinet to pick from, once she saw where they were. And dinner would be delayed until after the crisis was over, anyway.

Daniel returned to his cabin once everything was in the dishwasher and chugging away. Ndidi cleaned up the dining hall from what little mess the women had left, took off her mostly-clean apron.

She wasn't dressed in the same general uniform of the comitatus, but loose pants to mid-calf in a sturdy, green cotton denim and a gold shirt that resisted stains and flowed with her. She check her look and glasses in a handy mirror and decided she was presentable enough for now.

Ndidi went out and met him in the hallway as the time grew short. He would still need company, right up until the moment of truth. She could do that for him.

Into the nearest of the six elevators. Up to the hub of *WinterStar*, where they flew like pretty fish through the air. Aft, the corridors were empty, with everyone either at a damage control station, a weapon turret, or ready to launch their Spectres into combat.

They met the Commander at the rear airlock. Port side, if there was such a thing in the absence of gravity to provide a down element. Only out on the rim did you get downward pressure, which was why people who worked in the core slept in spin.

"You are prepared?" Kathra asked as they hung from bars and looked out a nearby portal at lines of stars.

It was an unnecessary question, as Daniel had changed fully into the bizarre costume he had inherited from Urid-Varg's last victim.

Ndidi watched Daniel quickly cycle through the stages of death, lingering on pain and anger perhaps longer than he should, and less than she expected. Finally, he nodded.

"There is no other way, Commander," he murmured. "At least none that does not introduce unacceptable risk to the rest of the tribe. I will succeed, and meet you, or I will die, and that will be that. Tomorrow, we will be renegotiating my contract to include hazard pay over and above the normal excitement of a starship kitchen."

She watched Daniel's face break out into as much of a grin as the weight on his soul would allow right now. The Commander shared it with him, and then sobered.

"Have you not always warned me that the most dangerous job in the galaxy is a professional kitchen?" she teased back. "Tattooed psychopaths with knives, I believe was your phrase."

"*Oui*," he agreed. "But today it might be *Untattooed Xenocides with Axial Megacannons*. Perhaps they can become as dangerous as an angry *Sous Chef*. We shall see."

"Good luck," Kathra sobered. "I will be below, ready to launch, so we can still talk on the comm until you step into space. After that, radio silence must be maintained."

"Understood," Daniel said.

"I will keep him company here as well, Commander," Ndidi interjected, meeting the woman's eye and communicating on a much deeper level.

He was tough, they knew that, but he was still just a male. Who knew what the silence would do to him?

Kathra Omezi nodded and pushed off to head forward. Ndidi knew the woman had prepared herself for an apocalyptic battle when they arrived, however much they were now just going to stay long enough to cast their favorite chef to the wolves and hope he could sing for his supper.

"Are you okay?" Ndidi asked after a few moments of solitude.

"Scared shitless," he grinned wanly at her. "There are so many ways this could go wrong, and only a few where it actually works out. But we have no choice whatsoever, and this is a duty that I cannot pass off to any of the rest of you."

Ndidi nodded.

"What does flying in space feel like?" she asked, mostly to distract him in the few minutes until the countdown reached zero and the stars turned back into points in the darkness, instead of streaks.

"Much like being here," he said, gesturing with the hand not holding on to a rail. "There is no gravity acting on me, nor inertia. I think, and I go. As you said, we are little fishies."

He took a deep breath and Ndidi watched his eyes focus on something a thousand light-years distant. He grabbed the pole with both hands and pivoted himself around to go feet-first into the airlock.

"And now, we must part," he said with stone in his voice.

Ndidi watched him, and came to a decision. She took a breath.

"I'm coming with you," she said. "You said you could probably wrap your field around more than just you, to carry things or even people through space."

"I was talking about rescuing someone from a broken

Spectre, if I recall," he replied. "Not attacking a Septagon in single combat."

"Nonetheless," Ndidi challenged him. "You need someone to come with you. Otherwise, you will be alone with your ghosts for however long it is until you catch up to *WinterStar* again. That would be bad for you."

She saw the bolt of pain that shot through the man. Yes, she knew his weaknesses now. Kathra Omezi had ordered him to share them with her and Ndidi, so they could keep him sane. Sane enough, anyway.

Ndidi knew what things brought him up from a nightmare, screaming as he woke. Solitude was nearly at the top of the list, behind only evil itself.

He studied her face now. They were on a plane right now, relative to one another and the corridor. He was weighing his options against his needs.

"You will get permission from the Commander," he challenged her back finally. "Otherwise, the answer is no."

Ndidi nodded and reached out to key a comm line open.

"Commander Omezi, this is Ndidi," she said simply, waiting.

"Go ahead," the Commander replied after a moment.

"I believe it would be best if I accompanied Daniel on his mission," Ndidi said in as firm a voice as a nineteen-year-old cook could, when challenging both her Commander and a male who might yet become the Mad God he feared. "He requires your approval."

There was a long pause as Kathra Omezi considered the situation. It ran long enough that Ndidi was expecting her to side with Daniel.

"Yes, you should go," Kathra said. "Daniel, she has my blessing."

"Understood, Commander," Daniel said, reaching out his free hand and closing the line. "Thank you, Ndidi."

"You haven't taught me everything you know," she teased him. "Can't have you escaping my clutches just yet."

He chuckled, and it looked like some pain disappeared, from the way his eyes got brighter.

"Come," he held out a hand.

Ndidi took it and let him pull her into the airlock and close by his side. It was not a sexual movement, rather he was holding her against his hip with an arm around her waist, side by side as he keyed the lock to close.

Cold water started at her toes and slowly rose up her calves. When she looked down, there was a faint, silvery glow engulfing her body from the bottom up, like the one around Daniel already. Quickly, it cocooned her before warming.

To do this, you must become me, and I you, Daniel said in her mind. *Perhaps the Conqueror had other methods, but he would have never allowed a peer this close, and he had no friends.*

What must it have been like to live so long and only have victims? To never have someone you could drink wine with, or enjoy a pleasant meal?

Ndidi looked around and realized that part of her was inside the being known as Daniel Quentin Lémieux, even as Daniel touched the points that were Ndidi Zikora. They could have no secrets from each other while it lasted, as they slowly merged into one being in some way that she could not explain.

They remained separate, though, even as they were not, like a swirled cake ready for the baking. The cake still had the vanilla and chocolate parts, easily identifiable even after it became a cake.

She looked, and felt him looking at her. He saw her as a woman, and thus ogled her body to a certain extent, even as she could not overcome the revulsion at the sexual touch of a man. But he understood evil, and she was safe. And he had Areen and a few others, if he needed.

They could be emotional partners without ever turning into something else. And he was old enough to be her father. At least that was the laughing phrase she heard from his side of the split.

Ndidi grinned at him and wrapped her left arm around his waist as well.

She watched him press the button and air slowly started pumping out of the space as the clock counted down to zero.

Shortly, it would be just the two of them against the entire Sept Empire.

But Daniel would not be alone when he faced them.

39

Walking into darkness.

Daniel tried not to hold his breath as the outer hatch opened and he could see the lines of nearby stars stretching to infinity before him.

And the endless night.

He had a firm hold of Ndidi's hip against his own, flying lightly towards the opening while remaining yet inside *WinterStar*'s safety, just to test how it felt to bring a second person with him. It had been only theoretical before, the possibility that he could rush out to a damaged Spectre and rescue the pilot by encasing her in the same shield that protected him from the cold and vacuum of death. But it was working. Ndidi smiled nervously at him, reaching up to absently push her glasses back into place on her nose.

Daniel did something and reduced the temperature around them a degree or so. Just enough to offset the mad heartrates and sweat of two adventurers about to threaten a Septagon.

The clock wound down the last few seconds as he

watched. When it hit zero, the stars returned to his world almost at exactly the same instant.

Daniel slid to the outer edge of the airlock, took a grip, and looked out. Nothing was immediately close enough for the naked eye to spot, so he carried them outside the ship, past the theoretical limit that the valence drive might accidentally pick him and Ndidi up when *WinterStar* jumped.

Cold, silent eternity.

Below, the green and gold banded marble shooter of a gas giant. Daniel knew that there were perhaps as many as a hundred moons in various orbits, some below but most still above them somewhere, along with the faintest wisp of rings seen nearly edge on. He drew a breath from somewhere and moved in the direction of the great storm in the planet's northern hemisphere, a grand upswirling of blue gas like an underground water line erupting upwards to flood out your kitchen and close the business for three days while plumbers and inspectors argued about minutiae of legal interpretations.

But it was still the perfect place to hide his ship. And it made a mad sort of sense to park a thing he always saw as an aquatic creature near an underground ocean. Or whatever that layer of blue gas underneath turned out to be. He was a chef, not a physicist.

A thought drew his attention back. It might have been Ndidi's desire to look, but she remained silent in that odd, metaphysical salon where they spoke. Still, he turned them as an entity to watch the great, graceful lines of *WinterStar* hovering in a high orbit.

The ship would not remain for long, if they spotted anything or anybody that gave them pause. It vanished as they watched, a soap bubble popping into nothingness and dooming Daniel to this mad feat he had undertaken.

Hopefully, Ndidi's death would not be on his conscience as well.

Forward and down, there was nothing they could do now. *WinterStar* would never return to this system. Or at least not for several years, when they might know safety after the Sept had left for good.

Daniel reached out with his various senses and tried to smell the scent of danger in the solar wind.

There.

And several other, smaller places.

They must have brought both a Septagon and more than one Patrol. One enormous collection of minds even greater than the largest TradeStation Daniel could imagine, surrounded by a swarm of silent fireflies, just waiting for the moment to light up and shatter the darkness.

You'll do fine, Ndidi told him.

Daniel smiled and tried to nod persuasively. If he could do that enough times, he might even convince himself. Pigs might fly, but he was alone in orbital space, without a suit, carrying his new *Sous Chef* to a rendezvous with a stolen starship, hidden in the clouds of a gas giant while hiding from a Septagon dangerous enough to destroy cities from orbit.

Could it get much weirder today?

Daniel moved to mask himself from the Septagon's eyes. He lacked a vocabulary to describe it, even to a woman inside his mind, but he envisioned a cloak around their shoulders, and pulled the hood up to shadow their eyes. The Septagon would still see them if they got close and they pounded the area with a scanner beam, but until then, they were just a small rock moving around.

Commander Omezi had once told him that orbital space in a gas giant's neighborhood was a messy place, filled with shattered remains of comets and old moons that had been destroyed. Or had it been someone else talking? One of his ghosts?

Daniel shuddered and pretended it had been Kathra Omezi. Any other conclusion was one step closer to madness.

Yes, Ndidi said. *I was there when she mentioned it, discussing with Kam where to best mine things for ForgeStar.*

Good, he was only slightly crazy, then. Or no more than usual.

And the Septagon was too busy looking up. They were not directly over the place where Daniel had hidden the turtle. Not far enough away that he could sneak the ship out without being seen, but had they known the location, they would have been closer to it.

Daniel focused on being a rock and falling into the gravitational depths of the gas giant.

40

Ndidi had to remind herself to keep breathing occasionally, even as she knew that it didn't really matter, as long as Daniel was doing whatever it was that carried them through space. None of the comitatus had ever had a view like this, as they were always either inside a Spectre, or at least looking out from a suit's viewport.

She was a goddess, reigning over the very heavens themselves. A hawk, starting to swoop down on a rabbit in the tall grass, aware of a great cat lurking somewhere nearby.

Have they seen us? she asked the other half of herself.

I do not believe so, Daniel replied. *Perhaps we will make it.*

Ndidi tried to relax and not distract the man as he flew. She was in his mind, listening to all the voices, some of which were other people and one of whom was just a male chef with what he thought of as a beautiful woman on his arm as he broke into the Bey's palace.

But Daniel had no secrets from her now, just as she had none from him.

Now she understood what the Commander must have gone through when she sentenced Ugonna. One entity, made up of thousands of parts, most of them small and quiet in the distance.

Daniel stiffened as she held him. They had fallen perhaps halfway to their destination, if she could measure such a strange distance. The planet had gone from a slightly rounded circle to a place where she could see the depths of clouds below her if she squinted a little.

An eagle comes, he whispered in her ear.

Ndidi looked around and knew that one of the patrol craft was approaching, although it was still just a brighter light against the sea of stars above them. Had they seen something? Detected two people dancing in orbit? Or was this just part of their regular patrol around the great behemoth that was only the suggestion of seven sides in the distance?

Daniel stepped from their mutual salon to a metaphorical window, perhaps, staring at a postal deliverer approaching up the front sidewalk.

Ndidi had never been on the surface of a planet, so it must be some memory of Daniel's as she watched those things unfold. In her mind, she saw a shadow appear against a cloudy day, slowly moving across the sky overhead.

Stupid machines, Daniel cursed. *Minds I can twist, but they would see something in their records later, regardless of how I cloud their eyes now.*

Can you make them see something on a nearby moon? Ndidi asked. *Convince them that the scanners are wrong and somebody saw a light on the surface?*

I can try, he offered.

She was alone in the room now, but also flying next to him as they both appeared like ghosts over the heads of the six men on the ship's bridge.

"I'm sure I saw something, Aspbad," one of the savaran said.

Aspbad. A Sept ship's captain, a rank below a naupati, but Ndidi wasn't sure how she knew that. Perhaps Daniel did, or read it from the men below them.

Savaran. An officer rank serving below the Aspbad.

Was this what it meant to share a consciousness?

"There's nothing on the scanners or the logs," the commander replied.

"Understood, sir. It was a flash of light from the surface of the moon. Could they have cloaked themselves against detection?"

"Notify Septagon Uwalu," the Aspbad commanded after a moment. "Tell them we are moving to investigate."

"Acknowledged, sir."

Ndidi blew out a breath. Sneakiness. Let the minds believe they have seen something the machines missed, and turn away from uncovering the truth. Hopefully, it would work for long enough. Daniel agreed with her and they resumed their fall into the clouds.

At some point as she watched, they crossed a threshold, and the sky above went from blackness to a pale salmon color.

This must be what it was like to live planet-bound. To have miles of atmosphere overhead, diffracting the light of the star into a haze. Blue on ancient Earth. Pinks and oranges at Azgon.

Are we safe? she asked him.

What is safe, child? he sent back, concentrating on the rapidly rising wind around them.

Even at this altitude above whatever depths lay below, they were engulfed in a hurricane, winds racing madly along from the warm side of the planet to the cold to redistribute the heat of the star and the interior. Visibility with her eyes fell to almost nothing, just an endless, pinkish fog bank around them.

But above, from orbit, a Septagon might notice, if they sent a beam this way. They had not, or Daniel would have noticed it, she thought, but what would they do when even the stupidest scanner ever built suddenly detected a massive object rising like Leviathan?

How powerful had the Conqueror been, ere he died? How much luck was involved at that moment when he had set out to command all the women of *WinterStar* as his slaves, never suspecting a male?

Perhaps merely her life rested on the answer. Maybe her soul.

Night fell. If you could call it that.

Shadows where there had been illumination before. Little fishies diving into the dangerous depths of the sea, rather than the shallow safety of the reef.

Down where the great monsters might swim.

The leviathan itself appeared suddenly before her out of the depths and darkness. Two great, gleaming eyes stared back at her as Daniel flew closer.

She had seen the images of the Star Turtle in space. Witnessed it out a porthole. But that was against the night.

Here, it was the great beast emerging into a nightmare as she watched.

And she had never been so happy to see something like it.

The maw opened and Daniel flew into it. The jaws could have snapped the core of *WinterStar* in half, had they bitten, but they were designed to gnaw on comets and asteroids from what Daniel had told her. Eat space debris, just as a sea turtle ate jellyfish and other things.

The throat looked big enough to fly a Spectre down easily, as it opened. She had no desire to go there herself and see.

Instead, Daniel took them to a small portal just below

the roof of the mouth, where the uvula might hang on another creature. Into the space he flew, depositing her onto the deck as gravity again appeared around her.

Ndidi did not understand how the turtle could have gravity. The great Septagons and TradeStations had grav field inducers, but they were huge things, enormously wasteful of power. Even the patrol ships used them, but they were the smallest things that flew with such devices, and they took up more than half the internal volume to work.

The turtle was a creature according to Daniel, and not a thing. But it generated gravity inside.

The thing she thought of as an airlock hatch closed behind them and the room seemed to gasp to life. Daniel looked around and lowered the shield that had protected them and they both took a sniff. Ammonia and other noxious things, but just enough to perhaps make her eyes start to water, and not enough to poison them.

An inner hatch opened and Daniel released the death grip he had maintained before.

Suddenly, she was alone with her thoughts again, a separate entity from Daniel.

Ndidi blinked and stared at the man.

"Yes," he nodded. "It is like that all the time. Welcome to my nightmares."

She didn't know what to say. He would know anyway, as they had been one person for long enough.

But she understood, perhaps in the same way the Commander did.

And yes, Daniel needed friends.

He set out at a brisk pace for what she assumed was the bridge and she followed.

They had only gotten halfway home.

Now they had to go confront Septagon Uwalu.

41

Kathra did not begrudge the anger that threatened to spill out from her soul. It should have been her battle to fight, not Daniel's. Not Ndidi's. But they had been left behind as *WinterStar* blinked back out of the universe, fleeing desperately to a place where the Concursion would occur.

At least the Mbaysey would be safe now, even if the day had cost her three chefs. That thought gave her pause. The comitatus were committed to serving her and fighting. Dying, if necessary.

Kathra only accepted those warriors who met her standards, regardless of the number that applied, which was why she only had twenty-two other women, rather than the twenty-five total Spectres that could fly in combat.

But this battle was to be waged by cooks, and not warriors, galling as she found that.

Kathra put on a happier face as she approached the mess hall, her warriors accumulating around her as she did. There had been enough leftovers to get everyone through dinner while she sorted out new duty rosters and hopefully only temporarily promoted people to take over the two kitchens.

Until Daniel and Ndidi returned. There was no other acceptable outcome. With the other woman, hopefully Daniel would not be overcome by emotions or Septagons and could meet them.

"He's more stubborn than you probably give him credit for," Erin said out of the blue as they entered the dining room.

"In that case, he would be second or third, behind me and possibly Ndidi, and just ahead of you," Kathra turned to her Second-In-Command with a teasing smile.

Erin's face broke into a smile that nearly erased the barcode tattoo on her cheek.

"Maybe," she laughed as the other women nearby chuckled as well. "Who would have imagined it from a male?"

"I might have gone a little deeper into his background than you realized, when it came time to offer him a job," Kathra said. "He was not too good to be true, but the man was most certainly a diamond in the rough, just waiting for someone to come along."

"No, he only became too good for us later," Erin sobered. "Will he return?"

"I believe so," Kathra said as she sat. "He has found a place here, and people who will protect him."

Someone else was busy in the kitchen, pulling bins from the refrigerator and letting the ancient autochef warm them up for now. Something that simple was within the robot's capabilities. Kathra would have helped, but Daniel had reminded her of the old adage about too many cooks, and there were at least a half dozen women at work already.

"Plus, Ndidi will protect him," Kathra continued.

"You might have to expand your definition of comitatus, Kathra," Kam said from across the table. "Those two belong."

Assents from the right and the left. That said more than Kathra could have. These proud, warrior women happily accepting a half-blind cook as their equal, to say nothing of a *Rabic* male.

"First, they have to make it home," she reminded them.

"And if they don't?" Erin asked in a serious tone.

"Then I will add that to the manifest," Kathra said. "We will be hunting the Sept after this. Those people owe me satisfaction, and I will claim it."

Around her, the women growled hungrily.

42

———

It was not his home. Nowhere on this ship was his, least of all this bridge chamber.

Daniel amended that as he glanced over at Ndidi and decided that he could tack on the word *today*. Tomorrow, perhaps.

This was just the place from which Urid-Varg had originally set out to conquer the galaxy, at least twice over, failing both times. In the first, the cost had been an entire species, while the second had only cost the galaxy several dozen planetary populations.

Daniel looked up and wondered what crimes had been committed in this room. Many of them haunted his nightmares, unwilling as he was to classify them as mere memories.

"Now what?" Ndidi asked as Daniel moved to that massive, green throne and stood before it.

He commanded the portals to open, so she could at least see something. Other than the organic lightstrips along the ceiling and Urid-Varg's chair, the room was empty. Blank, green walls that matched the floor and vaulted ceiling. The

Conqueror had commanded from this room, but his mind had been many other places while he did so.

Worse, he had become the turtle in many of the same ways that Daniel had become Ndidi or the Commander. One combined entity, save that the ship had no mind until he provided it one, merely the autonomous functions of a simple creature.

Daniel sat heavily and considered.

Outside the windows, the howling gales of the storms. In the distance, a blue tornado connected a deeper layer of gases with the outer edge of the atmosphere. Daniel had left the turtle in this place so it would be easy to find, not realizing that the storm itself might provide an indigo umbrella overhead, hiding them from rain and prying eyes.

"You move here," he said simply, pointing to a spot just behind him and to one side.

The back of the throne rose only to his shoulders, although Daniel knew he could adjust it, just as he had the clothing he wore right now. Making things fit you, rather than adapting to them.

There was probably no better description of the *salaud* known as Urid-Varg.

Ndidi took up a space at his left rear.

"Put your hand on my shoulder," he said. "That will let me bring you along."

At least she would understand what he meant. She had been him for long enough today.

Daniel felt her hand descend on his shoulder and connect a circuit. Together, they leapt outward, to become a Star Turtle, floating high in the atmosphere of a quiet gas giant.

There was no thought of engines igniting or thrusters adjusting their flight. Daniel flew as he might do himself, giving no more thought to such things as fins than he did to feet.

The horizon was suddenly below them, and the ship began to ascend into the skies.

Where are they now? the part of him that was Ndidi asked.

Daniel felt himself shrug. A Septagon could hide anywhere, as deep as they had gone to hide the turtle.

The head of the leviathan looked right and left, but the violet clouds yet sheltered them.

A light appeared from the darkness as they rose into wine-dark seas overhead. Daniel knew it for a scanner beam directed this way. An ancient spotlight seeking for submarines sneaking about in the dark waters.

Septagon Uwalu had found them.

Daniel found a growl rising from his own depths, similar to the turtle, but he could not tell which of the three of them originated it. It didn't really matter, as they were all one being right now. Images of Angel plagued him momentarily, ascending into the night on the arm of a professional Forceball player, aboard the skytaxi carrying her out of his life.

And carrying him into this one.

"Alien vessel, surrender or be destroyed," a voice came to them across radio waves. "This is the Sept Imperial Septagon Uwalu."

Should we reply? Ndidi asked the gestalt.

Non. *Let them fear something like Urid-Varg, and not two teenage chefs out joy riding in a stolen car,* he replied.

Her snicker gave him strength. Most of what he showed to the world was bravado today, but she already knew that. Saw it from the inside.

Daniel felt starlight on his skin as they climbed to the

final level of clouds. Solar wind played across the scutes of his back, tickling them with electrical charge.

"This is your final warning, alien vessel," the naupati of Uwalu challenged them as the massive Septagon began to close. "Heave to or face your destruction."

Daniel had never been a warrior. Fights in kitchens did not count, because nobody used knives in those situations. Too dangerous, there was always a risk of splattering blood on food and then you had to shut the whole kitchen down to get it cleaned and disinfected.

Fists were another matter, especially in back parking lots after closure.

As a small man, Daniel had been forced to act aggressively on more than one occasion, when some *connard* back home thought that height and perhaps muscle gave him an advantage that Daniel could not offset with rage.

Fools then. Fools now.

The Septagon hung in space, low in orbit as those things went, but still well above the plane the turtle rode. Ram Cannons opened fire, seven each on the facings that Daniel could see. Heavy Particle Cannons joined in the fusillade, eight of the fourteen on each side looking this way.

The range was extreme for the lighter weapons; and the depths of the atmosphere, however thin and attenuated at this height, still caused the beams to diffract too soon, either fading to nothingness or deflecting them in bizarre patterns as they ionized a trail from an induced magnetic field.

Daniel had no idea what he was talking about. Nor did Ndidi, so he presumed that perhaps the turtle contained this information, activated only when needed.

Such as when battle was imminent.

The Ram Cannons stung a little when they struck the hull. Like a sea turtle, the ship was covered with an armored shell, top and bottom, scutes and plates and tough hide.

The entity commanding pulled the front four fins back, close against the hull where they tucked in, mostly covered.

The rear two fins pointed straight aft and did…

Ndidi understood a gravity inducer as a machine that could create a field that mimicked the effect of walking on a planet. The tribal squadron did not have them, due to cost and mass.

The Star Turtle used something similar to fly. She did not understand it. Nor did Daniel when he looked inside himself.

His ghosts provided enough bits for now.

The gestalt of beings turned their attention to the Septagon.

Given enough time, the Ram Cannons might pound him into submission, but that value was measured in hours or perhaps days.

But everyone understood the meaning of the ship's mighty prow coming around to point at them.

The Axial Megacannon. The single greatest weapon ever invented, at least as far as the Sept had found. The tool that allowed them to conquer other worlds, able to destroy cities from orbit, and anything less than a Septagon in space.

Daniel had no concept of what the beam could do to them. His only exposure was from bad adventure vids, where music and excitement were usually more important than scientific accuracy.

Perhaps the shell could resist it. Perhaps the beam would open him up like a sushi chef wielding his sakimaru blade. Daniel had no interest in finding out today.

The turtle rolled elegantly onto his right side, like an aircraft in a war history, as a beam larger than the turtle's head lanced by, striking deep into Azgon's atmosphere and igniting a mushroom cloud of exploding energy.

The Ram Cannons began to miss as well, unable to

respond fast enough to something more maneuverable than a Spectre.

Somebody laughed with delight. It might have been him. Perhaps Ndidi. Many of his ghosts joined in.

Should we damage them? a voice broke into the gestalt.

Again, it was difficult separating them into beings, rather than consciousness, but the part that was Daniel thought the voice he heard belonged to the only woman in the stadium.

Let them know fear instead, he offered. *We have enough deaths on our conscience for now.*

He felt her nod as the turtle rolled onto another flank and pitched up.

They could not resist pointing the face of the turtle down at the Septagon as the ship began the slow twisting to perhaps aim the great beam at them a second time, after however long it took to recharge.

The turtle's eyes could fire beams back. Not as dangerous as the Megacannon, maybe, although the only test would be firing them to see. Destroying that vessel as an experiment in power, perhaps.

But they could make those same eyes glow with a terrible, internal fire as they looked the naupati in the face. Daniel screamed at Septagon Uwalu in pure rage as he did so, pulsing all the anger, pain, and despair of a thousand ghosts in his soul at the ship.

The Ram Cannons fell silent. The Heavy Particle Cannons did as well. Lights may have flickered across the face of the Septagon, seventy decks tall on the ring and thirty-two hundred meters on a ship-facing. Even the towers that rose from the top, like keeps atop a mountain, fell dark for a moment.

Daniel turned his snout and flared away from the mighty castle as he picked up speed.

Commander Omezi was out there waiting for him to return, and bring back her other chef.

He glanced back once to see the patrol ships swarming around the Septagon as the great ship's lights came back on and the engines began to thrust.

You will never catch me, they pulsed at the pursuers with as much dread as they could put into the words.

Daniel found the spot, the circle of night that was his goal, and the turtle leapt into the darkness.

READ MORE!

Be sure to read all five books in the Star Tribes series.

WinterStar
SeekerStar
SeptStar
SwiftStar
MorningStar

Available from your favorite retailers!

ABOUT THE AUTHOR

Blaze Ward writes science fiction in the Alexandria Station universe (Jessica Keller, The Science Officer, The Story Road, etc.) as well as several other science fiction universes, such as Star Dragon, the Dominion, and more. He also writes odd bits of high fantasy with swords and orcs. In addition, he is the Editor and Publisher of *Boundary Shock Quarterly Magazine*. You can find out more at his website www.blazeward.com, as well as Facebook, Goodreads, and other places.

Blaze's works are available as ebooks, paper, and audio, and can be found at a variety of online vendors. His newsletter comes out regularly, and you can also follow his blog on his website. He really enjoys interacting with fans, and looks forward to any and all questions—even ones about his books!

Never miss a release!

If you'd like to be notified of new releases, sign up for my newsletter.

I will never spam you or use your email for nefarious purposes. You can also unsubscribe at any time.

http://www.blazeward.com/newsletter/

Connect with Blaze!

Web: www.blazeward.com
Boundary Shock Quarterly (BSQ):
https://www.boundaryshockquarterly.com/

ABOUT KNOTTED ROAD PRESS

Knotted Road Press fiction specializes in dynamic writing set in mysterious, exotic locations.

Knotted Road Press non-fiction publishes autobiographies, business books, cookbooks, and how-to books with unique voices.

Knotted Road Press creates DRM-free ebooks as well as high-quality print books for readers around the world.

With authors in a variety of genres including literary, poetry, mystery, fantasy, and science fiction, Knotted Road Press has something for everyone.

Knotted Road Press
www.KnottedRoadPress.com